Kathryn Kincaid

Contents

To my fellow HSPs—
don't forget you're strong as hell for
shouldering the weight of your emotions

And to Roz for helping me learn to accept myself as I am.

Content warnings

For content warnings, please visit my website at https://www.authork athrynkincaid.com/.

Author's note

~Crying after losing a softball game or getting a bad grade.
~Fixating on something stupid I said.
~Feeling sick to my stomach when other people are upset.
~Needing alone time in a dark room under my weighted blanket after an emotionally taxing day.

These are some of my experiences as a Highly Sensitive Person (HSP).

I didn't know there was a name for how I experienced life until I went to therapy in college during a particularly challenging time. In that first session, hearing about what finally brought me into therapy, my therapist identified me as an HSP. I am so grateful to her for helping me understand myself better and for normalizing my emotions. Before then, I considered my emotionality a weakness.

Learning more about my trait opened my eyes. I never realized that what I liked most about myself was related to being an HSP. My creativity, for one. I started writing stories when I was in the third grade. The characters in my stories take on a life of their own inside my mind, whispering dialogue, scenes, and storylines when I least expect it. I love that I always have at least one story brewing in my head. I also am deeply affected by music and art, obsessing over fictional characters, playing the same song over and over again, grinning ear-to-ear at love stories on the page and the screen.

It took a long time for me to see my sensitivity as a strength, but now I'm grateful for feeling as deeply as I do. It's that acceptance that allowed me to tell Brenna Quinn's story. I hope you all love her as much as me.

I also hope to one day live in a world that doesn't shame us for our differences. It starts with each of us, learning more about how other people experience the world. In my opinion, the romance book community is at the forefront of helping people understand each other better. So thank you for picking up this book. It means the world to me.

PROLOGUE

BRENNA

Eight years ago

Nathan Sharpe backed me against the dugout wall, the cold sting of concrete searing my skin.

He'd insisted we end our last night of summer as we had so many others—side by side, backs on the infield grass, staring at the stars.

Except this time, we didn't make it there.

"What are you doing?" I whispered over the sounds of cicadas and crickets, the familiar soundtrack of summer.

He placed his hands flat on the wall to either side of my head. We'd been apart for only two months—the entirety of the summer before junior year of high school—but I could have sworn he'd grown a couple of inches.

"I want to kiss you."

My heart stopped beating. I blinked. "What?"

"Shit," Nathan hissed, his brow furrowing as he studied my face. His turquoise eyes were shining, even in the dark surrounding us. "Did I get it wrong?"

He traced his tongue along his lower lip, his eyes still trained on my mouth.

What the hell is this?

Not once had we ventured even close to exiting the friend zone... regardless of my inconvenient feelings. Feelings I'd long buried. Or so I thought. Apparently, all it took was Nathan crowding my space and spending a summer apart to make me forget I couldn't want *him*—my best friend—like this.

And yet, I slowly shook my head and smiled coyly, admitting what I'd painstakingly hidden from him since the beginning of high school. Nathan's face broke into a grin, and my knees nearly buckled. He leaned in, one hand moving to cup my jaw while the other twirled a strand of my caramel blond hair in his fingers.

"I missed you," Nathan murmured. His lips were so close, his exhale hit my face.

I sucked in my own breath, trying to calm my jackhammering heart.

My first kiss would be with Nathan—with *my* Nathan. The boy who, time and time again, I dreamed would look at me as someone other than his tomboy best friend.

Teen dramas had lied. Seeing me with makeup or in a tight-fitting dress hadn't altered his feelings. But tonight, while I was wearing my Brenna-est outfit of jean shorts and a Palmer City Owls T-shirt, some-thing shifted so quickly I didn't have time to process it.

Nathan placed his lips on mine, sure and steady and much softer than I'd imagined. He tasted faintly of watered-down beer and the strawberry bubble gum he liked to chew. I mirrored his movements, trying to conceal my inexperience... inexperience he clearly didn't share. My instinct was to hide that I had no idea what I was doing, but Nathan knew my entire history, knew this was my first kiss. Unless he assumed something had changed during his time at baseball camp in Florida.

He pulled back to stare into my eyes. "Are you okay?" He tucked my hair behind my left ear.

Those eyes. I'd lost myself in them before, but not like this. I'd never before let myself embrace the full weight of my attraction to him.

I swallowed involuntarily. "Yes."

"Yes?" His eyes searched mine, He needed reassurance to continue. I loved him for it.

I nodded and smiled as I moved closer. He met me halfway, recapturing my lips.

He would come to his senses in the morning when the buzz of alcohol wore off.

We would deal with it then.

1

 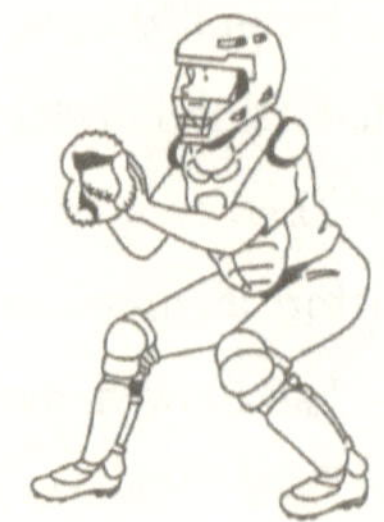

BRENNA

Now

I SLAMMED MY SUITCASE closed, desperate to make the week's worth of clothes fit.

Overpacking had always been a bad habit. Traveling tended to make me anxious, which manifested in checking the details of my flight a dozen times, wondering if I'd accidentally packed a firearm I didn't own, and confirming my license was in my pocket every few minutes.

I packed clothes and shoes for every scenario I could realistically—and unrealistically—encounter. I hoped my mom wouldn't realize my suitcase looked bigger than necessary for what was supposed to be a two-day trip to Middlebury. I'd already "betrayed" her by going to her ex-husband's funeral last month. As always, her needs superseded everything, even death. She was complaining less this time only because she thought he might've left me money in his will. Not that she would see a dime of it.

If she found out I planned to detour to Chicago to visit my fiancé before coming back to California, she'd throw a fit. Especially if this trip ended my relationship with Jack. She liked him more than I did.

Here I was, twenty-four years old, still hiding things from my mother.

It wasn't her disapproval that bothered me—I'd lived with that for as long as I could remember—but she could push me out of my half sister's life. I couldn't leave Molly alone to deal with our mother's instability and manipulation. Forcing that on a seven-year-old was unfair.

At least growing up, I'd had the Sharpes next door—a normal family, for a time.

I finished squeezing the suitcase closed and zipped it before letting out a deep sigh. This trip would give me a break from my mother, but it wouldn't be a vacation by any stretch of the imagination.

Two days, I reminded myself. *I can survive two days.*

The door burst open, and Molly trotted into the room, dragging her hockey stick behind her. "I don't want you to go!" She flopped face down on my bed. Her Goldilocks-blond hair sprawled around her head, half-submerged in the mattress.

"Aw, Molls. It won't be long. I'll be back before you know it."

She mumbled something into the blanket.

I sat down beside her and ran my fingers through her hair. "What was that?"

She pushed herself to a sitting position, her bottom lip jutted in a pout. "Why do you have to go?" She crossed her arms over the forest-green Palmer City Wolves lettering on her shirt.

Molly had lived in Middlebury, North Carolina, a small town near Palmer City, for the first half of her life. Though she was too young to remember most of it, she hadn't forgotten going to hockey games, and her love for the Wolves had stuck. She watched every game she could.

Over the years, I'd put her in front of baseball games, but she always complained they were *boring*. I tried not to let the comment sting.

"Molly, I told you," I said, taking on as patient a tone as I could muster. Normally, I didn't mind repeating myself, but this trip had me tied up in knots. Still, she didn't deserve to bear the brunt of my anxiety. "Someone I used to know they left me something."

When Gordon Sharpe died a month ago, I had the lovely experience of explaining death to her. Our mother was nowhere to be found.

"What is it?"

I shrugged, still as unsure as I was two weeks ago when I got the call telling me I was in Gordon's will. "It'll be a surprise, but I'll call you as soon as I know. Okay?"

She nodded solemnly. "Can you get me a present too?"

I ruffled her hair. "You got it."

When I looked up, my mom was in the doorway, watching us with narrowed eyes. Three months had passed since I moved in with Kathy and Molly, but it still took me a beat to adjust to this version of Kathy Quinn. Her unwashed hair and no trace of makeup were the opposite of how she'd composed herself for most of my life.

When I'd come for a visit, my little sister had been living off processed food, delivered to the house, for the better part of a month. She'd arranged her own carpool to and from school. The house needed a thorough cleaning, but Molly had kept the sink clear to avoid bugs. The laundry situation was another story; it sat piled high in her closet, her trove of clean clothes diminishing each day.

I helped as much as I could, then packed up my life in Chicago and put my physical therapy education on hold to move in with them, to care for my little sister. To get my mom to agree, I pretended I was down on my luck and needed her. I ignored her every time she threw the lie in my face. Her comments continued, even after I took on two jobs to support them while she sat at home. Every time, I wondered how much longer I could stand living in her delusion.

"Did you tell Jack about this trip?" Kathy asked, one side of her lips quirked in a sneer.

The tenor of her first words signaled her demeanor each day. I appreciated the warning to mentally prepare myself. Coping with negative emotions and combative environments was never my strong suit. When someone was upset, even when it had nothing to do with me, I couldn't ignore it. I *felt* it.

My mom never understood it. *Stop being so sensitive,* she'd say.

It took going to therapy while in college to realize this wasn't a defect. I nearly sobbed in relief when I found out there was a name for the way I experienced life. *HSP, Highly Sensitive Person.*

My mother called it bullshit.

I wondered if this trait made me similar to my father... not that I'd ever find out who he was. Kathy claimed their relationship was volatile, and she didn't feel safe bringing him into my life. Even if it weren't true, the fact that he never tried to find me was enough to forget his existence.

"Of course. Why wouldn't I?" I dropped to my knees and faced Molly, my back to my mother. "How about you go grab a snack? I'll meet you in the kitchen in a minute."

Molly nodded and moved around our mother without a glance. It broke my heart to see how she'd already learned to cope in Kathy Quinn's world. Mom scoffed as Molly wordlessly passed her but kept her attention on me.

"He wouldn't like it if he knew who you are going to see," she said.

"Jack's not worried, because he has *nothing* to worry about."

Well, not nothing. He'd worry *if* he knew the history between me and the two men I'd see in Middlebury. Or at least, it would worry him if our relationship continued, something I wasn't sure he wanted at this point. We'd seen each other a couple of times in the three months since I left Chicago. Between his job as a pilot and the two jobs I'd taken to keep this family afloat, we hadn't had much time for each other. I thought I'd miss him more—I *should* have missed him more—but part of me was relieved to have one less demand on my shoulders.

I couldn't continue a relationship my heart was no longer in, even if I didn't want to feel his pain.

My mom clucked her tongue. "You always loved that boy too much."

I didn't need her to clarify which boy—now man—she meant. My heart had been broken exactly once in my life. Eight years ago, when my mom's mistakes cleaved my relationship with Nathan Sharpe in two. My heart was like a broken vase glued back together—whole with visible but sealed cracks.

"You gave him the power to destroy you once." Disapproval dripped from her tone, the one she'd used whenever she found me crying and unable to stop. I'd felt weak for months when I was unable to move past it. *She* made me feel weak.

"Don't make the same mistake again."

"Your concern is heartwarming." I pushed past her, rolling my suitcase behind me.

The thought of walking out of this house and never returning shot through me like lightning. The temptation, as always, died as soon as Molly came into view. She sat at the kitchen table, nibbling a chocolate chip cookie, her legs swinging against her chair, her hockey stick beside her.

I took a seat, my heart squeezing at the sight of the meal she'd prepared for me—a brown sugar Pop-Tart and a glass of milk.

"I'm gonna miss you, Molls," I said, clasping her hand.

One week would pass quickly. It was okay to be selfish sometimes, to take a break from life. I *needed* this. And when I came back, I would be able to better care for Molly.

I could finish what I came here to do.

One day soon, Molly and I would leave together and never look back.

2

NATHAN

Now

I ROLLED OVER AND reached for my phone on the nightstand, a dull ache in my pitching arm flaring up.

A woman's moans echoed through the apartment. *Fucking Leo.* He hadn't brought a woman home from the club last night—at least not that I remembered—so he'd either gone back out after I crashed or summoned a booty call. A half-empty bottle of Jim on my nightstand was the likely culprit for my sleeping like the dead. I didn't even remember bringing it in here.

Sometimes I wondered why I didn't get my own place.

Living together had helped us create synergy on the field, but even after we synced, we never left each other. As minor league baseball players, neither of us earned enough to afford a place on our own. Living with me also gave Leo an easy out with women—either for them to leave after a one-night stand or for him to skirt the issue of moving in together if any woman deluded herself into believing that hooking up with him for six months meant something serious was on the horizon.

I waited for ten minutes after the woman's last *Oh my God, Leo* before heading out of my room and into the kitchen for coffee. Sure enough, within minutes, Leo walked a sheepish-looking brunette I'd never seen to the front of our townhouse, kissed her goodbye, and promised to call when his life calmed down. I rolled my eyes. During the offseason, we had no shortage of downtime, but women who didn't follow baseball were none the wiser.

"You're a dick," I said before taking a long pull from my coffee cup.

He leaned against the counter, shirtless as always. "As if you're better."

I was, but not by much. I especially hated the reminder today. My flight back to Middlebury this afternoon would bring me face-to-face with the woman who had once filled so many important roles in my life. Best friend. Neighbor. Confidant. Girlfriend. Teammate.

Brenna wouldn't respect the man I'd become. I dreaded seeing myself through her eyes.

"I don't make false promises." I tried to think of the last time I'd made a promise to anyone. Last season, I went on a couple of dates, and showing up for those was a promise of a kind. Outside of that, my last commitment had been to my ex, Beth, two years ago.

Two years ago. Jesus. Time flew while I single-mindedly pursued my goal to earn a permanent spot in the big leagues. I'd pitched some games there last season when the pitching staff had been decimated by illness, but I always ended back here. Triple-A, the minor leagues.

Leo opened the fridge, pulled out the OJ, and swigged directly from the carton before placing it back inside. "I'll call her… sometime," he said to be contrary.

I scoffed. "When? At three a.m., after your roommate passes out?"

He held up his hands, proclaiming innocence. "Hey, I tried to take away your booze, but you swung at me, so I gave up." He gestured at his face with a circular motion. "Can't have you messing with my moneymaker."

I'd heard women call him *stupid hot* too many times to count.

"Yeah, that's certainly not your arm." I attempted to elbow him as I passed.

Leo quickly darted away, dodging the contact. His laugh grew louder and louder until he stood in the doorway of my room. He ran a hand through his dark blond—*brond*, one of his women once told me—hair. "Ooh, something crawled up your ass this morning."

I didn't respond, depleted of energy. I couldn't deal with Leo while agonizing over this trip. The alcohol last night had kept my mind off it, but I couldn't be drunk for the entire weekend. I would have to face Brenna Quinn stone-cold fucking sober.

Avoiding her at my father's funeral last month hadn't been easy, but I'd managed. This time, there would be no escaping her. We would have to sit in the same room to listen to the reading of his will.

Dad's lawyer shocked me when he said we couldn't handle the paperwork without returning to Middlebury because I wasn't the only one listed in the will. What could my dad possibly have wanted to give to Brenna? Despite our tense relationship, I'd expected him to leave everything to me, his only son.

"Seriously, man, you good?" Leo asked.

He knew about my past, about Brenna. For years, I kept that part of my life buried deep enough, I could pretend it never existed. Then six months ago, I experienced the pure torture of watching Brenna Quinn get engaged during one of *my* games. All my bad karma had found its way to biting me in the ass that day. One of only a few games I played in the major leagues with the Nashville Blitz, and I had to see the woman I used to love promise herself to another man.

I held it together until I got back to Houston. When Leo picked me up at the airport, he saw the state I was in and drove us to the nearest liquor store. I spent the rest of the night drinking away the image of Brenna kissing the douche who got down on one knee for her. He should've known she'd hate being proposed to in public.

That night, I told Leo every single detail of my history with Brenna. He sat rapt, hanging on every word. I'd never expected him to be such a good listener. Maybe it wasn't only his good looks that drew women.

I looked up from my open, half-packed duffle bag. "I'll be fine."

"Do you know what you're going to say to her?"

I shrugged, moving to my closet. "*Hello. How are you? Goodbye.* It shouldn't take long to read the will, and then I'll leave Middlebury behind for good."

Leave *her* behind for good.

Six years since we'd gone our separate ways, and I still felt her absence.

At first, the pangs of loss constantly hit me—when I got drafted, my first paycheck as a minor league baseball player, my first pitch in the big leagues. The longing for her had dimmed over time, but now and again, I wondered what she'd say in certain situations.

Like last month, during the last game of the season, I left a curve ball hanging over the plate that the batter should have pounded into the gap. Instead, he sat on it, waiting for a heater. *That the best you got, Sharpe?* Her taunting voice had filled my mind, motivating me to get my head in the game and finish the season on a positive note. I struck out the remaining batters, even with my painfully throbbing arm.

"What if she wants to talk?" Leo asked.

I wondered how Brenna would act. It was our first meeting since our dustup at her high school graduation. I had no reason to assume anything between us would change, especially if I kept my comments short. But Brenna could surprise me; I didn't know the woman she'd become. Maybe this version of her had gained the confidence I always wished she'd had when we were kids.

"I'll tell her I don't think it's a good idea and wish her the best."

Leo tapped the doorframe. "I'd work on that plan if I were you. The girl you described doesn't seem like someone you can blow off."

"Real encouraging... thanks, man," I said with a sigh.

"How's the arm?" he asked abruptly.

I followed his eyes to my pitching arm, realizing I'd been absentmindedly massaging where my shoulder met the top of my arm.

Fuck.

To avoid his gaze, I refocused on folding clothes and tucking them into my bag. "It's fine. Just slept weird."

Concealing this injury from Leo was impossible. He saw me more than any other person in my life, and he caught every pitch of mine. He'd seen my usual pinpoint precision fail, up close and personal. At home, I frequently iced and heated my shoulder. Some days were better than others—there were times I felt nothing at all—but too often, a pulsating, painful heat gripped my shoulder until I stopped moving it.

Leo had learned when to strategically stroll to the mound to give me a rest. Even a few minutes could help me get through another inning before the pain flared again. Overuse injuries were like that, insidious bastards. All I could do was rest my arm when needed, keep strengthening my shoulder, and manage the pain with heat, ice, and ibuprofen. Anything stronger without a prescription would be flagged by a drug test.

Getting a prescription would mean disclosing my injury to the team, which was out of the question if I wanted to make the pitching rotation in the major leagues, if I wanted to live the dream I'd had since I was a kid. My career was all I had. If I couldn't play baseball...

I refused to finish the thought.

When I returned from Middlebury, I'd get my arm ready for next season.

Nothing would hold me back.

3

NATHAN

Eight years ago

THE FAINT SOUND OF Brenna's voice was pulling me from a deep sleep.

I should've napped during yesterday's two-hour flight, but the anticipation of seeing her had my stomach swimming with nerves. That and I'd sworn to myself I'd confess my feelings when I came home from baseball camp… if they were still there.

Scared shitless described my state of mind the first time I realized I wanted to kiss her. It paled in comparison to my fear on that flight, wondering if I'd waited too long and lost my chance. When she kissed me back last night, relief flooded me.

It hit me again, hearing her voice now.

"He's still asleep," my dad told her from the floor below. "But go on up, it's about time he gets his ass in gear."

The creak of the stairs forced me out of bed, and I stumbled to the mirror. *Not the worst she's ever seen me.* Still, I splashed water into my hands from a half-empty water bottle and ran them through my unruly hair. I took a swig of mouthwash, swishing it around for a couple of seconds before spitting it out. It'd have to do.

I opened the door before Brenna could knock and pulled her inside. She yelped as I shut the door behind us, then pushed her against it, all in one swift motion. Her wide eyes watched me, but she remained stock still.

"I'm glad you're here." I ran a finger along her forearm, leaving goose-bumps in its wake.

She swallowed. Her visible nerves calmed mine. Not surprising since we'd always balanced each other. I never hesitated to give her a pep talk when she doubted her abilities—on the field or in social situations. And Brenna could read me like no one else, instinctively knowing when to call a time-out to rush to the mound and talk me down before my frustration derailed a game.

But she hadn't seen this coming. I liked that we could still surprise each other, even after all this time.

"I thought you might want to watch the Owls game," she murmured, her eyes drifting to my lips. Her chest rose and fell quickly as I brought one hand to rest on her cheek.

"So you didn't come over to pick up where we left off last night?" I dipped my head, forcing her to meet my eyes.

"I wasn't sure you remembered."

I laughed quietly, my fingers tracing her soft skin. "Not something you forget, Quinn."

"You were drunk."

"Not *that* drunk... and I'm sober now, Bren." I wrapped my arm around her waist, pulling her closer to me. "Is this okay?"

It still didn't feel real; my best friend wanted me like I wanted her.

"Yes."

She fisted my T-shirt and surged forward to place her lips on mine. Last night, I eased us into the kiss, slowly crossing the line of no return with the caution it deserved. But now my lips moved against hers without an ounce of hesitation. Brenna easily shed her surprise, throwing her arms around my neck and meeting each movement of my lips and slide of my tongue. When I pulled back from her, she let out a small sigh of satisfaction.

I would never tire of that sound.

"Come on." I tapped a finger on the tip of her nose. "We don't want to miss the first pitch."

⸻⬛◆⬛⸻

BRENNA

Eight years ago

Our normal routine of watching Owls games broke the moment we sat on his couch. We ate our usual array of snacks and ordered a half-pepperoni, half-mushroom pizza from Ray's. We turned on the surround sound to create an immersive experience. We wore Owls merch—Nathan in a baseball cap, me in a loose tank top.

But instead of a healthy distance between us, Nathan took the seat right next to me and pulled my legs across his lap. In the same way he'd pulled me into his room and pushed me against the door, his movements were steady and smooth, as if we'd been this way with each other for years. This new frontier was thrilling and comfortable in equal measure.

"When did you realize how you felt about me?" Nathan asked during the commercial break after the first inning, his fingers moving in lazy circles on my calf.

I swallowed. It was surreal to talk with him about the feelings I'd kept secret for so long. "Do you remember that trip to Albany before high school?" I asked, staring into the turquoise eyes I loved.

"The tournament over July Fourth?"

I nodded. "That's when."

"Oh yeah?" He grinned, creating a set of parentheses on either side of his mouth. "What did I do?"

I looked away, nerves crawling into my stomach over sharing myself like this. Even if I was sharing with the person I trusted most in the world. "You didn't do anything other than exist. It's like the feelings were just... there one day."

I still remembered the first flutter in my stomach, when Nathan scooped me into his arms after he struck out the last batter and secured the first win of the weekend. I didn't want him to let go.

"What about you?" I prayed silently he wouldn't say last night. My heart couldn't take that.

Distantly, I was aware of the game returning from the commercial break, but Nathan maintained eye contact, ignoring the TV. "Last season Ax said he wanted to ask you out. He asked me about it, like he needed my permission or something. And it... pissed me off."

"That he needed your permission?"

He shook his head. "No, that he *didn't*."

The stomach flutter returned in full force. Any fantasy I'd ever had about crossing this line to being more than friends didn't come close to the reality.

"Oh, um... I didn't..." Ax and I had been friends for years. I had no idea about his crush. "He, uh... he never said anything."

Both of us turned back to the TV to watch the Owls try to score their first run.

"I told him not to, that it would mess with team chemistry."

My head whipped his way. "Do you think it will?"

I wondered what our teammates would think when they found out we were dating. Apparently, Ax would hate it. But everyone else, would it bother them to have their star pitcher-catcher duo become more than friends?

He laughed. "No, but it was the best I could come up with. I was... confused about my feelings. I had to be sure about how I felt, how you felt. So I paid attention until I left for the summer."

"How creepy of you, Nate."

He tossed a pillow at the side of my head, but I batted it away.

"You could have just asked me."

Nathan cocked his head. "Back at you."

"I did," I said, flashing back to a painful memory. "Um... homecoming dance, freshman year. I tried anyway." I took a deep breath, shedding the lingering hurt. "I put it away after that." Having Nathan in my life was more important than any specific role he played. "Sometimes it wasn't easy."

"Tell me about it," he groaned. "I thought about coming home and kissing you all summer."

"You did?"

He turned toward me again and placed a hand on the side of my head, fingers in my hair. "Yeah." He leaned forward to take my bottom lip in his. A small contented sigh escaped me as he pulled back. "Bren, can we keep this—"

My stomach plummeted. "You don't want to tell anyone?" My instincts screamed to pull away from Nathan before my heart cracked in two.

He raised an eyebrow. "Wait—is that what you want?"

"No, but you said—"

"I don't want to tell our *parents*," he clarified. "They'll start making us keep the door open and always want to be around when we're together."

A relieved sigh escaped my lungs. "Oh. Yeah, good thinking."

"Something is weird with them right now."

Those words were like a plunge into ice-cold water.

I considered telling Nathan what I saw when I came home early from a friend's house one night this summer. His dad and my mom, in my kitchen, flying apart from each other when the door opened, guilt written all over their features.

They swore it was a onetime mistake, that they had dinner together, drank too much wine. Mr. Sharpe rushed out of the house, leaving my mom and me alone.

She told me to stop being dramatic. She said it would never happen again because Mr. Sharpe was married to her best friend.

I chose to believe her.

Besides, I didn't want to mess with Nathan's baseball camp. He'd worked his ass off to get in front of scouts. If I said anything now he was home, it could make his parents' situation worse.

They'd sort it out. They had to.

"Why do you think I don't want anyone to know, Bren?"

I looked away from him. "I'm not the kind of girl Nathan Sharpe is expected to date."

"Fuck that noise," he said, tilting my face toward him. "You're the only girl I want, Brenna."

No sentence in the history of my life ever sounded so good.

4

NATHAN

Now

WE TURNED ONTO THE main road that traversed all two and a half miles of downtown Middlebury.

The first time I came back here after high school, I'd nearly doubled over from the onslaught of memories. Expecting it this time, I leaned my head against the car window and closed my eyes, ignoring locations that held some of the best times of my life. And some of the worst.

"Sir," my rideshare driver said, as if he'd repeated it more than once. "We're here."

The Sunshine B&B was a typical Middlebury house, not unlike the one where I grew up. Two stories, white siding, black shutters, wide front porch. The aging interior didn't resemble my childhood home though—a rickety wooden staircase, tuxedo floor tiles, green carpet, and so many floral patterns. I didn't mind the delicious smell of baked goods wafting into my room, which made the aging building feel cozy... like home.

Collapsing on the bed, I flipped through channels, finding exactly nothing to hold my attention. I considered calling my mom, but I didn't want her to know I was here. My parent's divorce traumatized her enough, so I tried to limit mentions of my dad. She'd come to the funeral to support me, but she didn't need to bother with the will.

I closed my eyes for a few minutes, hoping sleep would find me, but my ping-ponging thoughts wouldn't stop. After ten minutes, I knew it was a lost cause.

The basement of the B&B had a small gym, something the owner told me when I arrived. I slipped in earbuds and cranked my music, keeping my head down to avoid inadvertent eye contact as I descended two flights of stairs. The pounding of feet on the treadmill belt sounded louder with each step down.

When I reached the bottom and finally looked up, I nearly stumbled over my feet. The woman jogging on the treadmill wore black leggings and a familiar Middlebury Tigers baseball T-shirt. Her blond ponytail swung with each step.

She was still the most beautiful woman I'd ever seen.

I should have anticipated she might stay here, should have prepared for it.

My body moved closer on autopilot. She was focused on the treadmill screen. Soon, I stood close enough to see she'd run two miles at a healthy clip of six miles per hour.

Brenna's shocked expression met mine in the mirror.

Her steps faltered for a moment—long enough to lose her footing, stumble, and career off the back of the treadmill. I moved on instinct, rushing to catch her as she shot off the machine. Her body fell into mine, her full weight pushing into my chest.

Almost a decade had passed since I was allowed to hold her, but still, my arms instinctively wrapped around her. For a moment, I forgot our history. How we fell out of each other's lives. Every reason keeping us apart.

With our gazes locked, I was once again a kid in love for the first time. With her.

Brenna cleared her throat, eyes darting away from me. She pulled out of our accidental embrace... and then she just stared—pink lips parted, rich brown eyes wide as saucers, cheeks flushed scarlet.

I know the fucking feeling.

"Brenna Quinn," I said, pleased my tone didn't reflect the chaos brewing inside me. "It *is* still Quinn, right?"

She pushed away sweaty strands of hair matted to her face, her large diamond engagement ring glinting in the light. Taunting me.

"Y-yes."

"Not for much longer, it seems."

Brenna hadn't seen me the day of her engagement. She didn't even know I'd been there. My call-up to the Nashville Blitz, the major league affiliate for my Triple-A team, the Houston Sharks, had been last minute. Stomach flu had taken down the team, particularly the pitching staff. Not that an earlier call-up would've made a difference; I didn't expect Brenna to keep tabs on my career.

She followed my gaze to her left hand. "Wh-what?"

Brenna had never liked surprises and needed time to prepare for situations. I remained silent, giving her space to adjust.

Eventually she said, "I haven't decided."

"The ring says otherwise."

Her cheeks darkened. "I meant about changing my name."

Brenna carefully climbed onto the treadmill rails and stopped the belt. She sipped from her water bottle while I shamelessly stared at her ass, on full display in those pants. Thank all that was holy her reappearance in my life would be short-lived. Brenna Quinn was always beautiful, but these last six years had been more than generous to her. Calling her gorgeous did her a disservice.

I looked away before she caught me.

"Not that it's any of your business," she continued.

She'd stopped being my business a long time ago. Still, I pressed her, needing the reminder that she belonged to someone else. Being in Middlebury, with her, was fucking with my sense of reality.

"What would it be if you changed it?"

She remained atop the treadmill, looking down at me. Her right hand gripped her left wrist, the same nervous tick from our childhood. "Hayes."

"Brenna Hayes." I clucked my tongue. "Not terrible." When we were dating, we tried her first name with my last name to see how it sounded. *Better than Brenna fucking Hayes.*

"Glad I have your approval." She stepped down and strolled past me. "Treadmill's all yours."

I spun around. "That's it?"

Now that Brenna stood in the same room as me, I couldn't ignore her. Leo was right—she wasn't the kind of woman to be ignored. Not because she *demanded* attention. I was just a pathetic moth drawn to her flame, even if it burned me to death.

Brenna paused but didn't turn around. "What would you like me to say, Nathan?"

"You could start with *Thanks, Nathan, for stopping me from falling on my ass.*"

"Thank you," she said through gritted teeth, her back still to me, frozen to the spot.

"Your gratitude is overwhelming."

I walked to her. If she couldn't bother to face me, I would force it.

"You stopped me from falling over. It's not like you gave me a kidney."

Flippant wasn't ever a word I'd use to describe Brenna. Kind, patient. Smart. Shy, except on the baseball field—the only time she became competitive. I loved that side of her. It hurt knowing that girl didn't exist any longer, that this woman was someone I didn't know at all.

"Good to know I'd get a *thank-you* for giving you an organ."

"It's not like I'd ask you anyway," she replied. "No point in complaining about it."

I stepped in front of her. She still hadn't moved an inch.

"We haven't seen each other in six years, Bren." All the fight bled from my tone.

"There was a reason, Nathan. I know you haven't forgotten."

The memories were never far from the surface. All it took was being in this town, seeing her again to bring them—and my miserable feelings—back with startling clarity. I already wanted to get on a flight and get the hell out of here.

She breezed past me toward the stairs, making sure we didn't touch. "And don't call me that."

"I thought we could be adults."

"This is me being an adult, walking away before I say something impolite," she said a beat before I heard her weight hit the first stair.

I raised my voice. "See you at dinner."

She bristled. "I have other plans."

She could avoid me tonight. Tomorrow, she had to sit at the same table as me. To revisit our past.

5

BRENNA

Now

I BARELY SLEPT LAST night.

Nathan Sharpe was staying in the room across the hall. Each time I looked at the clock, another restless hour had passed, another hour bringing me closer to seeing him again.

I barely saw him at his father's funeral, only glances if the crowd around him shifted in just the right way. I'd gotten used to the way my body reacted to him—stomach flipping, heart pounding, breath accelerating—but *years* had passed. It should've created an immunity response to his threat.

Last night hammered home just how little my body had fortified itself against Nathan. At least that time, any reaction could be blamed on my run.

Not one part of me expected him to stay at a B&B. He played professional baseball—in the minor leagues, sure, but he made more money than I did. He could afford to stay at a hotel in Palmer City and pay for transportation. He wasn't responsible for supporting an out-of-work mother and a younger sister.

While I tried to disguise the dark bags under my eyes, I tortured myself with the memory of tripping over my feet at the sight of him. Blaming it on being startled helped save face, but I couldn't hide from the truth. It didn't matter how spectacularly our relationship had imploded, he still knocked my center of gravity off-kilter.

My phone rang as I was about to open the door. My stomach plunged at the name displayed on the screen. I took a deep breath. "Jack, hey."

"Brenna, I'm glad I caught you."

The relief in Jack's voice ramped up my nerves. "Uh... I was just on my way out, but I have a few minutes. Where are you today?"

"Home."

Chicago. My former home and the city where we met. Also the city Jack was pressuring me to return to. Two weeks in California had turned into three months in the blink of an eye. I understood *why* he wanted me home; he recognized the same thing I did—distance was slowly wedging itself between us. But he didn't seem to recognize his pressure made it worse. His questions shoveled more guilt to the mountain sitting on my shoulders.

"How was your flight yesterday?"

"Smooth," I answered.

The inside joke brought a smile to my lips. We met two years ago, on my way home from vacation. I didn't know what possessed me to thank him for the smooth landing—maybe I was a little tipsy, maybe his warm smile. When he saw me waiting for a ride in front of the airport, he asked for my number. We haven't looked back since.

"Smooth, huh?"

I could hear his smile. Was this all we had? Shared jokes, shared history? My feelings for Jack centered around having him there to take care of me, to be there when I needed someone. That had changed in the three months since I left Chicago. Some of it might've been on me, on my guilt. He was unhappy with the state of our relationship. It wasn't like I could ask him for anything when I wasn't holding up my end of it.

After a beat of silence, he added, "I miss you."

I swallowed. "You'll see me tomorrow." I adjusted my bag on my shoulder, suddenly desperate to get off the phone. "Sorry to run, but I have that meeting soon."

"Right." He cleared his throat. "I hope it goes well. Call me after?"

I opened my door, and my breath caught at the sight of Nathan staring at me from across the hall, his blue eyes gleaming in the sunlight that shone through my open door. His black suit, perfectly molded to his body, showcased his broad shoulders, his strength. And it covered the sleeve of tattoos he'd displayed yesterday. I hadn't gotten a good enough look to see anything beyond pictures of nature, but hot damn, he wore it well.

Once again, no part of me was prepared for him.

"Brenna?" I could barely hear Jack's voice over the sound of my pounding heart.

"Yeah…" I said to Jack, looking away from Nathan. His clean-shaven face didn't damper his appeal. *Dammit.* "I'll let you know."

"I love you," Jack said.

"You too," I mumbled, watching Nathan descend the steps. Annoyingly, his retreating form looked just as good as his front. I blamed his tailor.

"I can feel you watching," he called back to me, jarring me from my trance.

I'd lost my hint of southern twang years ago, but Nathan kept his. And it did a number on me. My face heated. I took a quiet breath, slowly in for a three-count before letting it out for four. Religion wasn't a presence in my life, but I prayed my face would drain its red hue before Nathan saw it.

"You probably think everyone is looking at you." I headed down the stairs behind him, hoping I wouldn't trip again. "It doesn't make it true."

Nathan stood beside the front door, holding one arm out wide to the outside. I stopped on the last step, hesitating to walk through the door he held open.

"We're going to the same place, Bren."

"It's Brenna," I replied curtly.

Nathan smiled lazily. "Whatever you say, darlin'."

The way the word rolled off his tongue in that accent, I nearly whimpered.

"No. You're not calling me that." Someone would need to scrape me off the floor if he did.

"What's wrong with that?"

I shook my head. "Think of something else."

He gestured to the open doorway, ignoring my request.

"I was thinking about grabbing something to eat," I lied.

"You don't want to be late. My dad's lawyer is a real prick."

I narrowed my eyes and gestured toward the kitchen, where I could hear Mrs. Callahan washing dishes.

Nathan shrugged off my judgment. "She's been alive for eighty years. She saw the Berlin Wall fall. I think she can survive the word *prick*."

"It's called being respectful." I pushed past him into brisk morning air, walking faster than usual. Nathan's long legs gave him an advantage, but I refused to fall behind, to have to watch him for the next five minutes. "And Derek is not a prick."

Nathan fell into step beside me, easily closing the gap between us. "He's a lawyer."

"So? Do you want to be judged by the stereotypes of *your* career?"

Nathan ignored my question. "You haven't seen him in years. He could be an axe murderer for all you know."

I huffed out a breath. "You'd love that, wouldn't you?"

People liked to say men—unlike women—never held grudges. They fought, then left their shit in the dust. But it wasn't true. Some men held tight to their grudges, for seven years and counting.

After a minute of silence, Nathan asked, "So... you going to tell me about him?"

My head snapped his way. "What?"

"Mr. You Too. I assume that was him." He gestured to my left hand.

The last thing I wanted to do was talk about my love life with Nathan Sharpe. "Why do you care?"

"I'm being *polite*," he said, calling back to what I told him yesterday.

"You're being nosy. Being polite is asking how I'm doing, not—"

"*Who* you're doing?"

I coughed, nearly choking on the implication of sex.

He winced as it dawned on him how inappropriate his words were. "Sorry, I didn't—"

I waved away his attempt at an explanation. "Let's stick to silence."

We waited for a car to pass before crossing the main road. After another block of silence, we reached our destination—a small building, home to a chiropractor's practice and a law office. Nathan reached for the door at the same time as me. Our shoulders bumped, which pushed me to the side.

He grabbed my forearm to steady me, sending a bolt of electricity to my shoulder. *No*, I ordered my brain, *not again*.

"My bad." He dropped my arm as soon as I was upright.

I smoothed my hair. "It's fine."

When I stepped toward the building at the same time as Nathan again, he deftly avoided me.

"Go ahead," I said at the same time Nathan told me, "You go."

He sighed, running a hand through his chestnut hair and ruining the clean-cut image he'd tried to project for whatever reason. He stepped back and gestured me forward with one hand.

I didn't hesitate and walked through the double doors, turning toward the law office without a glance behind me.

The receptionist looked up as we entered. *Be right with you*, she mouthed, gesturing to her headset.

Behind me, Nathan's presence was palpable. I tried to ignore it by studying the office walls. Most were plain white, but one was filled with photographs of men in suits in various pursuits—shaking hands with clients, speaking in court, standing in front of the building in a smiling advertisement. Seeing Derek dressed to the nines and without a trace of the boyishness I remembered from high school was another reminder of how much time had passed.

And yet, everything that happened back then was a wound that hadn't fully healed.

Nathan leaned toward me, his breath hitting my neck, which sent a shiver down my spine. "Imagining the life you could have had?"

"No." I shrugged my shoulder to push him away. "I'm wondering whether these lawyers could get me a free pass if I decked you right now."

He chuckled. "One of these lawyers would do anything for you."

I sighed, aggravated now... as Nathan intended. "That was a long time ago."

"Some things change, some don't. You'll see."

Nathan didn't need to remind me. Nearly vaulting off the treadmill after seeing his stupidly handsome face in the mirror had made that crystal clear.

"If it isn't my favorite ex-girlfriend."

I turned at the sound of Derek's voice—not loud or obnoxious, but strong. Confident. Soothing. His voice had grown to match him.

"It's good to see you, B."

6

NATHAN

Now

I WANTED TO PUNCH the cocky, self-indulgent smile off his face.

His favorite ex-girlfriend? Who even says shit like that?

Brenna clearly didn't share my opinion in the slightest and flashed Derek a genuine smile. A smile she'd not given me, even though I held the same title as Derek. A few steps, and they were in each other's arms. I hung back, arms crossed, watching our past play out in the present.

For some fucking reason, my dad had chosen Derek as his lawyer. He claimed it was proximity and familiarity. It was bad form to trash the dead... but goddamn, I was furious with him for putting me in the position of seeing Brenna and Derek together.

I thought I'd prepared myself.

I was wrong.

"It's great to see you," Brenna said as they separated.

The words stung like a paper cut. I wondered how many more I'd endure on this trip. I took a deep breath, reminding myself I only needed to survive this meeting. Thirty minutes. Then I could get back to my life. Leave Brenna to her fiancée. Or to Derek. It didn't matter.

She continued beaming at him. "You look so different."

"Growing up will do that," I muttered under my breath.

To me, Derek hadn't changed. Light black skin, black hair buzzed close to his head. He'd grown a couple of inches and probably could hold his own in a fight now, but otherwise, Derek Ellis was the same fucking guy. He looked at Brenna like she'd lit up the sky, like he would do anything she asked.

He glanced at me, finally acknowledging that someone besides Brenna existed. Hatred simmered in his eyes. "And yet, you're still an insufferable ass."

"It's been a shitty few months." I used the dead dad card in the most shameful way I could. Call it penance for how Gordon Sharpe messed up our lives.

Derek's body went ramrod straight. "That was insensitive of me. I'm sorry for your loss, Nathan."

He'd always been the better man—smarter than me, more patient, kind. I'd wanted that for Brenna. Still did. She deserved to be treated well, but it would have been easier if the guy she dated right after me hadn't been so fucking *good*, more deserving of her than me.

"Should we go in?" Brenna asked Derek, continuing to ignore me.

He led us down the hall, passing several offices before entering a corner conference room. Derek's paralegal, Tiffany, already sat at the table with a stack of papers in front of her. She smiled shyly before telling me it was great to meet me and her dad was a big fan. I doubted her dad was a "big fan" of a Triple-A player on an out-of-state team, but I let myself pretend. At least someone in this room liked me.

"Based on what I know of your... history," Derek started, shuffling papers in front of him, "the terms Mr. Sharpe laid out might not be easy for either of you to hear."

I sighed dramatically. "Enough preamble. Just spit it out, Ellis."

"*Really,* Nathan?" Brenna snapped.

Derek pressed on, realizing how quickly this room could ignite thanks to our *history*. "Gordon left everything to both of you."

I leaned back in my chair. He watched me, no doubt waiting for a fiery reaction. Most family members would hit the roof if they didn't inherit it all, but I didn't *want* any relics of my painful past.

Brenna leaned forward, resting her elbows on the table, her caramel blond hair momentarily rushing into her face with the movement. "I don't understand."

Derek cleared his throat. His gaze shifted between Brenna and me. "Gordon left his house and his business to the two of you. After settling his affairs, there wasn't any cash left, though it would have been divided evenly as well."

His affairs. Best euphemism for gambling debt I'd ever heard.

Courtside Café had belonged to both of my parents until the divorce. Mom relinquished her rights to it when she couldn't stand to be in Middlebury any longer. Instead of selling it, he ran it alone. Maybe out of some misplaced idea that she would come back to him, though he never admitted it.

"To *both* of us?" Brenna repeated, staring into the distance.

I wanted to ask what she thought my father left to her during our walk this morning, but then I stuck my foot in my mouth. Clearly, she hadn't anticipated this outcome.

"Why would he do this?" she asked, looking to Derek for an answer.

I laughed humorlessly. "Because he's an ass."

My dad knew he was the reason my relationship with Brenna ended. He hadn't understood how we hadn't reconciled over the years, as if repairing a fractured relationship was so easy. With his multiple divorces, he should have known better than anyone.

Sometimes I thought he used my relationship with Brenna as a proxy for my relationship with him—something else irreparably ruined because of his selfish actions. And now, he had the last laugh, forcing his wishes on us in death after I'd ignored his prodding while he was alive.

"Nathan," Brenna hissed, an action reminiscent of when we'd been friends.

Derek and Tiffany looked at each other, probably wishing a hole would open beneath our feet to free them from this situation.

"Just because he's dead," I said finally, "it doesn't make it any less true."

I swallowed when Brenna turned her stare on me, unaccustomed to the full weight of her attention.

"What makes him an ass? That he didn't leave everything to you? Or that he left something to me?"

That he tethered us together, reminding me of what I lost and can never have again.

I ignored the question and turned to Derek. "Can I sign everything over to her?"

Brenna flinched. "It's... *your* childhood home, *your* family's business."

"I don't have a lot of good memories there," I said quietly. More accurately, every good memory was tainted and painful. Before Brenna could say anything more, I told Derek, "Just give her the house and the business."

The words pained me. I could use the money from selling them. Minor league pay paled in comparison to the major leagues, and my wages during the season funded my year-round life. I also didn't know how many seasons my arm had left. I'd been ignoring the real possibility of a torn labrum, which for pitchers was more than likely a career ender. When I'd strained it as a kid, physical therapy healed me. But this was worse. I'd been reticent to admit to myself that my baseball career could end because I didn't have a backup plan. This inheritance could've been a backup plan.

But I needed a clean break from her.

Derek sighed, sneaking a glance at Brenna. "The terms of the will are forfeit unless both of you remain owners."

"And if we don't?" Brenna asked.

"The house and business will be auctioned and proceeds will go to charity."

"Can we sell the house and the business together?" Brenna asked.

Derek had become Brenna's protector in high school when her life was turned upside down. I knew he'd use this as an excuse to take up that mantle again, regardless of the ring on her finger. She broke his heart at graduation, and here he was, willing to hand it back to her.

That had always been Brenna's power. People *wanted* to tell her their stories, their deepest secrets, things they never admitted to anyone. Because she cared, even about strangers. She didn't anxiously wait to turn conversations back to her. She liked to listen to people's problems, to help them. She put them at ease, made them comfortable enough to open up to her. Ironic, since she rarely opened up to anyone.

"You can't sell until April," Derek said.

Six months from now.

I turned to him, crossing my arms over my chest. "What's with the asinine rule?"

"Your father set it as a condition in the will."

I let out a string of curses as I launched out of my seat and walked to the window.

"So in six months, Nathan can sell me the house and the business?" Brenna was taking this remarkably well for someone who hated surprises.

I fought the instinct to turn toward her. Would she *want* the house and the business? There were just as many bad memories for her as there were for me.

"No. The only way for you to retain ownership is if Nathan does, but you could sell to a third party in April."

"Why?" I asked, returning to the table.

Derek pulled two envelopes out of his stack of papers. "Maybe these letters will explain. He didn't tell me why he did any of this, but he wanted you to have these." He handed one to Brenna and slid the other across the table to me.

Brenna slipped the envelope into her purse, but I immediately ripped mine open, needing to understand why he'd force us into a past neither of us wanted to revisit.

Inside was my father's messy scrawl in black marker. Three lines. Fourteen words.

I AM FIXING WHAT I BROKE.
I LOVE YOU, SON.
DON'T REPEAT MY MISTAKES.

7

NATHAN

Eight years ago

My body sagged in relief when I spotted Brenna behind home plate.

She turned at the sound of the fence opening, and her face broke into a bright smile. It faltered when she took in my expression. She wrapped her arms around me, resting her head on my shoulder. My hands settled in the back pocket of her jean shorts, her breath whooshing out at the contact.

Her reaction to me would never get old.

I hoped it would always remain this way.

"They're fighting again," I whispered. Four weeks since coming back from baseball camp, and the tension between my parents simmered. At first, they'd limited arguments to when they thought I was asleep. Tonight, they didn't wait.

Brenna tensed but kept holding me tightly. "I'm sorry, Nate. Did you hear what they were saying?"

When the yelling started, I texted Brenna that I needed her, and she appeared without question. I took a deep breath, filling my lungs with the familiar, comforting scent of honey and peach. Brenna had carved a spot in my life when she became my neighbor, but now it was more than that. I had no idea why it took so long to figure out I was in love with her, but since admitting it to myself, there was no going back. Brenna owned my heart.

"I think my dad cheated on my mom."

She pulled back to look me in the eye, sliding her hands down my arms until they clasped mine, her eyes widening with surprise. "What? Why do you think that?"

"I heard bits and pieces, and my mom kept referencing a *she*. What else could that mean? They've been weird since I got back. Maybe he met someone over the summer? You were here, did you notice anything?"

Brenna worked at my parent's café, and my dad coached the summer league team we usually played on together. She saw him more than anyone, because my mom was with me. A car honked loudly, and Brenna jumped, turning toward the noise. There wasn't a sound that wouldn't startle her.

When she turned back, her lips were drawn together. I hadn't kissed them since this morning, after we turned off our street on the way to school. Sometimes I thought my parents knew about us, but they hadn't said anything. Too consumed with their own shit. Ordinarily, my mom would have cornered and questioned me. She'd teased me about Brenna's crush when we were kids, back when I thought kissing was gross.

Now, I barely thought of anything else.

Thoughts of my complicated home life left as I pulled Brenna toward me again. She rewarded me with one of those smiles that did me in. I kissed her with every emotion—gratitude, fear, amazement, love, desire—rushing through me. Her lips moved frantically against mine. She was as desperate for me as I was for her.

I would never get over the way she made me feel.

A chuckle escaped my lips as I dragged them away from hers. "And to think, how long we could have been doing that if—"

"If you weren't such a dumbass?" She laughed, leaning forward until her forehead rested on mine.

"I'm sorry *who's* the dumbass?" I playfully shoved her back.

Her hair flew behind her like a cape. Brenna motioned to herself with both hands—a taunt. "Can't wait to hear what's worse than waiting *years* to kiss."

On second thought... "You thought you weren't the kind of girl I would date."

"No," she said, raising a finger. "I said I wasn't the kind of girl you were *expected* to date. Do you see the looks I get when we walk down the hall together?"

I scoffed. "We've always walked down the hall together, Quinn."

"Not hand-in-hand."

"There's nothing anyone could say that will change how I feel about you."

Brenna's lips quirked into a half smile. She was still shy when I expressed my feelings. I stared into those eyes that had gone soft at my admission, wanting her to see how much I meant my words.

"You'll always have me, Nathan." She gripped my hand tighter. "No matter what happens."

The underlying meaning of those words didn't go unnoticed—something bad *could* happen—but I didn't want to focus on it. Not while I had my best friend here, the person I loved more than anyone in the world.

"Do you need to get back home?"

She shook her head. "My mom isn't there." She paused a moment, weighing her next words. "Do you... would you want to come over?" She chewed the side of her lip. We hadn't talked about our different experience levels. I wanted to go back to her room and pick up where we'd left off moments ago, but I didn't want to rush her. We had all the time in the world.

"Obviously, yes." I flung an arm around her shoulder, tugging her to my side. "But I had something else in mind for tonight, if you're up for it."

She peeked up at me. "Is it what I think it is?"

I grinned at her. "What do you think?"

"But... you don't even like that tradition."

We momentarily moved away from each other to leave the diamond.

"I never said that."

"You're always like, *Come on, Quinn, let's go home and watch the game*," she said, her voice a poor imitation of mine.

I huffed out a laugh. "I thought maybe now we're dating, you'd lay off me."

"Keep dreaming," she said in a sing-song tone. "Seriously, we don't have to go. I'm supposed to be making you feel better."

"You already have. And maybe I want to see if I like this tradition more now..."

"Now that we can kiss?"

Brenna and I walked two blocks to the only convenience store in town. We were frequent fliers, especially during the hot southern summer. She opted for her usual strawberry slushy, and I stuck to peach lemonade. We sucked down our drinks on the short walk to Brenna's favorite spot in town, a small pedestrian bridge over a creek. For the rest of the night, we sat side by side, legs swinging off the bridge, talking about nothing and everything.

Here, with only the two of us, I could pretend nothing else existed.

8

BRENNA

NATHAN'S EYES WERE GLUED to the piece of paper in front of him, the last words from his father.

"When did he change his will?" I whispered to Derek.

It couldn't have always been this way; Molly must have been included once. Gordon had thought Molly was his daughter for the first half of her life, until my mother asked for a divorce. When he sued for custody, she revealed Molly wasn't his biologically. He wanted her anyway, but the courts sided with Kathy. She claimed she didn't know who fathered Molly, but I didn't believe her.

"To add me, I mean."

"Six months ago."

When Gordon got sick.

I hadn't known he was sick, and at the funeral, I learned I wasn't the only one. By the time Gordon found out about his diagnosis, treatment options were limited. He opted to quietly tie up his affairs in the time he had left rather than put his body through treatment with low odds.

And this—Nathan and me taking over his house and business—was his dying wish.

"We can sell in six months," I said, addressing Nathan. "We'll hire someone to clean out the house and fix it up. Same with the café. It'll take a few days to arrange everything, then we can both go home and deal with the rest by email."

Derek cleared his throat. "You can't. Gordon stipulated that any efforts to flip the house or business would need to be directly overseen by the owners."

Owners. Nathan *and* me.

Gordon made me a co-owner with his son—my childhood best friend, my first love, the boy who shattered my heart. I'd cried myself to sleep every night when our relationship ended. Running was the only time my thoughts didn't succumb to sadness, because I was too focused on trying to breathe to remember Nathan was no longer in my life.

"Jesus Christ," Nathan muttered. "This keeps getting better."

"Derek, how is this legal?"

Derek rested a hand on my forearm. I tried—and failed—to ignore Nathan's eyes tracking his movements. It transported me back to dinners with the two of them death-glaring across the table during senior year of high school.

"You can fight it if you want, but it'll be expensive and take longer than dealing with the stipulations."

Move back to Middlebury for six months and leave Molly to fend for herself or give up ownership and the possibility of getting enough money to fight my mom for custody of her. I couldn't leave Molly to fend for herself again, but I also didn't know how long I could live with Kathy Quinn. Pause my life while I built a case against her.

Relive the emotional torture of growing up with my mom.

"I don't know if I can stay here," I said finally after untangling my mess of thoughts.

"Can't stand being parted from Mr. You Too?" Nathan asked.

I hadn't even been sure he'd been listening these last few minutes.

I wasn't about to bring Molly into this conversation. She'd always been a sensitive topic. Instead, I answered, "I have responsibilities I can't leave behind. Not all of us have offseasons."

Nathan scoffed. "Look, I don't want to be stuck in this situation either. I want to be back in Houston tonight... but that's a lot of money to turn down."

My heart squeezed at yet another reminder he wanted to be through with me as soon as possible. Even though it was better this way. Nothing good could come from the two of us being in the same place.

"You want to work... together?" My voice wobbled.

"What choice do we have?" Nathan shrugged, unaffected. I hated that I couldn't hide the way he affected me. "I'll reschedule my flight to tomorrow morning. If I don't hear from you tonight"—he turned his attention from me to Derek—"this mess is all yours to deal with."

"I hope you stay," Derek said, his gaze locked on me. It was partly to get under Nathan's skin, but I also detected truth, surprising given the way we ended. Like Nathan said, *Some things change, some don't.*

"Are there any more bullshit conditions you haven't told us about, Ellis?" Nathan asked.

Derek shared a nervous glance with Tiffany.

"Just one."

"Are you all right?" Derek asked me as soon as we were alone.

Nathan had stormed out of the conference room after learning we'd also inherited four cats from his father. If we agreed to the inheritance, Derek would arrange to have the cats brought from their foster homes to *our* house. It was the last straw for Nathan and sent him from the room, muttering about how fucked this entire situation was.

"I'm okay." I forced a smile, but Derek's frown deepened. I must not have been convincing. "Mostly just in shock. This isn't at all what I expected."

"I wish I could have given you a heads-up about what you were walking into but—"

"No, I get it." I lifted my hand to silence him. "I might not have come here if you'd told me."

He nodded, assuming as much.

"I always knew you'd make a great lawyer."

I still remembered the day he approached me in the lunchroom after transferring to Middlebury High School. He'd found me at my lowest point, my loneliest, but he didn't hesitate when I told him he'd do better sitting somewhere else. He took that seat over and over again, persisting even when I barely gave him anything to work with. He slowly helped me return to a sense of normalcy amid my devastating heartbreak.

"*Great* might be overselling it. But I'll do anything I can to help you."

"Yeah?"

"Of course," he said, nodding. "But there's not much I can do. My hands are tie—"

"There's something else." I rushed to speak, relieved to have a sounding board. "I want custody of Molly. My mom is a mess. I've been living with them for three months, trying to collect evidence to prove she's unfit. She wasn't taking care of her, Derek. Molly deserves better. *I* can give her better."

He ran a hand over his face. "Courts don't like taking kids from their parents."

"I know… I know," I said, my gaze falling to my folded hands on the conference room table. "That's why… I mean, it will help if I have a house and a business… or more money to show the court I can provide, right?"

"You have to prove you're the better option," he agreed. "Not just emotionally, but also materially."

"Then I've gotta stay."

"I'm sorry." He sighed. "I know how hard this will be for you. If there's anything you need, I'm here, all right?"

"Thank you." It would help to have an ally and friend as I undertook this project.

As soon as I got back to my room at the B&B, I stripped off my clothes and settled into bed to eat takeout and watch daytime soaps. I waited a couple of hours before texting Nathan, making him sweat my decision.

> **Brenna**
>
> I'm going to accept the inheritance.

His reply didn't take long.

> **Nathan**
>
> Meet me at the house tomorrow at 10 am.

I flopped back on the bed, my breath whooshing out of me. I hoped I wasn't making a huge mistake.

NATHAN

Now

Twenty-four Hart Drive was untouched by time.

The unassuming two-story house with gray siding, black shutters, and a bright red door held so many memories. So did the house next door, where Brenna used to live. Aside from the fading red brick, it also matched the house of my memories.

I didn't understand why my dad never left Middlebury. Maybe he wanted to remain haunted by everything he'd screwed up in his life. I shook my head at the thought before using the key Ellis gave me to enter the house.

It was like stepping back in time—same furniture, same painted walls, same wall art. Some of our family pictures had been replaced by more recent photos that didn't include my mom. My dad lived in a tomb of our old lives. It *almost* made me feel bad for him.

The door swung open behind me.

"You're late," I grumbled without even turning.

"Wow, this place is the—"

"Same," I cut her off. "I know. We have our work cut out for us."

For a minute, Brenna wordlessly assessed the space. I wondered if she had the same sinking feeling in her gut as I did in mine. When she turned to me, our eyes met, and my gut sank even further as we stood there in the remnants of our childhoods.

Brenna's presence hung over every inch of this place. Her home life had never been steady. Her mom worked inconsistently—to excess when things were going well, and not at all when something went off the tracks. That *something* often had to do with whatever undeserving man she let into her life... and Brenna's.

My parents loved Bren and had opened their home to her. She always hated it when she had to leave.

"Well, I'm here. As commanded." She crossed her arms over her chest. "I assume you have a plan?"

I fought the urge to respond to the *as commanded* comment—I didn't need distractions from the topic at hand—and cleared my throat. "Divide and conquer. One of us takes the business, the other the house."

After a sleepless night, this was the best I could come up with to accomplish our goals without losing my mind. We couldn't sell the properties for six months, but if I had anything to say about it, I'd leave Middlebury in three. Even if a sale couldn't go through, we could still look for buyers while Brenna and I returned to lives hundreds of miles away from each other.

A safe distance.

"Fine," she said.

Still as agreeable as when we'd been best friends. *Go along to get along.* Having a mother like Kathy Quinn made rolling with circumstances a necessary skill.

"I worked at the café more than you, so I'll take the business."

Leaving me with this fucking house. It made sense, but I didn't have to like it.

"Fine," I echoed her, squaring my shoulders. "But we both have to meet with my dad's girlfriend who used to run the place. She's expecting us in"—I glanced at my watch—"forty minutes."

"*Forty* minutes? Nathan, I'm not dressed for a business meeting, and with traffic, it'll take at least thirty-five—"

"You look goo—I mean fine. You look fine." I cringed. *Jesus fucking Christ.* Ten minutes with her, and I was already making an ass out of myself.

She pointed to the T-shirt beneath her zip-up hoodie. The design included the text *Talk Sports to Me* and the image of a girl with her finger over her lips surrounded by different sports balls. "Did you not notice what's on my shirt, Nathan? It's hardly professional."

How did she expect me to answer that? *Yes, of course, I noticed because the words are written across your chest, which I couldn't ignore if I tried.*

I rolled my eyes and suppressed a smile. "I can't believe you still have it."

She blinked. She either hadn't expected me to remember or forgot she got that shirt in high school. Brenna's T-shirt collection was so large, she ran out of drawers and had to hang them in her closet. Every time her mom complained that she never tried, Brenna doubled down by buying more T-shirts.

I wouldn't want her any other way.

Shit, I'm screwed.

"Did you know he had a girlfriend?" she asked, bringing the conversation back to easy waters.

"Yeah," I said on an exhale, drawing the word out. "She's... an experience. You'll see. Anyway, we should get going. Where are you staying, by the way?"

Brenna hiked her purse higher on her shoulder and followed me to the door. "Derek has an extra room. He said I could crash with him."

My footsteps halted. "You're not staying with Ellis."

Watching him put his hands on her yesterday had been almost more than I could stand. Thinking about her living with him... *for months...*

She narrowed her eyes. "Why not?"

Fuck. This was why having Brenna in my life wouldn't work. I lost all sense of myself, rattled by her mere presence. Stuck reliving memories, rendered speechless by her breathtaking beauty, fuming with jealousy. This was why I needed to keep my distance.

But I wouldn't be able to concentrate on what we needed to do if she went home to Derek Ellis every night.

I didn't need her to suspect my jealousy and make this situation even more awkward. Scrambling for an excuse, I said, "We can get more done if we stay here together. You want to get out of here as quickly as I do, right?"

Brenna flinched. She still wore every emotion on her face.

"And I can't imagine Mr. You Too would be happy with you living with your ex."

Her eyebrows rose. "But he'd be fine if I live with *you*?"

"I hardly count."

Not true, my mind rebelled. Brenna and I dated for only a couple of months, but our connection spanned years, before and after. We couldn't rewrite our history, but maybe we could ignore it.

Brenna turned her back on me and ignored my comment. "I'll stay at the B&B."

"Mrs. Callahan is heading down to Florida tomorrow for the rest of winter."

"How do you know that?"

I smirked. "She told me at the dinner you skipped because you were embarrassed about falling off the treadmill."

Her gaze fell to the floor, studying it, as if something there caught her attention. She didn't retort as expected. My strategy to get through this required her to be on the same page as me, and she wasn't playing along.

"I don't know if I want to stay here." Her voice was thick with emotion as she fiddled with the strap of her purse.

And dammit if her emotions didn't put a massive crack in the front I put on around her.

My hand landed on her elbow before I could give it a second thought. The barest of contact, not even skin to skin, and my body screamed for more. Brenna's eyes tracked my hand before slowly making their way to my face.

Time stood still. I waited for her gaze to lock with mine.

When it did, all the air was sucked out of the room. Brenna's chocolate brown eyes held a softness I hadn't seen since we'd reunited. I hadn't had a chance to study her closely like this. My eyes hungrily took the opportunity to reacquaint themselves with their favorite view.

Her throat bobbed.

Such dangerous territory we navigated.

"Neither do I," I said finally before opening the front door and gesturing her out. "But we'll have to do a lot we don't want to do in these next few months."

I was less worried about what I'd have to do. The single thought in my mind was what I *wanted* to do but couldn't.

10

BRENNA

THE NEIGHBORHOOD SURROUNDING THE Courtside Café vibrated with activity—residents leaving condos in small expensive cars, pedestrians frequenting newly opened stores and restaurants, the cacophony of a city bursting around us.

And there our business sat, exactly as I remembered it. Gordon either had a fixation on the past or he was very, very lazy.

"Palmer City has changed," I mused, looking in all directions as I walked beside Nathan.

I didn't know how I expected him to respond, but it wasn't with silence. Though after our *moment*, I shouldn't have been surprised. Nathan had filled the car ride with a baseball podcast, saving us from having to talk. Not that I digested a damn word. I was too focused on replaying how Nathan's eyes had roamed over my face in a way that was anything but appropriate.

But now, the silence wrapping around us provoked my insecurity. When I was younger, I assumed silence meant the other person found me uninteresting or weird. That they would rather be anywhere but in my presence. That I was *lacking*. Therapy helped me realize I created the narrative, and it likely didn't exist. All part of feeling more deeply than people who weren't HSPs. I now recognized my thought patterns and could combat them... most of the time.

Not today.

"Do you remember how this street was so empty, we'd play catch on our breaks?"

Nathan and I both worked at the café in high school because it accommodated our baseball schedule. It forced me out of my comfort zone. I'd hated it at the time, but it helped me become more comfortable making conversation with people I didn't know. Nathan liked working there far less than me. He agreed to work only when I was there.

"No. I don't." He opened the café door.

Our new business was already unlocked, and Gordon's girlfriend stood inside, arms crossed, foot tapping, as if we were late. Her sharp-angled face, piercing blue eyes, and thin impatient lips added to an intimidating sight. Surreptitiously, I glanced at Nathan, but I couldn't read his expression.

"Well, if it isn't the prodigal son," she crooned in lieu of hello.

So this is how it's going to be.

Nathan matched her stance, squaring for battle. Quickly, I stepped to her and stuck out my hand, desperate to cool the rising tension.

"I'm Brenna Quinn," I said, my hand still lingering in the air.

The woman clucked her tongue. "I know who you are. Who your *mother* is."

I dropped my hand, a wave of shame rolling over me. I shuffled to the side, wishing I could blend in with the walls, away from her appraising gaze.

Lacking, my brain chanted.

"Don't talk to her like that," Nathan said.

My eyes snapped to his, but his focus remained entirely on the woman. "How did you get in here?"

"How do you think?" The woman, who still hadn't told us her name, shook a ring of keys, jangling them loudly in the surprisingly quiet space. The lack of noise from the street had to say something about the sturdiness of the building. "I used *my* key. I've been running this place for the past year."

Gordon had never mentioned this woman, but her protective feelings toward him and this place were unmistakable. Maybe she resented that he hadn't left the business to her, opting instead to pass it to his less-than-present son and a random girl who used to live next door. Anyone would struggle to adjust to the loss of their significant other and livelihood in one fell swoop.

I tried again. "It looks great," I said, my gaze wandering over the space.

The sportcentric inside of the café hadn't changed. A basketball hoop hung in one corner of the room. A baseball dangling from the ceiling in the center of the café looked as if it had been hit by a baseball player painted on a wall. A quarterback painted in another corner had a football cocked behind his shoulder, ready to throw. And the Palmer City Wolves had a wall of pictures with a replica hockey goal for people to pose in front of for photos.

"Not all of us need the newest, latest thing." The woman waved a hand, her gesture a knock against the bustling neighborhood. "Some things should be kept the same for posterity."

Nathan scoffed, motioning around the room. "I'm surprised my dad never sold this place to pay his gambling debts."

"He wasn't gambling this past year," she retorted. "He was too busy dying."

"I'm well aware." Nathan remained stoic, unfazed by this interaction. Meanwhile, my gut tangled itself in knots. "You weren't the only one here, Allison."

"You came home?" The words shot out of my mouth before I could stop them.

It had broken Nathan, watching his father's affair with my mom tear his family apart. But the worst part was the deep stab of betrayal from the man he'd revered, who had been his biggest supporter. The man who took Nathan to pitching lessons and tossed baseballs in the batting cage. The agony of not being able to understand why *he* wasn't enough for his father to stay away from my mom.

I knew the feeling all too well, having wondered time and again how my mom could prioritize subpar men over me.

"Not to his home," the woman—Allison—jumped in. "*My* home. I opened my home to Gordon."

Nathan ignored her and responded to me. "He's my dad."

"But you said yesterday…"

"That he's an ass? Both can be true, Bren."

I needed him to stop using my nickname. Every time he did, my mind surfaced another time he'd used it. Laughing while he showed me some stupid trick with a baseball, like rolling it up one arm and down the other. Intently staring at me, memorizing my face before placing his lips on mine. Sharply hissing my name from the mound to get my attention on the field.

All of it was too much.

"He never mentioned you came home."

Not that Gordon and I talked about Nathan, not recently. In the early years after Nathan and I fell apart, I would ask, *How's he doing?* Eventually, I learned the answer never felt good.

Nathan's eyes narrowed. "Why would he tell you?"

Allison cut in, a smug smile gracing her lips. "Gordon talked to her more than he talked to you. Didn't you know?" The remaining words were left unspoken. *Didn't you wonder why she was in the will?*

Nathan stared at me, and I could see gears turning in his mind while he tried to make sense of this revelation.

"We kept in touch after... after the divorce. The one from my mom." With a shrug, I added, "I kept him updated on Molly, let them chat when I could. Holidays, mostly."

Nathan's father was the only person who understood the pain of losing Nathan. There was a time I needed to talk about my devastation, to come to terms with my new normal. I wished I had a mother who would listen to me, who wouldn't judge me, but since I didn't, I found a substitute. A man who I partially blamed for Nathan's loss. Beggars couldn't be choosers.

"You just couldn't leave him alone," Allison said. "You forced him to feel the pain over and over."

"That's not what I was doing... or what I meant to do..." I rambled, biting the inside of my lip to hide a swell of emotion.

"You got yourself a house and a business out of it. Hope it was worth it."

"Because this is what dreams are made of?" Nathan took a step forward and gestured around the room. "This *thriving* business? A house full of useless crap."

"No one forced you to accept it," Allison said coldly. "Just... walk away."

"We don't need to justify ourselves to you." Nathan turned his back on Allison and stared out to the street. "Now if you're done with this melodrama, we can get to the real reason we're here."

"You ungrateful—" Allison hissed before I blocked out the sound.

"I need to step outside for a moment," I managed to say, fighting a sick feeling in my stomach.

I didn't wait for them to respond—had no idea if they even did—before striding to the door. Once outside, I heaved in a breath, feeling the weight on my chest lessen. Leaning against the building, I closed my eyes and started a breathing exercise to slow my racing heart. Inhaled for two seconds, exhaled for four, paying attention to how the release of breath untangled the tension in my limbs.

Feeling too much sucked sometimes.

"Hey, are you all right?" A perky feminine voice came from my right.

My eyes snapped open. A pregnant woman whose belly seemed on the verge of bursting stood outside the business next door. Her pink apron, covered in specks of flour, popped against her dark skin. Beneath it, she wore black leggings and an oversized white tank top. Her hair was pinned above her head, strands falling out of a haphazard bun. *Hidden Gem Bakery* read the sign above her head.

"I'm Gemma." She gestured behind her. "I own the bakery."

"Brenna." I let out a nervous laugh, turning to look behind me. Nathan and Allison still stood in the same spots. "I guess I own the café here."

"I was wondering when this place would be scooped up," she chirped, her hands finding their way to her bump. "It's an amazing location."

"It's different than I remember. I grew up here but haven't been back in years."

Gemma's smile brightened her friendly face. "Well, if you ever want to talk about how tough it is being a small business owner or to gossip… or whatever really, I'm here. And I have sweets."

"Thanks—" My voice cut off when Nathan burst through the door.

"We're leaving." He tossed the words over his shoulder, not breaking stride.

Gemma's eyes widened. Hers had been the most comforting presence I'd experienced in days. That must have been the explanation for what I said next. "I'm going to stay."

Nathan's steps hesitated as he half turned to face me. "Are you sure?" he asked, his voice less brusque than a moment before. At my nod, he said, "I'll see you at ho—" He caught himself and violently shook his head once. "Later."

I watched him leave, wondering what happened between him and Allison. I had enough self-preservation instinct not to follow and ask.

Gemma whistled after Nathan moved out of earshot. "That man is *fine*. Good work, girl."

Relief flooded through me at seeing rings on her finger.

Not that it mattered. Nathan could do what he wanted with whoever he wanted, but I didn't want to see it.

"Oh, he's not… we're not…" I rushed to clarify. She eyed my engagement ring. "I'm with someone else."

Her eyebrows rose. "You know, I just took a batch of brownies out of the oven, if you want to come in."

"That's the best invitation I've had in days."

Gemma opened the door to the bakery for me. "I can already tell we're going to be good friends."

11

BRENNA

Now

MY PHONE RANG AS I climbed up the porch steps.

The call I'd dreaded all day.

I sighed deeply, wishing I could ignore it. After the fight at the café this morning, talking with Gemma for hours, and dinner with Derek, my social battery was depleted.

But this conversation with Jack couldn't be avoided. He was supposed to pick me up from O'Hare about now. I texted earlier to tell him I wouldn't be on the flight and said it'd be easier to talk by phone.

And apparently, now was the first break in his busy day. I dropped onto the steps, feeling cold seep through my jeans.

"Hey, Jack."

"Brenna." His tone was clipped. "I'm not bothering you, am I?"

I fought a sigh. "No, of course not. Sorry, this trip has been... a lot. I didn't expect—"

Jack cut me off. "What happened? What's keeping you from our plans?"

I swallowed hard. I knew he'd be upset I wasn't coming to Chicago. We hadn't seen each other in person in more than a month, and during that time, our communication in general had tapered. Sometimes, it didn't feel like I was even in a relationship, more on my own than supported by a partner. I wished Jack could see this wasn't easy on me, but he placed the blame for our separation solely at my feet. And now with this canceled trip, he couldn't see beyond how it affected him.

"It's a long story." I launched into a recap of the will reading and the stipulations Gordon placed on the inheritance. I spared no detail, except that I was living in the same house as my first love and hanging around with another ex-boyfriend. It wasn't as if I had much choice in the matter.

"Just say *no*," Jack responded as soon as I finished my explanation.

"What?"

"You don't need a house or a business in your hometown, so say you don't want them and be done with it."

"I can't," I blurted out but then remembered Jack didn't know about my long-term plans for Molly. "I mean, the money would be helpful, you know... with my family."

"You're staying with them until they're back on their feet. That's what you said."

The massive guilt—that I was letting Jack down, that I was withholding information he'd hate—settled in the pit of my stomach. He deserved the truth. He deserved someone who would be there for him, someone committed to building a future with him. This was why I'd needed to go to Chicago in the first place, to talk to him about our relationship. His disappointment in me, my unhappiness.

It was easier to have it out on the phone thousands of miles apart, but I owed him more. I agreed to marry him. I committed to him. I took that seriously. I wanted to give us one last shot at getting back to a good place. We'd been good once. He pushed me out of my comfort zone. He helped me come alive when I was struggling. He'd made me happy, but now the guilt over not being enough crowded out those good feelings.

I bit my lip, willing my emotions to remain under control. "This would help them get on their feet *faster*."

"How long, Brenna?"

I opened my mouth to answer, but apparently, the question was rhetorical.

"How long are you going to prioritize every other person over me? I am your *fiancé*. I deserve more than a couple of text messages and a call a week. Don't blame my job or your job. You would make time if it was important to you."

My lip wobbled. "I know. I'm sorry. I'm just overwhelmed. I never meant to hurt you, Jack. Please believe me."

"It'd be easier to believe if I knew when you were coming home. Can you tell me that?"

I couldn't, especially not with this new wrinkle. I wasn't sure how long I needed to stay in Middlebury, something I still had to tell my mom and Molly. They didn't expect me back for a few days, so I kept putting it off. Mom would want to know how they'd get by without my income, who would take over the chores, drive Molly to hockey practice, something I signed her up for when I moved in.

I was letting every single person in my life down.

Even today at the café, I wasn't able to back up Nathan with Allison. Their argument had me retreating to a less emotionally draining location. For all my work, all my strategies, I still failed at the most basic of human interaction and relationships.

"We need space, Brenna," Jack said after a minute of silence. "*I* need space. To figure out what I want. You should do the same."

"Okay," I whispered, relief washing over me that this fight was ending and I'd have a reprieve from the discomfort of our relationship.

Jack let out a heavy sigh. I'd said the wrong thing. I didn't say what he wanted to hear.

"I'm sorry," I said immediately, hating the feel of his pain.

Jack ended the call.

12

NATHAN

Now

By the time Brenna walked through the front door of the house, I was well into my third beer and the Palmer City Wolves had a 1–0 lead in the second period.

Seven fucking hours after I left her outside the café.

If she'd come home sooner, she would have found me hard at work, sorting through my childhood bedroom, reliving the happy years before everything went to hell. The shitshow of a conversation with Allison had motivated me to get to work. The quicker I worked, the sooner I could leave.

"I didn't know you were a hockey fan." Brenna came into the room and parked herself on the large comfy chair in the corner. She curled her legs into a pretzel, apparently still her preferred position for relaxation. I took note of her puffy eyes, but the last person she'd want to confide in was me.

I shrugged. "I like it enough. It's the only game on right now. But we don't have to watch—"

"No... I want to watch," she said quickly. "I've been watching games with Molly. My sister."

"I know who Molly is."

Brenna inhaled sharply. "Right."

Molly had been a sensitive issue between us from the time her mom became pregnant to our last conversation at her high school graduation. We thought we shared a half-sibling—it was years later we learned it wasn't true—and Brenna resented me for keeping my distance.

When I grew up and realized how badly I'd bungled the entire situation, I understood her anger. It wasn't Molly's fault she was born into a messed-up family. I should've put my feelings aside and understood that bonding with someone I thought was my sister didn't mean I was being disloyal to my mom.

But I was a kid. I screwed up.

Brenna said she'd never forgive me for it, and I didn't blame her.

"Are you... okay?" I asked, unable to take the silence or resist my need to know who hurt her. Every limb in her body was locked with tension. For so long, having her back was my role, and it was hard to shed the protective feelings.

Brenna let out a watery breath. "No." Her voice was barely audible over the goal horn on the TV.

I muted the volume. "What's wrong?"

She shook her head. "You don't have to ask me. I know you don't care."

My head fell back, resting on top of the couch cushion as I let out a pained sigh. "Not caring about you has never been a problem. Talk to me, Bren."

"I-I'm a disappointment," she choked out, fighting to swallow a sob. "I can't be what everyone needs me to be. Someone always gets hurt because I'm too weak to manage it all. And I feel guilt... all the time for letting the people I care most about down. I'm so... tired."

"Hey," I said, leaning forward, resting my elbows on my knees. Brenna didn't turn. "Listen to me, all right? You're not disappointing me, Bren. You got that?"

The words *I couldn't do this without you* sat on my tongue, but I didn't offer them to her. They would complicate this situation more than the sudoku puzzle it already was.

Brenna nodded into her knees, her legs pulled into her body. Those sad brown eyes killed me. Whatever we were—friends, lovers, enemies, strangers—it would never matter. I would always have this instinct to comfort her. It was why it was so difficult to be around her after our relationship fell apart. I was furious at her, and so hurt, and every step of the way, I had to remind myself to hold onto those feelings. Because if I didn't, my innate need to protect her would consume me, would push out all logical thought.

We watched the rest of the game in silence. The Wolves scored a few more goals. Brenna's breathing gradually evened out. I was inching forward on the couch, preparing to stand, when Brenna broke the silence.

"Are you going to tell me what happened with Allison?"

Are you going to tell me where you've been? I swallowed the question I had no right to ask. Asking it might disrupt the copacetic vibe that, by some miracle, had settled between us.

I fell back on the couch, keeping my eyes on the screen. "Nothing that hasn't happened before."

"She was *such* a bitch."

Bren was one of the kindest, most forgiving people I'd ever known, but she had a line. When someone crossed it, she revealed a usually hidden side. The other side of the line might as well exist in another dimension for how far it sent a person from her good graces. I knew better than anyone.

I swiveled my head toward her, still leaning against the couch cushion. "Because she didn't shake your hand?"

"All of it." Then she added, "She said I made your dad's life worse by keeping in touch with him."

"I heard what she said."

"Do you... think she was right?"

I turned my gaze back to the TV, needing a break from her sad, guilt-ridden eyes. "Hell if I know. I didn't even know y'all were still in touch."

Brenna blew out a breath. "I hated what he did, but your dad was the only person who understood how it felt to lose you. He didn't make me feel bad for missing you."

Her voice was low, tentative. It couldn't have been easy for her to admit this. I wasn't sure why she did.

I shifted in my seat, wanting to jump out of my skin at the reminder that I hurt her. If there were ever a sign I never deserved her, it was this. She could still access the feelings of friendship and love for me after I purposefully hurt her, time and time again. And back then, I couldn't even manage to find any of my feelings for her beneath the boiling rage consuming every thought.

Brenna continued, "Even though my mom would've killed me if she knew, I wanted to help him stay in touch with Molly. I knew how I would feel losing my sister. I thought I was helping."

I clicked the TV off and set down the remote. "You shouldn't let Allison get to you."

"So I should follow your example?"

There she is.

"What did she say to make you storm out of the café?"

"It doesn't matter. We're going to have to learn to ignore her, all right?"

"What? Why?"

"She's going to work with us to reopen the café." This was why I stormed out on Allison. Rather than transfer her knowledge, she blackmailed me to give her a job in exchange for help. All because my father *left her with nothing*. Not surprising, but fucking infuriating all the same.

Brenna launched out of her seat. "Nathan, you can't leave me alone with her. I know we agreed on divide and conquer, but that was before—"

"I know," I cut her off. Allison would eat Brenna alive if I left them alone. I knew it before Brenna came home twisted in knots over a couple of snide comments. My dad's girlfriend was not a nice person. If I hadn't already suspected she stuck it out with my dad to get the business, I did now.

"We'll have to pull double duty. Café during the day, house at night." Because my life wasn't fucked enough—Brenna Quinn would haunt my days and my nights, and I had no idea how to survive it.

She nodded, looking the picture of defeat—shoulders drooped, lips in a tight thin line, forehead creased. "Okay."

Her less-than-enthusiastic response twisted the knife deeper.

Her right hand reached for her left forearm, and she held it across her body. "Allison said you came back... at the end. I'm sorry. That must have been hard."

Hard was an understatement. My father moved in with Allison in his final months. I visited as much as I could between games. There'd been a wedge between my dad and me since high school. We talked periodically and saw each other on holidays—never in Middlebury—but we never got back to the closeness from before he betrayed my mom. It all fell away at the end though. And it hurt, to lose him. He was a flawed man, but he was my dad and I loved him.

"I gather he never told you."

She shook her head. "No, and with everything going on those last few months, we hadn't been in touch. I tried a couple of times, but we never connected."

"It's not your fault. He wanted to go quietly. We had time, in the end... to just watch baseball like we did when I was a kid. It was as nice as it could be, I guess." I stood from the couch and motioned to the stairs. "I'm going to head to bed. I moved your bag into my dad's room. Probably not your first choice, but I changed the sheets and aired it out this afternoon. He turned the old guest room into an office. And obviously, I'll be in my room."

She nodded. "Okay, thanks."

"Oleander's is in the fridge."

Her eyes grew wide. "But you hate Oleander's."

Like a fucking jackass, I ordered from Brenna's favorite diner because I knew how today must've affected her. She stepped out of the café because of our fighting. Extreme emotions were always hard for her. I thought the food would lift her spirits.

And then she didn't come home. I didn't want to think about where she'd gone.

I tapped the wall with an open palm. "It was convenient. And it was better than I remembered."

One day with her back in my life, and I was already feeling my control slip. With that thought in mind, I headed to my room and continued sorting through my stuff, desperate to complete our work as quickly as possible, to put the woman downstairs behind me for good.

***

I slept like shit, tossing and turning all night, waking up and falling back to sleep at half-hour clips.

I waited until a decent hour to call my mom—four a.m. my time, but nine a.m. for her in London. After I graduated high school, she moved there to take a job as a business management professor. Before she met my dad in college and got pregnant with me weeks after they graduated, she'd planned to pursue an MBA. She sacrificed her dreams to move to Middlebury, to raise me, though she wouldn't describe it that way.

The phone trilled twice before her warm, eager voice came through the line. "Nathan! This is a surprise. I'm so happy to hear from you."

There wasn't even a tinge of resentment in her voice, but guilt tightened my chest all the same. How long had it been since we'd talked? Weeks? I hadn't known what to say about coming back to Middlebury for the will reading, so I didn't say anything. Something else my father took from her, but I wouldn't let it continue. That was why I picked up the phone, to explain what had happened and where I'd be the next couple of months.

"Mom, hey," I said, sinking into my pillows. "I'm sorry to call early."

"You know I've always been an early riser." A fork clanged in the background. "Wait—is something wrong, sweetheart?"

"No, no, nothing's wrong. I just haven't talked to you in a while. How's school?"

My mom laughed. "You're calling me to ask about school?"

"Yes."

She laughed again. "All right, if you say so." She spent the next ten minutes telling me about three classes she was teaching this semester, complaining about an asshole student in her operations management course and the annoying head of her department who insisted on forced bonding time among the underpaid and busy professors.

"Other than that," she concluded, "it's going well."

"And Louis?" I asked.

"Still married."

I snorted. "I wonder how he'd feel about that description."

"He'd say it's accurate."

My mom met Louis the year she moved to London, at some faculty event at the university. He taught English literature and spent his free time at the theater and art or history museums. All the places my mom wished my dad would've enjoyed instead of dragging her to endless base-ball fields, even though she said watching me play was one of her favorite activities. I was glad she found someone more her speed. Buttoned-up Louis also needed someone like my mom to breathe excitement into his life. Their wedding last year was low-key, just the way the two of them preferred.

"Louis was just promoted," she went on happily. "And we're going to Greece after the semester to celebrate."

I couldn't picture Louis in Greece. I couldn't picture him in anything but a dusty suit from the 1960s. "That sounds fun. What—"

She cut me off. "Nathan, I think it's time you admit what has you up at four in the morning."

Right. The fucking time difference. Maybe my sleep deprivation stopped me from realizing the time of my call would give me away.

"I'm in Middlebury," I replied in a rush. "Our old house. I inherited the house and the business."

She went quiet. "I figured."

"With Brenna Quinn."

The line went deathly silent. I waited her out, needing to know what direction to take this conversation. They'd divorced, and she moved on with her life, found happiness. At the funeral, I thought a tear flowed down her cheek during my eulogy. Still, I didn't talk to her about my dad after their separation, so this was new territory.

"He did *what?*"

I laughed nervously. "Yeah, I was surprised too. He left everything to both of us. Neither of us gets anything unless we both agree to the inheritance."

"That *sonuvabitch.*"

"Mom, it's fine. Bren and I worked it out." I flinched as I realized my mistake—the casual use of her nickname. I hurried on before my mom could point it out. "We're both staying here for a couple of months to flip the properties and split the profits. People want to live in Middlebury, so it shouldn't take long."

"Here *where* exactly?"

"What?" I asked, hoping she meant something different from my interpretation of her question.

"*Where* are you both staying?"

"The house."

"*Together?*"

"Yes."

"Hmm."

Silence stretched on. It was too early to make an excuse about needing to do something else... unless I could feign sudden sleepiness. Worth a shot. I forced a mild yawn from my lips.

"Oh no, Nathan Alexander Sharpe. Do not try to fool me with whatever that was."

Of course she read through it.

"I don't want you to worry about me," I said. "Everything is under control. Brenna and I came to an agreement, and—"

"She's engaged, you know," my mom interrupted.

"How do you know that?"

"I talked to her at the funeral."

Right.

"Her engagement ring tipped me off."

My mom drew in a breath. "Don't do this to yourself, Nathan. She's moved on."

The words struck me, sharp and painful, in my chest.

"You'll get hurt if you let yourself get attached again."

"I know," I whispered. "You don't need to worry. There are clear boundaries. We have a plan."

"If you say so..." Another clatter of dishes sounded in the background. "I'm sorry, Nathan, I've got plans—"

"Of course. I should probably try to sleep."

"If you need anything, call me, all right? Any time."

I nodded, the pressure in my chest easing with her reassurance, her support. "I promise. I love you, Mom."

"I love you too, sweetheart."

There was no way I'd get any more sleep.

13

BRENNA

Eight years ago

TAP, TAP, TAP. THE faint sound pulled me from my sleep, thanks to me being the lightest sleeper in history.

I shot up, looking at my window. The outline of a hand positioned on the glass, ready to knock. My heart hammered so loudly I could feel it throughout my body.

I stumbled to my feet, to the window, preparing myself to see an unfamiliar face. It'd be fine. I'd bolt from the room, scream for help. But throwing open the curtains revealed Nathan in a dark hoodie that shaded half his face. I heaved a sigh of relief before I unlocked the window, pushed it as high as it would go, and carefully popped the screen out so Nathan could climb into my room.

"You woke me up," I grumbled. "And scared the shit out of me."

Even grumpy and tired, my body responded to his presence. Heart pounding. Stomach swooping. Mouth dry. Nathan made me comfortable in a way no one else could, and he always had. But the devious smile he tossed my way also sent delicious anticipation zipping through me. For the rest of my life, I would chase this thrill. No other feeling could rival it.

"Care to explain why you're lurking outside my bedroom window?"

Nathan straightened to his full height, towering over me. I still hadn't gotten used to it. I'd hit my growth spurt earlier than him, so for a while, we'd been eye-to-eye.

"I'm not the one who keeps my window latched."

I scoffed. "Someone could break in."

He laughed. "Bren, we're in Middlebury. Nothing bad ever happens here."

I leveled him with a look. "I'm going to keep locking my window."

Nathan took a step toward me, then another, pushing me back until my knees hit the mattress. "And I'll keep leaving mine open." He winked.

My knees buckled.

Nathan leaned down, his hands resting on either side of my head, caging me. His eyes traced my face, the anticipation of him kissing me becoming unbearable. The moonlight shining through the window illuminated us, allowing me to admire those turquoise eyes.

"Nate, are you okay?"

He shook his head, one brief, slow movement. "Sometimes, I can't believe how long it took me to see what was right in front of me."

"You were so into yourself, you couldn't see the obvious."

The joke broke his serious expression, his face cracking with a grin. "I take back everything I said," he replied in an overly dramatic tone, pulling back from the bed.

I hooked my legs around his waist, keeping him in place. He could have easily broken through my resistance, but he remained close.

"You can't stay away," I taunted. "You're totally obsessed with me."

Nathan let his body weight partially rest on me before brushing his lips over mine. "Bren..." He ran his fingers along my cheek, then sighed deeply, turning his face to the side.

"What is it?"

"There's never enough time," he said, still avoiding eye contact. "It's why I'm here now, in the middle of the fucking night, creeping outside your window. I couldn't sleep because I kept thinking about..."

I placed my hands on his cheeks and turned his head until our eyes locked. "About what?"

"I've been trying to tell you for days... and every time, I find some excuse to put it off. But I was lying in bed, turning the words over in my mind, and if I didn't come over here to tell you, I wouldn't be able to sleep and—"

My stomach dropped in the thrilling way it did on a looping roller coaster. Maybe I should've been worried about how quickly our relationship was advancing, but it took years to get to this moment.

"I'll say it back," I interrupted him.

Nathan placed his hands over mine, bringing them down from his cheeks and resting them in the small space between our bodies. "Yeah?"

"Without a single doubt."

"Brenna, I love you," Nathan said on an exhale of breath, as if relieved to get out the words.

"I love you too," I said, warmth blooming in my chest.

Instead of kissing me, he pulled me tight to his chest, shifting us onto his side. His heart pounded against my ear, a steady, soothing rhythm.

"You are my favorite person," he whispered into my hair.

I'd never forget this moment for as long as I lived.

—◦—

Now

My eyes opened as I bolted upright in bed before taking in my surroundings.

Sunshine drifted through the gray blinds, a sliver covering my pillow. The digital clock on the nightstand showed it was seven in the morning, hours before Nathan and I needed to get to the café. I flopped back on the bed, fixing my gaze on the popcorn ceiling. I sighed, hoping my exhaled breath carried away the memory of the dream.

It had felt so *real*. I hadn't dreamed of Nathan since I was a kid.

Last night, he comforted me, offering words I needed and hadn't gotten from Jack. I wasn't disappointing him. I was doing my best. It was enough. And despite our history and less-than-ideal circumstances, he cared that I was upset.

And then after Nathan went to sleep, I ate my favorite meal from Oleander's—a Greek salad with extra hard-boiled eggs—while watching sitcom reruns. The kind gesture and his consideration of my feelings were so like *my* Nathan, it must've jogged memories loose from deep in my subconscious.

I hopped out of bed and into workout clothes before any more inconvenient memories could push to the surface.

Movement in the backyard caught my eye while I was grabbing a glass of water in the kitchen. "Fucking hell," I groaned, grateful no one was around to hear my breathless utterance.

Nathan was doing arm exercises with resistance bands, wearing only black baggy basketball shorts low on his waist and a backward baseball cap on his head. I watched as his pitching arm, bent at a ninety-degree angle and tucked tight against his oblique, grasped a green band and pulled it away from his body. His bulging bicep flexing with each movement froze me to the spot, mesmerized. Well, that and the sweat gleaming on his toned back. My eyes ravenously studied the skin on display.

The doorbell rang, saving me from any truly abhorrent behavior that would ruin my dreams tonight.

Who the hell would drop by this early?

Derek waved through the side window as I approached the door.

"Well, this is a surprise," I said, smiling.

Yesterday, after the messy meeting with Allison, my body felt out of my control. Gemma seeking me out while I tried to wrest back control of my emotions had distracted me enough for everything to settle. Seeing Nathan fly off the handle as he left the café nearly upended it again, but it was up to me to decide whether I would allow it.

I would always feel things deeper than other people. I couldn't change it. But I could determine which situations I put myself in, and when I needed to retreat to a quiet place to recover.

"I was planning to leave this on the steps, but I saw you through the window," he said, holding my sweater out to me. This time of year was unpredictable, so I kept one on hand, my body always running a bit cold. "Up early working?"

"I was about to go for a run." I gestured to my body covered in leggings and a loose T-shirt. "Thanks for bringing this, but you didn't have to—"

"I know, but—" Derek stopped abruptly, his gaze locking on something behind me.

A glance over my shoulder, and I was met with piercing blue eyes fixed on Derek and me. There was that damn swooping sensation deep in my gut again. Nathan leaned on the kitchen doorway, annoyingly still shirtless, sipping a glass of water. He wasn't even trying to hide his eavesdropping.

Derek directed his attention back to me. "Since you're both here, mind if I come in and talk to you about something?"

I pushed open the door and stepped aside, then trailed behind Derek as he followed Nathan who had retreated to the kitchen. I thought starting my morning by dreaming about Nathan meant my day could only get better, but like with most things lately, I was very, very wrong.

"You make early house calls to all your clients, Ellis?" Nathan leaned on the counter, gripping the edge with both hands. His toned forearms were obscene this early in the morning.

I glared at Nathan. One side of his lips tugged up in a wry smile.

Derek ignored the bait. "I've been in touch with the cats' foster homes, and they are each willing to bring their cat to the house, so you don't have to drive all over to collect them."

Nathan sighed. "Can't they just stay there? We're trying to sell this place."

"They're all separated?" I squeaked. The thought of being ripped away from everything familiar without explanation made my chest ache. "They're probably scared and miss your dad."

Nathan scoffed. "God, you're such a bleeding heart."

"You used to like that about me," I said quietly, staring at the floor, refusing to look at him. Or at his sleeve of tattoos. Or his abs.

Fucking hell, is he going to be half-naked every morning?

Derek cleared his throat. "They can't keep them. It was a temporary arrangement. If you can give me a window when you'll be home, I'll arrange it. They've all offered to bring over supplies for a couple of days until you can get to the store."

"Thank you, that's nice of them," I said.

Nathan turned away from us, busying himself by starting a pot of coffee. The decision was left to me.

"Any time this week will work fine. In the evening."

"I'll let them know." Derek pointed over his shoulder. "I should..."

I nodded. "Right. I'll walk you out."

When we got to the door, Derek took my hand and led me through it. He kept his voice low. "Are you sure you're okay staying here?" He'd expressed the same sentiment yesterday when I told him what happened at the café. "I have room—"

I waved a hand. "I'm fine. Really. I've known him my entire life."

Except this is new territory, the voice in the back of my mind frustratingly reminded me. Nathan and I had a lifetime of being teammates, but we were friends then. After our falling out, we never had to work together. Live together, yes, but his dad and my mom provided a buffer. This time, I was alone with a man who would rather be anywhere than in this house with me. But after last night, I had hope we could get to a good place.

Derek's assessing gaze remained on my face. "You know how to find me if you change your mind." He clasped my forearm and gave it a single squeeze.

"I know."

"I'll text you later to finalize arrangements with the cats."

I nodded. "Thank you, Derek."

He smiled and a wave of comfort washed over me. I wasn't alone here. If something went wrong, if I needed someone, Derek would show up for me. This was all I'd wanted from my fiancé these past few months.

Maybe if he'd been concerned about me as much as his own needs, we wouldn't have fallen apart. Maybe.

"So that's where you were yesterday." Nathan was sitting at the table when I returned, a coffee cup and a plate with two slices of toast in front of him. "I should've figured."

I poured myself a cup of coffee. "It wasn't a secret."

Nathan's jaw ticked. "He moves fast, I'll give him that."

I groaned loudly. "Nathan, this isn't high school."

"He still has a thing for you."

"I'm engaged." I wiggled the finger on my left hand. "And he's in a relationship."

"Doesn't make it any less true."

I spun toward him, a familiar surge of anger blazing through my blood. "And what? I should go for it? Because a thing like marriage won't stand between me and what I want?"

Nathan's eyes flared. "I didn't say that."

"You didn't have to."

My mother had made a mess of her love life since I was a kid. I couldn't defend what she did to Nathan's parents. The implication that *I* could do the same because of shared genes was more than unfair.

But you did do it once, the hateful voice at the edge of my mind whispered. I fought the memory of a night with Nathan in this house that I wished I could undo. I still resented him for showing me I had the same capacity for moral failing as my mother.

"I'm going for a run," I announced before turning on my heel and heading out the door.

14

BRENNA

Eight years ago

PURE CHAOS GREETED ME when I opened the door to my house a few days before Thanksgiving.

I stepped over broken glass in the hallway, heading toward raised voices. I could have picked those three out in any crowd. And I knew—I *knew* without anyone telling me—what I was walking in on.

"He's *my* husband, Kathy!" Nathan's mom shouted at a volume I'd never heard from her before. "*My* husband."

"You've been separated for months," my mom responded evenly.

Heels clacked on the floor, and I imagined Mrs. Sharpe pacing the room. "You are my *best friend*. How can you even live with yourself?"

"Leah, I'm sorry this is how you found out," Mr. Sharpe began, his voice thick. "I was going to tell—"

"Tell me what?" she demanded. "You're *together*? We were married for twenty years, and I know it wasn't perfect... but *her*? You think you'll be able to make it work with *her*? This woman who runs through men like tissues? Who doesn't give a shit she wrecked our lives? Our children's lives? Who had no problem stabbing her best friend in the back? Is that what you want to tell me?"

"We're having a baby."

Curt. Smug. This was the woman who raised me. She'd passed half her DNA to me, but I couldn't find a trace of myself in her.

"This isn't some fling. We're in love, starting our own family. I'm sorry this hurt you—"

"Oh fuck you, Kathy," Mrs. Sharpe screamed.

I tiptoed my way to the stairs, unable to stomach listening to their argument any longer. Gently, I eased my bedroom door shut, taking a deep breath and willing my body to relax. It did little to loosen my tense muscles or settle my knotted stomach. Not that I expected it to. I always needed extensive alone time to recover from bursts of emotion, even when they came from other people.

"Did you know?"

I gasped, quickly flipping the light switch. Nathan sat in the bay window, arms crossed over his chest, his hair askew.

"Oh my God, Nate. You scared me. How long have you been here? Why are you sitting in the dark?"

Nathan rose from his seat but remained on the other side of the room. I wanted to close the distance between us, wrap myself in his arms, and pretend what happened downstairs was a nightmare, not reality. But I wouldn't be able to stand it if he refused me, and with the anger radiating off him, I thought maybe he would.

"We got home early from my doctor's appointment. My mom wanted to see your mom. I wanted to see you. They were kissing in front of the window... like they didn't care if they were caught. Do you know how fucked-up that is?"

I pinched my arm to wake from this nightmare, but it was real.

My mom lied to me. Mr. Sharpe betrayed Nathan's mom.

How could they do this?

"You get what this means for us, right?"

A tear slid down my cheek. "It has nothing to do with us."

Nathan laughed hollowly. "Your mom and my dad are having a kid. They're going to move in together, maybe get married. You think my mom will want to stay in Middlebury now?"

After Nathan's parents separated, his mom moved in with her sister for the waiting period to divorce, a full twelve months in North Carolina. In the interim, they worked on a custody arrangement and his mom searched for a house. His parents wanted him to stay in Middlebury so his life wouldn't be upended. He'd blamed both his parents for the separation, convinced they hadn't tried hard enough. But this changed his mind about who was to blame.

"She's never going to move back now," Nathan continued. He violently ran a hand through his hair. "And I won't leave her alone. Not now."

My heart squeezed to the point of pain. "You would leave?"

You would leave me? The words sat behind my lips. I was afraid of the answer. Not that I would hold it against him if he had to leave for some time. I'd understand it. But I worried it wouldn't stop there, and Nathan would end our relationship because of this development. My mother was the root of his parent's divorce. Neither of us had a car, or even a learner's permit. How could we stay in a relationship if we never saw each other?

It wasn't as if his mom would facilitate visits to her ex-husband and his new girlfriend's house.

"What other option is there?" Nathan's voice broke on the last word.

I moved quickly to him, wrapping my hands around his. "It doesn't mean anything needs to change between *us*."

Distantly, I heard a door slam, and Nathan dropped my hands. I tried not to let the sudden movement sting; he was dealing with a life-altering change.

"You never answered my question." Nathan locked eyes with me. "Did you know?"

The question was a punch to my gut. "Why would you ask that?"

"Something your mother said."

My heart kicked into overdrive. "What did she say?"

"She was surprised I didn't already know, given how close we are. Why would she say that, Brenna?"

I hate her. There was no way she didn't realize this secret would drive a wedge between Nathan and me. She'd never been his biggest fan, but I didn't think she'd hurt *me* like this.

I believed her when she told me the kiss with Mr. Sharpe was a mistake, something never to be repeated. *I'm such an idiot.*

If I told the truth, Nathan would categorize me as another person who hid things from him, even though my intentions were noble. His baseball career hinged on a successful camp this past summer, and bothering him about drama at home could've thrown off his game. Nathan's dreams were too important.

"You knew," Nathan whispered, his eyes studying my face, reading me as he always could.

He might believe me if I lied convincingly enough, but it wasn't a skill I'd ever mastered. And I didn't want to start lying to him now. We'd told each other the truth our entire lives. He loved me. I had to trust in that, trust he could forgive me eventually.

"I-I saw them once over the summer, but they told me it was a mistake. That they would stop. I believed them. I trusted them—"

His hand flexed into a fist. "How could you not tell me?"

"It would've been a distraction—"

"Un-fucking-believable," Nathan shouted, turning from me and tossing his hands in the air. He moved to the window, and I followed.

"Please stay," I pleaded. "*Please* don't leave me, Nathan. I love you. You know I wouldn't hurt you. I was doing—"

He held up one hand. "Don't. Because you did. All those times I talked about how my parents were fighting, and you never said a fucking word. If you had, maybe there would have been something I could do to stop this. To save my mom from the embarrassment of catching them in the act."

This felt like the last moment of *us*, as if his climbing out that window would mark a point in our story when everything changed. Like when he kissed me that night on our walk home from the party. Except this time, it would undo the best thing in my life rather than begin it.

"Nathan, there was nothing you could do."

"You're right," he fired back. "This is on you, Brenna. I *blame* you. I can't have anyone else in my life who I can't trust."

Tears streamed down my face. I swiped at them, but they kept coming. I couldn't keep up.

"I'm s-s-sorry," I choked out. "I'll do anything to make it up to you."

"Anything?" he asked, teetering on the bay window, about to leave the room. "Leave me alone."

I moved toward him but stopped at the glare he sent my way.

"We're done" were his only words before he left me.

15

NATHAN

Now

Brenna and I beat Allison to the café this morning, which wasn't an accident.

Allison thought she could take charge because she knew the business better than we did. This morning, I'd remind her that she answered to us. The next three months would be difficult enough without battling this woman for power.

Allison pushed her sunglasses onto her head, pausing to survey the scene in front of her. Brenna behind the counter of the café, typing furiously on her phone. Me standing with my arms crossed in front of a whiteboard with a list of tasks written on it. Brenna's focus remained on her phone, as it had since we got in the car. She muttered clipped responses when necessary, clearly still upset about this morning's argument over whether Derek was pursuing her.

I had no damn idea who she was giving her attention to, and I wasn't about to ask.

"We have a lot to get done," I said, gesturing at the to-do list. While Brenna was on her run, I'd gathered supplies and prepared for the day. "Today, we'll make a plan."

Allison quirked an eyebrow. "The boy wants to work."

I huffed. "Don't patronize me, Allison. I'm your boss now."

She flung her bag onto the counter. "You dodged a bullet with this one," she said to Brenna in a low voice. I heard her clearly, exactly as she intended. When she turned back to me, she wore a smug smile. "Well, go on. It sounds like you have a little presentation for us."

I gritted my teeth so hard it hurt. Part of me wanted to tell her to get lost, but Brenna and I needed her to reopen quickly and earn revenue. We couldn't afford to keep this place afloat without income, and we had no idea when we'd find a viable buyer.

Brenna continued staring at her phone, not paying attention to us. My morning had been positive before Derek showed up. My shoulder held up during strengthening exercises, enough that I decided to try pitching for the first time since the season ended. I held onto that victory now to keep me grounded.

"We need to get this place open, so we'll tackle the tasks necessary for that first. Once we're up and running, we can work on the other improvements."

"Other improvements?" Allison repeated. "Because you plan to sell?"

I slipped my hands into the pockets of my jeans, avoiding Brenna's gaze. "It hasn't been decided."

Not a lie, exactly. Brenna and I agreed to sell, but we didn't have any buyers so *technically*, plans to sell weren't final. If Allison knew we'd only given her a job until the two of us could peddle the business, she wouldn't want to help us.

Allison huffed out a breath, but before she could spit another retort, Brenna asked, "What do you need me to do?"

She was asking me for direction? What the hell was going on with her today?

"I was going to take the books"— I tossed her a cheeky grin—"since we all know how well you do math..."

Nothing. No reaction. She kept her focus on me, waiting.

"Allison knows the vendors and former employees better than we do, so she can figure out who we should hire back and what we need to do to resume our existing contracts."

Brenna scanned the list. "Which leaves... what? Cleaning?" She shrugged, then took out wireless earbuds and placed one in each ear, twisting a bit to find a comfortable position. "Fine by me. Allison, can you point me to the cleaning supplies?"

My phone buzzed with a message.

> **Leo**
>
> Miss your flight??

I sighed audibly.

He didn't know my exact plans, but he'd expected my trip to Middlebury to be short. I wasn't ready to explain. It would mean too many questions I didn't want to answer. I also didn't want Leo to fly here to help. He needed to focus on preparing for the season, not the drama in my life.

> **Nathan**
> I need to be here longer than I thought.
> Mind sending some clothes?

My phone rang immediately, and I let out a groan. Brenna stared curiously as she and Allison emerged from the back. I answered, moving outside as quickly as possible, away from them. "Couldn't do this by text?" I said instead of hello.

"You take too long to text," Leo replied. The sound of silverware clanging against a plate echoed in the background. *Ten a.m.* The time he usually got out of bed. In the offseason, he picked up a job as a bartender around the corner from our place, so he often didn't get home until late. "I figured I would have follow-up questions. You're fucking her, right? That's why you're staying?"

Of course he'd think that. "Not even close."

"But you're working on it?"

"For fuck's sake," I grunted, then glanced around to make sure no one heard my outburst. The activity outside the café had calmed down after rush hour, so no one was close by. I lowered my voice anyway. "I told you I would keep my distance."

Not that I have, but it wasn't in my control. Mostly.

"Come on, man. That's bullshit and you know it." He released one of the haughty all-knowing laughs women loved from him. "You're hung up on her. After you told me about her, everything made sense. You're not like me. You *want* commitment, but you never seem to find it. Wonder why."

"Are you forgetting that I saw her get proposed to?"

He made a disbelieving sound, *pshh.* "Does she seem over you?"

I watched Brenna spray tables and chairs. Her caramel blond ponytail swayed as she gracefully wiped away cleanser with a microfiber cloth. Her jean shorts were molded to her ass and covered half her thighs, and when she leaned over like that... *fuck*. My attraction to her was out of my control. It wasn't anything deeper than a chemical reaction. And unlike Leo, who succumbed to every impulse, I wouldn't let it run my decisions.

"Yes," I said. "She's engaged to another man."

"Say she wasn't—"

I rolled my eyes even though he couldn't see me. "She is."

"And you were both single. What does her behavior toward you suggest?"

Such a dangerous question to consider. I thought back to when we saw each other in the gym—the way she'd stumbled at the sight of me, the way she momentarily leaned into my touch when I caught her, the way she raked her eyes over my body when she was back on stable footing.

This attraction wasn't one-sided. Her eyes had greedily fixated on my bare chest this morning, even while we were in a disagreement. But it only meant we were human. It didn't change the fact that she was going to marry someone else.

"That she's not happy to be here either. She avoids me. Her words are clipped, her tone exasperated."

"So she still cares," Leo said, satisfied.

"Can you send me clothes or not?" I bit out, done with his psychoanalysis.

"Yeah, yeah," he said. "Text me the address. And hurry the fuck up with whatever you're doing and get back home so we can get to work."

"Is this place reopening?" An older man strolled up beside me as I ended the call. A thin layer of white fuzz covered each side of his head. His glasses hung from a lanyard around his neck over a dark brown jacket. He held a half-eaten French cruller in one hand and had a rolled-up newspaper tucked under the opposite arm.

I slipped my phone into the back pocket of my jeans. "If all goes to plan."

Next door, the bakery door opened. "Bertram," a heavily pregnant woman called as she waddled to us. "You left your wallet."

He smacked his forehead. "It's your damn sweets, make me lose my mind."

A slow smile overtook her face, and she turned to me. "Is this old geezer bothering you?"

Bertram cut in before I could reply. "I'm not *bothering* the young man. He should be nice to me, considering I'm a future customer."

"Lord help you," the woman remarked. "I'm Gemma, owner of the bakery."

We shook hands.

"Nathan Sharpe. You probably knew my dad."

"You're Gordon's kid?" Bertram asked, raising his bushy gray-black eyebrows. "Sorry for what happened to him, and not only because he still owed me money."

"Of course he did," I muttered under my breath as Gemma hissed, "Bertram!"

Midbite of his donut, the old man responded, "What? He did. Do you expect me to lie to the boy?"

Gemma blew out a breath in exasperation. "He didn't ask!" She turned her attention to me. "I'm sorry for your loss. Your dad was always nice to me when he stopped in."

"Nicer than that C-U-next-Tuesday." Bertram gestured toward the café. Gemma hissed at him again.

This man was growing on me. "Not a fan of Allison's, huh?"

"She's always trying to kick us out. Gordon never cared how long we stayed."

"That's because he was part of your group of gamblers," Gemma argued. She cocked an eyebrow. "Generally, raucous guests are not good for business, but Allison could handle it better."

Bertram huffed. "That's an understatement."

"I met your fiancée the other day," Gemma said, skillfully navigating the conversation away from Allison. "You're a lucky man."

"She's not... we're not..." I stuttered, scratching the back of my neck. "Did she say that?"

I wanted to slap myself across the face. *Of course,* Brenna hadn't said that.

Bertram laughed, unfortunately not oblivious to the way the incorrect statement threw me. "I need to meet this gal. She inside?"

Gemma rolled her eyes and pointed to Bertram with her thumb. "Do not let him in. You'll never get him to leave. Strict boundaries are crucial with this one."

"If he makes Allison mad, he's fine by me," I said, looking back inside. At least Allison was making calls. Maybe putting up with her attitude would be worth the value of her input. "It'll be at least a month before we're ready to reopen."

Bertram returned his glasses to his face, then fumbled through his pockets for his phone. "A month," he repeated. "I'll let the guys know."

Gemma slowly shook her head. "You have no idea what you just did."

I shrugged. "He seems harmless."

"I should get back inside." She flashed another bright smile. "I told your f— I told Brenna you're welcome any time. At least until I pop." Her hands massaged her baby bump.

Her almost calling Brenna my fiancée again grated. The ring on Brenna's finger flashed at me often enough, and I didn't need other reminders.

"When's the big day?" I asked, nodding toward her belly.

"I'm a month out, and I can't wait. I want to meet her and get her off my bladder." She laughed. "Anyway, it was great meeting you." She tottered toward the bakery.

"Yeah, you too. Let us know if you need anything."

She gave me a salute before heading inside. Bertram took off after confirming he'd return on opening day.

I stepped back inside the café, and it took a moment for my eyes to adjust to the dim light.

Brenna's hands sat on her hips. "If one of our jobs is to make nice with our neighbor, I'll trade you." She shook the bottle of cleaner as if to say, *This could all be yours.*

"No need. She's already a big fan of you."

"Amazing how people warm to a person who doesn't have a permanent scowl on their face."

"I don't remember seeing *Lay into Nathan* on our list this morning."

She sighed. "I don't remember you being this grumpy."

"Well..." I paused my retreat to the back of the café, stopping beside Brenna. "You always did view me through rose-tinted glasses."

Her throat bobbed. She turned her head to meet my gaze. Only inches separated us; up close like this, I could see a light brown freckle on her left cheek. Somehow I'd forgotten that detail... or blocked it, more likely. But now it was all I could focus on, remembering how I used to place my finger there when we'd lay side by side, staring into each other's eyes.

I wondered what she thought now as she looked at me, seemingly at a loss for words.

Her lips parted briefly, like she wanted to say something.

Anything would ruin this moment, so I tossed her a half grin and took off to the back office before she could say a word.

16

BRENNA

Now

I slipped on Nathan's sweatshirt and settled onto my bed.

After a week of nonstop cleaning in the café all day and working in the house at night, I looked forward to a relaxing evening. My clothes, packed by Molly and shipped by one of my coworkers, hadn't arrived yet, and I ran out of clean clothes yesterday. Nathan took pity on me and loaned me a sweatshirt until my stuff arrived. I forgot how the weather here could turn on a dime—one day, ninety degrees, the next in the forties.

I regretted accepting the sweatshirt when Nathan's scent surrounded me—fresh laundry with a hint of the strawberry bubble gum he apparently still chewed. I was already shutting my eyes, feeling peace...

The doorbell rang, jarring me out of a deep sleep. I wasn't sure how much time had passed, but it was dark outside. *Shit*. I scrambled out of bed, realizing this must have been one of the foster cat families.

"Brenna!" Nathan hollered up the stairs as I slipped on leggings.

I didn't dignify his shout with a response. I didn't need him to beckon me downstairs.

I took a deep breath and pulled open my bedroom door. Nathan stood there with his arm outstretched, fist about to knock. I gasped loudly, adrenaline shooting through my body.

Nathan cracked a smile. "Still so jumpy," he teased.

But then he realized what I was wearing—*his* sweatshirt—and all traces of humor fell away. He swallowed, his gaze lingering on my body before meeting mine. Our eyes locked, and my skin heated, suddenly making the sweatshirt too heavy to bear.

"I like that you haven't outgrown it," he murmured, looking away from me.

I never would. I jumped at loud sounds and unexpected presences, even when I anticipated them. I avoided horror movies for this exact reason. The moment when the volume diminished to pin-drop silence, then blasted creepy-ass music as someone popped onto the screen? Yeah, that was my version of hell.

Nathan cleared his throat, pointing to the foyer behind him. "One of the cat foster families is here."

Over the next hour, a parade of cats moved into our house. The tortoiseshell cat, Mia, booked it as soon as she was free of her carrier, taking off up the stairs. A tuxedo cat—Mojo—meowed loudly, swiveling his head around the space, as if looking for someone. *Gordon*. My heart broke watching him, knowing he'd never find his person. A three-legged cat named Bebe arrived next, and she was *pissed*, hissing when anyone approached. Her behavior was the exact opposite of the orange cat, Cappie, who flopped at my feet and stared up at me with soft eyes.

"They are your responsibility," Nathan said, doing that infuriatingly hot wall-lean. Didn't he know any other pose?

"Don't listen to him," I cooed to Cappie, running my fingers under his chin as he stretched his body to its full length on the carpet.

Nathan scoffed. "I'm more of a dog person."

I pretended to cover Cappie's ears. "He can hear you, you know?"

Nathan shook his head, a trace of amusement on his lips. He pushed off the wall and settled beside us on the floor. "I never knew you liked cats."

"Look at their faces." I used a sweet, higher pitched tone. Cappie's excitement bubbled over as he launched himself at my arm, trying to pull me into a game that would only end with an array of scratches. I pulled back, glancing at Nathan. "My mom told me I was allergic to cats. I learned it wasn't true after spending time with a boyfriend who had one."

Nathan's jaw clenched. I thought it was the revelation about my mother until he asked, "Mr. You Too?"

"His name is Jack," I corrected. The reminder of his existence made me feel queasy. Even though we were taking time apart, at Jack's request, the unresolved issues in our relationship hung over me. I'd been relieved to avoid the tough conversation, but I also didn't like having loose ends like this. "And no, it was someone else. In college."

Nathan winced while pushing to his feet. Earlier this week, the same expression had crossed his face when he reached to clean the top of a window. He'd caught me staring and asked, *What?* The pinched skin between his eyes made me say, *Nothing.* He didn't want me to worry about his well-being.

But I couldn't curb my instinct. The place within me that wanted to protect Nathan wasn't an empty well. "What was that?"

Nathan didn't pause his movements. "What was what?"

"The look on your face," I pressed, getting to my feet and following him to the kitchen. "Is your shoulder bothering you? Is that why you're up at the crack of dawn to do physical therapy exercises every morning?"

During freshman year of high school, Nathan injured his shoulder—an overuse injury, they said. For six weeks, he took a break from baseball and went to physical therapy. He was miserable, but he didn't experience another issue for the rest of high school. At least as far as I knew. It was this injury that inspired me to pursue physical therapy. I liked how someone could stitch people back together without cutting into skin, to impact individuals in such a profound way.

I always loved baseball, but I only played for as long as I did because of Nathan. Becoming a physical therapist for a sports team seemed like a great way to stay in the world I loved without having to become the first woman to make the major leagues.

"It's called maintenance." Nathan swung open the refrigerator and took a swig from the milk carton. I raised an eyebrow. He wiped residual milk from his mouth with the back of his hand. "What? You don't drink regular milk."

He remembered.

"Why did you grimace then?" I asked, returning to the issue at hand.

"Maybe I don't like hearing about your college boyfriend."

I rolled my eyes. "Don't try to distract me. I know that's not it."

He stepped toward me, backing me up until I hit the counter. "Do you?"

I swallowed hard, trying to ignore the butterflies taking flight in my stomach thanks to Nathan's proximity. "You were also in pain while working in the café earlier this week."

"Someone's paying close attention," he replied, tilting his head to the side. "Why is that?"

My stomach dropped when Nathan's gaze flitted to my mouth. He wouldn't act on it, but oh, how my body craved his kiss. I turned around and closed my eyes, giving myself a break.

I walked through life as a ball of barely concealed emotion, and it didn't take much to see what pulsed beneath the surface. Having these feelings didn't make me an awful person. It only mattered how I chose to behave.

I stepped away from Nathan and leaned back into the counter. "Have you seen someone about your shoulder?" I asked, refocusing on my original point.

The teasing smile fell from his face. "There's nothing wrong with my shoulder."

"Then explain what I saw."

He crossed his arms over his chest. "Have you never slept wrong, Brenna?"

I matched his stance. "Not so wrong that my arm hurt for *days*, Nathan."

The ringing doorbell interrupted our conversation. I headed to the front of the house, wondering if it was one of the cat owners. "It's Derek," I said, pausing in the formal dining room connected to the kitchen.

"Fucking hell," Nathan groaned, tossing his head back. "How many fucking times is this guy going to show up at our house?"

Our house. It didn't mean anything—this was our house. We owned it. And yet, my mind raced with unsaid implications in those words.

"What do you have against Derek?"

"You didn't *seriously* just ask me that question as if you don't know?"

"I know it was awkward in high school when we dated, but that was a lifetime ago. You can't still be holding a grudge. So what is it?"

"He got all the moments I was supposed to get with you, Brenna. You can't blame me for disliking the guy."

Everything else in the world fell away—the sound of the doorbell ringing again, the cats meowing in the other room, the hum of the fridge, even my rapidly beating heart pulsating in my ears.

He got all the moments I was supposed to get with you.

His pained tone played over and over in my mind. Nathan broke up with me in high school. He left Middlebury with his mom after finding out his dad and my mom had an affair. He transferred to another high school. He told me he couldn't forgive me for hiding what I'd seen while he was at baseball camp—his dad sharing a romantic moment with my mom. He blamed me. He shut me out of his life.

Only once since then did I think Nathan regretted doing so. Until now.

The doorbell rang a third time.

"You should get it," he said, his voice gruff. "Before he burns your name in candles in the backyard."

I watched Nathan retreat upstairs. At the landing midway up, he looked at me, hitting me with the full weight of his emotions. The feeling of his regret and sadness weighed on my chest. I wanted to go to him, to soothe the ache, to fix our past. But I didn't trust that I could manage my own emotions if I did. I couldn't guarantee Nathan wouldn't push me away again if I tried.

We'd made significant progress on the café and the house this week, but we were nowhere close to finished. I refused to jeopardize our working relationship. Successfully flipping the house and relaunching the business were too important to derail.

So I turned my back on Nathan and walked to the front door to let Derek inside.

17

NATHAN

Now

THE MORNING WE REOPENED the café, two weeks later, I was in the back office trying to get a passable accounting system in place.

We were selling coffee to bring in needed revenue while we got our ducks in a row. Despite working diligently every day, I'd only managed to go through two years of the receipts my father "filed" in a shoebox. At least he had one shoebox for each year, or I might have torched this business on the off chance insurance would pay for the damages.

Shit. I needed to ask Allison about insurance coverage. I pulled out my phone and added it to my ever-growing list.

"Brenna Quinn!" A familiar booming voice pulled me back to reality. "I haven't seen you in these parts since high school. How the hell have you been?"

"Hey, Ax," Brenna greeted him cheerfully in the practiced customer service tone I'd heard all morning.

That's right. I spent the morning sorting receipts and listening to the former love of my life chat with every customer who stepped through the door. Asking each person more questions than she'd bothered to ask me since we reunited. *Not that I had made it easy on her.*

I left the back office, moving toward the counter. My body tensed, seeing the way Ax looked at Brenna with the sky-blue eyes that had made him popular with girls at school. With her beauty, I couldn't blame him.

Ax's shirtsleeves were torn at the shoulder, and his faded blue jeans were covered in grass stains. I'd heard he took over his father's landscaping business after playing college ball. He had designs on making it to the major leagues—all of us did—but it was like hitting the lotto.

"And Nathan fucking Sharpe!" Ax said when I stepped behind Brenna. He shifted the baseball cap on his head, pushing his blond hair over his ears. "Never thought I'd see you here."

I shrugged. "Circumstances change."

"I'm sorry about your dad, man. I always liked him."

"Thank you," I said, falling silent when Brenna's hand connected with mine. I didn't know if I was even still breathing as she intertwined our fingers and squeezed. It lasted only a few seconds, so short I wondered if I dreamed it.

"Hey," Ax continued, unaware of anything between Bren and me, "you should join our baseball league for a game. Freeze, Stark, and Cafferty are on the team. The rest of the guys are from my crew. They're cool."

"Nathan." Brenna's warning tone. Her eyes narrowed, concern etched between them. I would not entertain this conversation with her. I thought I'd already made that clear.

"Quinn, you're welcome to join us too."

"I don't know if it's a good idea, Nathan," Brenna said. "You're supposed to be resting."

"Sharpe, don't tell me you've gone soft." Ax leaned his elbows on the counter. Brenna glared at me, trying to silently communicate the seriousness of her point. "Do you remember the game you played with a high ankle sprain?"

Brenna sighed loudly. "*I* remember. From behind home plate, I could see him *grimace* every time he took a step, but he refused to acknowledge it."

Ax laughed, unaware of the callback to our earlier argument. "He was always a tough motherfucker."

I loved playing baseball, so I played regardless of injury or illness, outside of the stint in physical therapy that my parents and Brenna forced on me. This game had been the most consistent part of my life ever since I picked up a rubber baseball at two years old. I loved it, and I didn't know what I would do without it.

"Stubborn motherfucker is more like it," Brenna muttered under her breath, turning away from us and moving down the counter to clean one of the coffee machines.

Ax gave me a mischievous half smile, nodding toward Brenna. "So you finally locked her down, huh?"

"Brenna's engaged to someone else." The words were like sandpaper on my tongue. I punched him playfully in the arm. "Don't get any ideas."

Ax mock-saluted me. He'd backed off in high school too. By the time Bren and I got together, he'd moved on to someone else and didn't hold a grudge. It wasn't like our relationship surprised anyone. People recognized what had taken me far too long to realize—our connection was deeper than any friendship.

And then I fucking lost her.

I shook my head, needing to forget that thought.

Brenna and I reached a good place these last couple of weeks, slipping into a comfortable routine. I made coffee in the mornings while I maneuvered around the cats swarming me for food. Brenna came downstairs an hour or so later, and we ate breakfast together. We drove to the café and worked until midday when we ate lunch with Allison to strategize next steps. After lunch, we headed home, and Brenna disappeared for hours in her room, resurfacing to tackle the to-do list for the house. Sometimes we had dinner together, sometimes Brenna left.

Most nights, we watched a movie or a hockey game. Every time Brenna smiled at me or observed me in what she thought was a surreptitious way, I tried not to let hope take root in my chest.

"See you at the next game." Ax handed back my phone after entering his number.

Brenna would raise hell when she found out I planned to play. It shouldn't have surprised me she noticed my shoulder pain, even when everyone on my team—except Leo—missed it. From behind home plate, Brenna had learned to read me, picking up every tell.

It was disconcerting that this particular ability of hers hadn't vanished in the years since we shared the field.

"Are you done working for the day?" Brenna asked, abruptly pulling me from my thoughts. She still wore a green apron, one hand positioned on a popped hip.

I sighed. "Sure, yeah. It'll all still be here tomorrow."

Tonight, Brenna and I would continue painting the house. Usually I liked the time we worked together at home, just the two of us, the rest of the world shut out. It was then we almost felt like friends again.

Although I didn't look forward to being pressed about agreeing to play baseball, not that she could sway me.

"You know, you used to love that I was a tough motherfucker."

She crossed her arms over her chest. "Nathan, I worried about you *all* the time."

I took a step toward her and leaned in. "Don't pretend you didn't also find it hot, darlin'."

She stilled, like she'd expected an off-speed pitch and instead was hit with a heater. I couldn't resist stunning her, soaking in her self-conscious expression, the way her cheeks blushed. A risky game, but I couldn't help playing.

I couldn't help a lot of things when it came to Brenna Quinn.

"I'll be ready to go in fifteen minutes," I said over my shoulder.

18

BRENNA

Seven years ago

My entire body froze when Nathan Sharpe entered the athletic training office.

The trainer, Ms. Williams, waved at him a beat later. "Good to see you, Mr. Sharpe. How's the arm holding up?"

"It's fine," he said. "Just coming by for some ice for the bus ride home, if that's okay?"

Nathan hadn't seen me yet, didn't even know to look for me here. Five months ago, after the showdown between our parents, Nathan and his mom moved to Pillsner, a neighboring town whose high school baseball team rivaled ours. I hadn't seen Nathan since the night he told me we were done. He hadn't answered any of the daily texts I sent him.

And now he was here.

"Of course," she said. "I'm in the middle of something, but my intern... Brenna, can you set up Mr. Sharpe with a bag of ice?"

Nathan's gaze swung to mine. His mesmerizing blue eyes widened then turned to ice. His once smiling expression tightened to a frown. I barely recognized my happy-go-lucky best friend. I hoped his reaction was because of me and not because the last five months had irreparably changed him.

Not one thing had changed for me in our time apart. My heart rate sped as I appreciatively scanned Nathan's body in his baseball uniform—gray pants clinging tightly to his thighs, short sleeves of his jersey displaying strong, suntanned arms, black baseball cap sitting backward on his head. Every single instinct shouted to move close to him, remembering how, by some miracle, Nathan had once belonged to me. He had loved *me*.

I managed a nod and gestured to the table closest to the ice machine. "Sure. Take a seat."

I turned my back on Nathan, focusing on shoveling ice into a plastic bag. The air chilled my hot cheeks. But it didn't take long to tie off the bag, which meant facing Nathan at a closer distance. My body was a livewire with emotions surging through it.

"I expected to see you on the field," Nathan said as our eyes met again. Neither of us was in control of the instinct to stare.

I moved to his side, carrying the bag by its neck. "No one told you I'm not on the team?"

Nathan arched a brow. "Who would have told me?"

Right. Nathan wasn't talking to his father. I thought he would have kept in touch with our teammates, at least the ones he considered friends, but maybe he avoided them too. Or they knew better than to talk about me.

"Put your arm at your side, please." I broke eye contact to focus on the task at hand. He obliged and allowed me to place the ice pack on his shoulder. "Adjust it if you need to, and then I'll wrap it."

Nathan shifted the bag. His hand brushed mine, awakening every nerve in my body, each one craving more contact.

My sharp intake of breath gave away exactly how that brief touch affected me.

He cleared his throat, then said roughly, "Go ahead."

At least I wasn't the only one affected by our closeness.

I placed one hand on the ice, concealing my wince from the cold, and pulled a wrap across his body. "Can you lift your other arm?"

Nathan followed my instructions. I reached across him, deftly swapping the hand holding the gauze with the one securing the ice. The move brought me closer to Nathan. His bubble gum scent consumed me, dredging up a thousand memories of us. The sound of his breath hitching sent an ache of pure longing deep into my belly.

"Why aren't you playing this season?"

"I didn't want to." I continued wrapping gauze around his body, over and over, ripping my scabbed heart open each time.

"Because of me?"

"I'm not popular with the team." Most of them blamed me for Nathan leaving Middlebury. I'd lost them their shot at state. It wasn't Nathan's fault no one wanted me on the team. And even though he'd cast me from his life, I couldn't find one part of me that wanted to hurt him. I loved him too much. I would forgive him if he asked.

"Besides, playing baseball isn't as fun without you." I fastened the gauze with a piece of metal, tugging to confirm it was secure before adding, "And interning here will look good on college applications."

"I think it's less fun without you too," Nathan admitted.

A tear slipped from my eye and slid down my cheek. I reached to wipe it away, but Nathan beat me to it. His fingers lingered on my jaw after drying the tear.

My stomach bottomed out when I met his gaze, already on me.

"I'm sorry," I rushed to say.

Nathan immediately dropped his hand from my face, the reminder of our circumstances breaking whatever spell he was under.

"I'm so sorry, Nathan. If I could go back—"

"But you can't." He shifted his legs over the table, then stood.

I looked up at him, his face all hard lines, his expression shuttered. "Will you ever forgive me?"

"I don't know." Barely a whisper, but I heard pain in his tone all the same.

I stared at the floor, unable to take the sight of the face I'd never kiss again.

"Thank you for the wrap."

He left, and I fell to my knees as my swallowed-down sob finally escaped.

19

NATHAN

Now

A STRIP OF LIGHT streamed into the hallway from the cracked-open office door.

I reached through the door for the light switch, inadvertently nudging it open wide enough for *her* to come into view. I stopped, mesmerized by Brenna's hips swaying to the song playing through her earbuds. Gray cotton shorts barely covered her ass, leaving her toned legs on full display. Bren always had great legs, thanks to all the squats she did to get into her catcher's position. Her caramel blond hair, secured in two braids, fell over her shoulders as she rolled paint on the wall.

I swallowed, fighting two opposing instincts. Brenna's back was to me, so she'd have no idea I saw her if I left now. I also couldn't pry my eyes off her. During this past month, we spent plenty of time together but nothing so unguarded as this. I snuck glances when I could, and too many times to count, Brenna's gaze snagged on my own. She watched me too.

And there was always that second when I *forgot*. That Brenna and I weren't here by choice. That there was a long list of reasons why we weren't in each other's lives. That she was engaged to another man. That second of only her and me broke my heart every damn time. I wished I could live in that second, go back in time and do things differently.

What right did I have to tell her about my feelings? She'd moved on, found someone who loved her. Revisiting our past would resurface a lot of hurt, and I didn't want to cause her any more pain. Brenna had chosen someone to spend her life with. Confessing my feelings would be selfish, and it would shatter whatever peace we'd managed to establish between us.

I couldn't do that to her.

Brenna's earsplitting scream jolted me from my inner conundrum.

She dropped her paintbrush to the floor, splattering cream paint. Thankfully, we'd covered the carpet before we started painting the room. She clutched her chest, and yep... she wasn't wearing a bra. *Fucking hell.* My gaze darted away from the nipples visible through her thin pink tank top.

"Nathan," Brenna panted. She pulled her earbuds out, resting them on one of the steps of the ladder. "What. The. Hell?"

I stepped into the room. "I didn't know you were in here. I thought we left the light on..."

Brenna used a stray cloth to wipe paint from her legs. "What are you doing up?"

"What are you doing *painting*? It's three a.m."

She tossed the cloth aside, then shrugged. "I couldn't sleep. What's your excuse?"

"I needed water." I lifted my bottle. "Haven't you heard of watching TV or reading a book? Or are you just so desperate to finish, you decided to work around the clock?"

Her eyes flickered with an emotion I couldn't name. "It hasn't been so bad," she admitted, picking up the paint roller again. "When you're not being grumpy or scaring me half to death."

I snatched another roller off the floor and strolled over to her. "So you mean 3 percent of the time?"

She flashed me a smile, one I recognized as genuine. God, I never thought I'd see that from her again.

"Give yourself some credit. It's a solid 10 percent."

I tapped her ass with the paint roller, which sent her scampering away from me. She angled her head to see if I left a mark, but no paint was on the roller.

She tensed her face into a stern look. "Don't make me kick you out of this room."

"So," I said, looking around the half-painted room, "you *don't* want my help?"

She dipped the roller in the aluminum tin of cream paint on the floor, tapping it gently against the side, then lifting it out. "I was doing fine before you got here, Nathan."

I smirked. "Yeah, it looked like you were having a great time."

Her head snapped to me. "How long were you watching?"

"Long enough to see that your dance moves haven't changed since high school."

"Shut up!" She smacked my arm before quickly returning her hand to the handle of her brush. "This is why I don't dance in public... at least not sober."

I laughed. "Probably for the best."

"I hate you," she grumbled, but I could see a smile tugging at her lips.

I swallowed. "You should, Bren." I focused on my roller, skimming up and down the wall. "You looked good. I've always liked it when you let your instincts run wild."

She tucked a strand of hair behind her ear. "I only ever felt like I *could* with you."

I raised an eyebrow. "Not with Mr. You Too?"

The question brushed the healthy boundary I set. But dammit if the thought that I made her feel something no one else could didn't have me greedy.

"*Jack*," she corrected, swiping hair out of her face. That's when my eye snagged on her finger—her *ringless* finger. Maybe she didn't want to get paint on it. Or maybe she always took it off at night. Regardless, I liked seeing her finger bare.

"Not with *Jack*?" I pressed, unable to stop myself.

She turned away to gather more paint on her roller. "No." The word was so quiet, I almost didn't hear her.

But I did hear, and I couldn't ignore it.

I wanted her to relax again. People tended to view Brenna as reserved, but when she was comfortable, she let her goofy side show. I missed hearing her wild laughter, seeing the spark in her eyes.

This was why I didn't want to come back to Middlebury, why I didn't want to *stay*. Remaining angry with Brenna took effort. It always had. I held a ridiculous number of grudges, for small and large things, but with her, my instinct was to forgive, to let things go.

Because I never wanted a life without this woman. Even when I was angry with her, I hadn't wanted to permanently push her away. When I realized I had, it gutted me. If all I could have was friendship, I'd find a way to make it work. It was worse to not have her in my life at all.

I bent down and dipped my finger in the paint. "Brenna," I said softly. When she turned to me, I ran my finger across her flushed cheek, smearing paint in one thin line.

Her eyes widened. It took a second for her to grab her own handful of paint and toss it at me, spattering it across my chest and neck. She broke into laughter, loud and unrestrained and ending with an adorable snort. Her true laugh. I wanted to hear it again.

"You're asking it for it, Quinn."

"You started it, Sharpe."

We lunged toward the can at the same time, both of us coming away with globs of paint dripping through our fingertips. We faced each other, readying for the fight.

"It's not too late to surrender," I said, "before I make an absolute mess of you."

Brenna's chest rose and fell rapidly. "And let you get away with this?" She motioned to her face. "Not a chance."

She flung a handful of paint at me, breaking our standoff. I shut my eyes before it hit my face and neck.

"Oh, you're going to regret that!"

I charged toward her. Brenna screamed, running from me while flinging paint over her shoulder. I caught her around the waist with one arm and pinned her to my body.

"Surrender," I whispered into her ear, and she shivered. These little signs of her attraction made it hard for me to put away my feelings.

Brenna writhed, trying to loosen my grip. She kicked backward, but I blocked it before her foot could connect with my nuts.

"That wasn't nice, darlin'."

Despite her strength, she didn't stand a chance against me, not unless I gave an inch. Since I didn't want our game to end, I did. I brought down a handful of paint onto her head using both hands. She let out another high-pitched yell, then dodged around me to grab more paint. We kept flinging paint at each other, trading the role of chaser and chasee.

Both of us were out of breath, loudly huffing and puffing when we flopped onto our backs in the center of the room. Paint was everywhere—in our hair, all over our clothes, streaked across the walls, some of which we'd need to redo tomorrow.

But I didn't care because Brenna was smiling at me like I wasn't the boy who broke her heart.

"We made a huge mess," she said.

I couldn't stop myself from reaching toward her, brushing my fingertips over her cheek. She didn't move. I showed her a gob of paint I'd wiped off her skin. "And it's going to be a bitch to remove this."

She mirrored my movements, bringing her fingers to my chin, stealing paint from my skin. My entire body ignited at the simple touch.

"Worth it."

20

NATHAN

Now

THE SOUTH WAS MADE for baseball.

Brenna and I made our way through the backyard to the baseball diamond in Hart Park, where we played as kids. The atmosphere was perfect. We had unseasonably warm weather with a slight breeze to keep us cool while we played. The sun was setting, brilliant reds and oranges peeking out from behind wispy clouds.

"If I see you grimace even once—" Brenna started.

I turned, placing my finger an inch from her lips to silence her before she could finish the sentence. The air from her gasp hit my fingers.

"I'll be fine."

Ever since our paint fight a week ago, all I could think about was touching her again. Even though she was engaged to another man, completely off-limits, and hadn't forgiven me for our past. This was my punishment for treating her the way I did when we were kids.

I wondered if this unending temptation was what my dad had endured for Brenna's mom when he was still married. My dad was the villain in my parent's marriage and in my life following their divorce. I never wanted to be like him, to succumb to moral weakness.

Yet here I was, admiring the long column of Brenna's neck as she pulled her hair into a ponytail. The paint had finally faded from both of us after a few days of diligently following removal techniques we found online. *Worth it*, Brenna had said that night. With each passing day, I agreed with her more. That night alleviated the strain between us, and we'd slipped into a version of friends—not what we used to be, but something we could build on.

"Sharpe! Quinn!" Ax shouted when we stepped through the opening in the chain-link fence to the baseball diamond. He halted catch with one of our old teammates, Vic Stark, and jogged over from first base. Brenna stiffened at my side when Vic, one of the more bitter teammates about not going to state, came into view.

"It's water under the bridge," I whispered. "He won't say anything."

She nodded once, weakly.

I locked eyes with her and vowed, "I won't let him."

Ax held his hand out for me to slap, then opened his arms to Brenna for a hug. It lasted as long as any platonic hug, but the seconds dragged as they embraced. "Glad y'all could make it."

"I haven't played in years," Brenna said. "Hopefully, I won't ruin your chances."

Ax shoved a thumb in my direction. "We have a major league baseball shortstop and pitcher. We'll be fine."

"Minor league pitcher," I corrected.

Freeze was the only one from our high school team with a permanent spot on a major league roster, playing for the Palmer City Owls—the team I always dreamed I'd play for. He got his nickname when we were kids because he stopped hits no one else could. People joked that he could slow down time, something that hadn't changed in the years since I'd known him, at least from what I saw on *SportsCenter*.

Ax introduced us to the team. Most of the guys worked on his landscaping crew, but there were a few familiar faces, including our high school team's centerfielder, Cafferty, who had once been a close friend. Brenna stood behind us, her left hand gripping her right forearm while her eyes warily bounded around the group.

I reached for Brenna's arm, lightly tugging her to my side. "Y'all remember Brenna, right?"

Her eyebrows squished together. I shrugged. Trying to break the ice with dumb humor never hurt anyone, except maybe by embarrassing the person who said it. Making her feel comfortable was more important than how these guys perceived me.

Brenna waved shyly. "Hey."

"Quinn." Freeze spoke first. His presence was more intimidating in person than on TV. About my height—six feet—with an intense stare, dark eyes, and thick eyebrows. He'd amassed more tattoos than me, and both of his olive arms were covered with artwork.

Brenna had thrown the ball to him at second base thousands of times, and they'd been closer than many of the guys on the team. But his competitive streak rivaled my own. Not getting a shot at state drove them apart.

"It's good to see you out here again," he continued. "I thought about you over the years, about how I fucked up. I was a dumb kid."

Stark stepped forward, towering over all of us. His imposing frame was perfect for a first baseman. "We were all dumb kids. We should've never made you leave the team. None of it was your fault."

Brenna's shoulders sagged with relief. The way she wore her emotions like a blinking neon sign was one of the things I loved most about her. She'd always been self-conscious about being emotional while growing up. She missed out on seeing her strengths. The depth of her loyalty exceeded anyone I'd ever known. There was nothing like the feeling of having Brenna Quinn on your side.

"It was a long time ago," she repeated my words from earlier. "Thank you for saying it though."

Ax threw an arm across her shoulders, sending a zing of jealousy through me. "Time to get serious about this game. Let me tell you about our batting signs." He tossed me a look over his shoulder. "You too, Sharpe."

He walked us to the side of the field, out of sight of the opposing team. Ax told us this was a light-hearted game, but I doubted it, given the seriousness with which he concealed information from the other team.

"I assume y'all will use your own pitching signs?" Ax asked.

I looked to Brenna for an answer, to see if she remembered them.

"You want us"— she gestured between her and me with one hand—"to pitch and catch?"

Suppressing my smile took effort. "I throw faster now, so I understand if you don't feel comfortable..."

Brenna straightened, her eyes sparking with her familiar competitiveness. "That's not it. I'm just surprised. This is our first game with the team."

First game. It implied there would be more.

"You two are our secret weapon," Ax said, his eyes swiveling between us. "So you'll work out your own signs?"

"We're good," I confirmed before snatching Brenna's hand and leading her to the dugout. I cursed myself for breaking my vow to keep my distance, for taking any excuse to hold her hand.

I sat on the bench as Brenna started fastening catcher's equipment to her body—two shin pads and a chest protector. She held the helmet under her arm, pressed into her hip. The sight of her dressed for the game took me back to long weekends together, playing baseball or hanging with friends. Nights under the lights, the two of us locked in, shutting down the other team.

Kissing each other, hidden from teammates and coaches, any chance we got.

I liked seeing her in baseball clothes and catcher's gear. *She's fucking engaged, you twit.*

I cleared my throat. "You remember our signs?"

"Of course I do. We've used the same ones since we were kids."

Even when in high school, our coaches never made us change them. They realized Bren and I had our own language, and it was best not to mess with that magic.

"All right." I clapped her on the shoulder as I passed her on the way out of the dugout. "Let's go."

21

BRENNA

Now

NATHAN'S FIRST PITCH STUNG my hand.

His velocity had increased since I'd last squatted behind home plate for him. I'd also forgotten Nathan threw a "heavy ball," meaning it moved late and often landed in a suboptimal spot in my glove.

In other words, it hurt like hell. I used to wear additional padding in my mitt, and I usually ended up having to ice my hand after games.

But this sting... I relished it. I was at home, not only behind home plate but also on the receiving end of Nathan's pitches. We'd always made sense on the diamond.

"You good?" he asked from the mound while I tried to covertly shake out my hand.

I took my helmet off. "Never better," I called back with a smile.

A shift happened after Nathan found me painting in the middle of the night. So much had been forced on us. Co-owning a house and business. Remaining in Middlebury to get it up and running. Living together to work on the house.

But no one made Nathan watch me dance or start a paint fight. Our routine didn't change after that night, but it *felt* different.

Sometimes, Nathan's hand would brush mine while passing me in the kitchen in the morning. Instead of disappearing to my room in the afternoon, I stayed on the first floor, playing with the cats or reading a book in the same room as him. At night, we sat closer together on the couch while watching TV.

"All right, let's show them how it's done," Nathan said. He caught the ball I threw to him, and full-on grinned, making my chest tight.

I missed this—being on the field, part of a team. It was why I wanted to pursue a career in sports. Growing up, I spent so much time alone before moving to Middlebury. Nathan introduced me to this sport I loved and made me his partner. Baseball gave me a feeling of family I never got in my own house.

Something that was again absent from my life.

It wasn't until the sixth inning—the final one in this shortened game—that Nathan's face contorted in pain. I stood, whipped my helmet off, and stalked to the mound.

He lifted his arms in the air. "Throw me the ball, Brenna."

I ignored him, keeping the ball in my mitt and continuing toward him.

"You're making a scene."

"I told you what would happen if I saw you grimace."

He put his non-gloved hand on his hip. "I didn't."

"Are you saying I'm lying?" I narrowed my eyes.

"Course not," he said, taking a step forward. I moved my glove behind my back. "But you're *looking* for a problem. There's no problem." He held out his glove, waiting for me to drop the ball into it. "We need two more outs, Bren. Let's finish the game, then we can talk about what you saw. For hours, if you want."

The place those words sent my mind.

I stepped close to him, then spoke into my mitt so no one else could hear or read my lips. This game had no real significance, but Nathan and I easily slipped back into the childhood versions of ourselves, competitive as all hell. "Is your arm fine?"

Nathan's lip twitched before he raised his glove to cover his mouth. "Why don't you go back behind home plate, and I'll show you how fine it is?"

He managed to make the sentence sound dirty.

"You're shameless," I said, rolling my eyes.

"Walk slowly, please."

So he can watch me go.

I considered spinning around to hit him, but then I saw the expression on his face. I walked slowly, swaying my hips more than usual. An echo of laughs sounded around the infield from Ax, Freeze, and Stark.

"All right," I called to the team, standing on home plate and lifting one finger in the air. "One out."

Nathan's next pitch resulted in a ground ball to Freeze, who quickly zipped it over to Stark for the second out. Nathan tilted his head to me as if to say *Told you I was fine.*

The next batter went the distance in the count—three balls, two strikes. He was the only player who'd been able to get the better of Nathan, and in the serious lines on his face, I could see he wanted this strikeout. I stuck two fingers down—a change-up—followed by one finger, signaling for him to throw it over the outside corner, but Nathan shook me off. He would hear an earful from me later about letting fear make his decisions. I stuck one finger down, followed by my middle finger which was our sign to throw close to the batter. Nathan nodded his agreement. He lifted his leg in the air, then planted his foot, and hoisted the fastball toward me with everything he had.

The batter swung too late. The pitch landed in my glove with a satisfying smack. I didn't even care about the sting as I rushed to the mound and into Nathan's arms.

"I bet I felt just fine," he said into my ear, sending a shiver down my spine.

He meant his last pitch, but in each other's arms like this, I couldn't ignore how good his body felt against me. I inhaled his strawberry chewing gum scent, and it transported me to my childhood when Nathan centered my world.

The prospect of the past repeating itself didn't seem far-fetched any longer, and it scared the shit out of me.

I wriggled out of Nathan's arms. My stomach dipped when my gaze met his—the devastating smile, those turquoise eyes, the scruff covering the lower half of his face. *This*—feeling all hot and bothered for Nathan—was half the reason I kept wearing my engagement ring. I didn't want to do something I'd regret... like remind myself about the feel of his lips.

If that was all it was, my stomach wouldn't have felt like it was tied in constrictor knots. I could fight physical attraction—I wouldn't enjoy it, but I could do it. Without my permission, though, my old feelings for Nathan resurfaced and tangled with my lust for him.

You always loved that boy too much. My mother was right; I'd been powerless to those feelings before. Without a single doubt, Nathan still held me in the palm of his hand.

"Brenna?" a voice called behind me.

I turned toward home plate, and the knots in my stomach tightened painfully. Jack leaned against the chain-link fence, forehead scrunched, watching me. Derek stood beside him, hands in his pockets, his expression unreadable.

What the hell are they doing here?

Nathan's heat surrounded me as he leaned in to whisper, "Is that—"

"Jack," I cut him off. "Yes. Jack is here."

22

NATHAN

Now

I DRAINED MY BEER in one swig, then motioned to the bartender for another.

"You okay man?" Ax eyed me with concern.

Brenna Quinn's fiancé showed up at our baseball game tonight with Derek Ellis in tow. *Of course* I wasn't all right. After the most incredible time on the field with her, a heavy dose of reality kicked me in the balls.

My feelings for Brenna didn't matter. She would never be mine.

"Never better," I muttered, snatching my second beer off the bar and heading to the tables the team had commandeered in the corner of the room.

Ax reached my side seconds later, holding a beer bottle in one hand. "Because if you're not okay, I can make an excuse for you. Like you need to water your plants or wash your hair or something."

I scoffed. "I'm not leaving."

Bolting out of the bar would reveal how much seeing Jack wrap Brenna into a hug bothered me. I watched them together for far longer than I should have, but I needed the fucking reminder. There was *nothing* there for me. I ruined my chance a long time ago.

"Your funeral, man."

I hated the way Ax saw through my facade. If *he* could tell how much I cared for her, Brenna probably could too. I wondered if she pitied me... or worse, she only played nice because of my dad and his stupid will. The institution of marriage obviously hadn't held significance to him, but *I* respected other people's relationships. I took them so seriously, I refused to commit to a relationship if I couldn't give it the attention and care it required. I refused to start a relationship that would fail.

I used to think I held back because of me, but now I suspected it had something to do with the gorgeous blond sitting across the table from me.

Brenna studied her menu while her fiancée sat rigidly beside her, keeping his hands to himself. They hadn't seen each other in over a month. I didn't know how he could stand not touching her.

Ax nudged me in the ribs, as if to say *What the hell is going on here?*

I cleared my throat, speaking before Ax could. "So, Ellis, I didn't expect you at the game tonight."

He looked up from typing quickly on his phone and pinned me with a glare. "Jack came to my office, hoping to get Brenna's address. We stopped by the house, and no one answered. But the baseball lights were on. Took a wild guess I might find you both there."

"That's, what, the third time you've been to my house in a month?" I took a swig of beer. "Such dedication to your job."

Ellis glowered. "It was nice seeing Brenna play. By the time I met her, she'd quit... as you well know."

Brenna's eyes snapped to Ellis, but either he didn't see or refused to acknowledge her. She hated the way we'd fought in high school. Never physical, though one time did come close. We both mastered the wielding of underhanded barbs instead.

Jack spoke quietly. "I didn't even know you played baseball."

Ax choked on his beer. I shot him a look, urging him to keep his mouth shut. For once, he followed my silent direction.

"It was a long time ago." Brenna tore her straw wrapper into smaller and smaller pieces.

"I heard you were good." Ellis's finger circled the rim of his bottle; his words were still for me. "Too bad you had to give it up."

I could read Brenna's discomfort. I wanted to cut Ellis down to size, but I didn't want her to feel worse.

"So, Jack," I said, taking the reins of the conversation and pivoting it away from the past he knew nothing about. "How did y'all meet?"

He glanced over at Brenna, a frown on his face. "I see you've talked a lot about me." To me, he said, "We met on a plane. I was her pilot."

Ax laughed, tipping his glass in their direction. "That's romance novel shit right there. Did you ask her out over the intercom?"

Jack shook his head, a smile starting to bloom. "No, I waited until the plane *wasn't* in the air."

"You didn't even see me until I was exiting the plane," Brenna piped in.

"No, I saw you board." He placed a hand on hers, staring at her with stars in his eyes. Brenna pointedly kept her gaze away from him. "You were laughing with your friend. I stood with the flight attendants to bid the passengers farewell so you might see me."

"You never told me that." Brenna's hushed voice was barely audible.

He pulled his hand back from hers. Silence descended around the table, turning our presence into an intrusion. The lack of physical contact might have been an aversion to public displays of affection, but neither of them making eye contact or showing a single trace of happiness after being reunited hinted at something wrong between them.

Had they argued on their way to the bar? Ellis drove them, so it didn't seem likely. Maybe Jack was pissed about our hug after the game? I chanced a look at him, and he caught me, but no malice crossed his features. If it wasn't my past with Brenna, what the hell was causing this awkward-ass vibe?

"I bet you did something crazy romantic to propose." Ax broke the silence in the worst way possible. He still hadn't developed the ability to read a room.

Jack gripped his glass tighter, his knuckles turning white. "I proposed at a baseball game."

"No shit," Ax said, smacking me in the arm. "Nathan plays professional baseball."

"Triple-A," I deflected.

"He's so modest. You played ten games in the majors this year."

A wave of guilt hit me for not keeping in touch with Ax. He'd followed my career and rooted for my success while I barely knew anything about his life. I shoved Middlebury into the depths of my mind as soon as I graduated.

"There was a stomach flu," I explained, trying to move the conversation off me. "They were desperate."

Brenna's gaze found mine, her eyes sparking with realization. She didn't follow my baseball career, but she would never not watch the sport altogether. The stomach flu news was widely known because it took down a significant number of popular players. Brenna knew the story.

I could tell from the way her mouth fell open when she figured out the timing. She knew the Nashville Blitz played the Chicago Monarchs while I was in the major leagues. When she was proposed to.

You were there? she mouthed to me.

I nodded imperceptibly, not wanting to tip anyone off to our silent conversation.

Brenna's mouth slackened. She ran her hands over her arms, as if she needed to inject warmth into them.

I wanted to jump out of my skin, relieving the memory of watching the only woman I'd ever loved say *yes* to another man's proposal. Her mouth had tipped open in shock that day, but it quickly gave way to a dazzling smile. She wanted to marry the man sitting at this table.

My father's note said *Don't repeat my mistakes.* He meant letting my mother go, his way of urging me to fight for Brenna. But that wasn't his mistake. He'd let his desires get in the way of what was best for the people in his life. I wouldn't do that.

I was about to announce I was going home when Jack beat me to the punch. "Why don't we get out of here?" he asked Brenna.

She finally pried her gaze away from me. "Sure, okay."

Ax began booing while the two of them stood.

"I'll see you at the next game, Ax."

"Quinn, that's a promise." Ax pointed at her.

"I'll see you at the café in the morning, Brenna."

She blinked, her right arm crossed over her body, held by her left hand. "Good night, Nathan."

23

BRENNA

Now

"My car's around back," Jack said, reaching for my hand.

"I'm staying in Palmer City, only ten minutes from here."

I stepped back from him. "Your hotel room?"

"Brenna, I didn't mean *that*. We need to talk. Somewhere private. And because you're living with another guy, we can't go to your place, can we?"

For the last two hours, I'd dreaded this moment, his airing of grievances. Those had continued to pile up since he arrived. Seeing me in Nathan's arms. Finding out I'd been living with him for a month. That we used to play baseball together... that I used to play baseball at all. We needed to have a long overdue conversation about our relationship, but I wasn't in the best shape for it.

My mind wouldn't stop replaying the earlier conversation. *Nathan saw Jack propose to me.* I couldn't imagine the agony I'd feel watching Nathan propose to another woman. Why hadn't he said anything?

"I can't afford to live in a hotel," I explained.

"I would've given you money if you'd told me."

We were separated, I wanted to retort, but I also didn't want to escalate this fight.

The bottom of my stomach dropped with dread when I saw Jack earlier, making it clear what I needed to do. Seeing my fiancé shouldn't fill me with panic. I should've missed him these last few weeks. Instead, I'd been consumed with memories of my past, with thoughts of Nathan.

I flashed him a disbelieving look. "That is a waste of money when I can stay in *my* house. I've known Nathan forever—"

Jack sneered. "Yeah, that's real fucking clear, Brenna."

My eyes roamed the handsome golden face of the man I'd agreed to marry. When he met me, I was scared, lonely, and unsure of my future. I'd been studying for the GRE to pursue a physical therapy degree. I worried about taking on debt to pay for school, having witnessed the way money created imbalances in my mother's relationships. She put up with poor behavior because her boyfriends contributed materially to our lives. I never wanted to put myself in debt to someone else. Jack had been so solid, there when I needed him.

But it wasn't like that any longer. The distance strained our relationship, but so did his inability to understand the importance of me being there for my sister.

"Is *he*"—Jack pointed his finger toward the bar—"why you canceled your trip to see me?"

"What?" I shook my head vigorously. "No."

"But you used to date him, right?"

I sighed, helpless to the way this conversation was spiraling away from what we needed to discuss. "Nathan has nothing to do with our issues. They existed long before I came here, and you know it."

"Yeah, but fucking someone else certainly doesn't help."

"I'm not fucking him!" I shouted as the bar door swung open and Nathan strode outside.

There was no way he hadn't heard me. I wanted to plunge through a crack in the sidewalk.

Jack tossed his hands in the air in exasperation. "Perfect."

"Are you okay, Bren?" Nathan asked.

Jack glared at him with more hatred than I'd ever seen from him. It wasn't for Nathan though. It was for me. Jack didn't want to admit we were over and it was *our* fault. No one else's.

"We're fine," I replied tightly, wanting Nathan to leave. I couldn't have this conversation with him here.

"Are you sure?"

"She said we're fine," Jack snapped. "Leave."

Nathan took a step toward Jack, and I lunged for his arm, pulling his attention to me. "Please just go. I promise I'm fine."

Nathan kept his blazing brown eyes on me. "I'm inside if you need anything, all right?"

Under his breath, Jack muttered, "How sweet."

I nodded, encouraging Nathan to go back inside. He watched us through the window.

"You were saying..." Jack extended his arm toward the bar.

I wouldn't convince him of the story he wanted to believe. So I took a deep, steadying breath, and pivoted to the real issue. "Our relationship hasn't been working for a while."

"Since you moved to California."

My reason for moving to California was overshadowed by how it affected him. Our relationship worked when it was on his terms, when he got everything he wanted. When he was happy.

Maybe it took distance to show me what I'd been too close to realize before.

There had been times I caught myself wondering if I *should* feel something more than I did, even before I moved to California. I chalked it up to my favorite pastime of overthinking. There was never anything *wrong* with our relationship, but there was something that didn't feel exactly right.

"This isn't working," I murmured.

"Wait, Brenna... are you *breaking up* with me?"

The question asked so plainly made me hesitate. Finality never came easy for me. Permanence flooded me with too much emotion. Jack took my momentary silence as hesitation over this decision.

And I realized in that moment, he'd never really known me. I'd never let him.

"Brenna, the distance has been hard, but when you move back to Chicago—"

"I don't know when I'll move back to Chicago," I cut him off, the words stunning him into silence. "I've got the house and the business here, and my sister to think about. If this was right, we should be able to survive the distance."

"We would've survived the distance if you prioritized our relationship," he said. "You couldn't even bother to make the one trip you planned, which was apparently to break up with me."

Why had I lied to myself for so long? I knew what being desperately in love felt like. The rush of warmth and safety. The torment when I, rightly or wrongly, perceived we weren't on the same page. But with Jack,

I stopped being affected. The absence of feeling for an HSP was glaringly and unmistakably obvious, because all we did was *feel*. It spelled the end of our relationship.

"I'm sorry," I whispered, not sure what else to say.

Jack and I had tiptoed around our unhappiness for so long, it dismantled our relationship. My therapist once told me it was important to take out the trash in a relationship, to not push down the unsaid words and feelings to the point it breached the top and overflowed. Like it was now.

I fought the heat stinging my eyes. Jack wasn't a bad man; he just wasn't who I needed. I was doing the right thing, but breaking his heart made me sick to my stomach.

"You don't get to play the victim here, Brenna." Jack's tone was colder than I'd ever heard. "I've been more than understanding about your… issues. I was so careful about what I said so I wouldn't strike a nerve. I can't even talk to you like an adult without you breaking down. Grow up."

My teeth pressed painfully into my bottom lip, and I willed myself not to cry.

"Nothing to say?" Jack prodded.

I shook my head, needing this conversation to end before I broke down and proved his point.

His head bobbed once, his lip curled in distaste. "Seems about right. I'll take my ring now."

"I don't have it with me. I didn't want to damage it playing baseball."

He laughed hollowly. "Of course." He held out his arm to the sidewalk leading to the parking lot. "Well, let's go. I'm not leaving without it."

Every ounce of my energy was focused on not crying as Jack drove us back to the house in the most painful car ride of my life. I retrieved my ring and brought it to him while he sat in the car. He didn't say a single word before driving out of my life.

Tears overwhelmed me as I crawled into bed. Hours later, my body jerked awake, my mouth parched, in desperate need of water. Nathan stood in the upstairs hallway when I came back from the kitchen. I stumbled the moment I saw him, water sloshing my hand as I grasped the banister to stay upright.

The misstep didn't happen because he startled me. My temporary loss to gravity rested squarely on Nathan being shirtless.

Did it make me a terrible person, being so affected by him only hours after breaking up with my fiancé? Probably. Go ahead and reserve a spot for me in hell, because I had zero control over my reaction to Nathan Sharpe.

His brow furrowed. "Is everything all right?"

"Yes." I didn't trust myself to look at him, so I fixed my gaze on the stairs as I ascended. I forced a yawn, not able to carry on a conversation with him right now. "I'll see you in the morning."

I closed the door behind me, heaving a sigh of relief to shut out the world.

Minutes after settling into bed, though, I saw a shadow beneath the door. *Nathan.* I held my breath while he debated whether to knock.

I wanted him to knock.

But the shadow soundlessly retreated.

Keeping my distance from Nathan was for the best, but disappointment washed over me all the same.

24

BRENNA

Seven years ago

THE CRYING STARTED AGAIN, loud wails that ripped me from sleep.

I held a pillow tight to my head to drown out the noise. Even with earplugs and a closed door, some nights I could hear her screams from down the hall.

Noise could send my head careening into blackness, unable to think until the volume came down. My complaints were ignored. Mom said we all had to make sacrifices. In other words, *suck it up*. I'd heard some version of the phrase so many times, she didn't have to say it anymore.

Over time, I developed ways of coping when overwhelmed. Retreating into a quiet dark room. Slipping beneath a weighted blanket, letting its heaviness calm my overstimulated body. I carefully chose the situations and environments I put myself in, learning when I could push and when to hold back.

Like tonight, when Molly's piercing screams wouldn't stop, my mom's and Gordon's voices layered on top, lashing out at each other due to sleep deprivation. I wouldn't get any sleep here.

I rolled out of bed, opened my window, and climbed onto a ladder propped against the side of the house. Once on the ground, I moved the ladder to the Sharpe's house and climbed to Nathan's old, perpetually unlatched, bedroom window.

The room remained unchanged after he left. It wasn't healthy for me to sleep in his bed, but when I felt abandoned and alone, being in his room gave me comfort. So I slipped under his Palmer City Owls comforter and let out a small sigh of relief.

Quiet.

My eyes closed, and sleep took me.

⸺◆⸺

My eyes fluttered open to find Nathan leaning over the bed, his hand on my cheek. I jerked away from his touch, startled by his sudden presence.

After eight months without my best friend, without the boy I loved, I thought I was dreaming him.

"Nathan, what are you doing here?" My voice was clouded by sleep. Even through the haze, relief at seeing him zipped through me.

He straightened to his full height, swaying on his feet. "This is *my* bed. What are *you* doing here?"

"I couldn't sleep with the crying and the yelling... and you don't live here anymore."

"So you thought you could break into my room and sleep in my bed?"

"It wasn't like you were using it." I greedily took him in, desperate to memorize the way dark strands of longer hair fell on his forehead, the way his cotton shirt clung to his toned abdomen, the shadow of dark stubble lining his jaw. "Why are you here, Nathan?"

He let out a humorless laugh, sinking onto the bed beside me. "They didn't tell you?" He pushed a strand of hair behind my ear, his cold fingers brushing my skin. The move surprised me, so reminiscent of when we were dating. A bite of alcohol tinged my nose with him this close.

Well, that explained it.

"The custody agreement is finally in place," Nathan went on. "I have to come back to this hellhole twice a month."

His fingers trailed down my face, and my body trembled. He broke my heart, but I still craved him.

"I should go." I needed time alone to process his return.

I'd cried myself to sleep every night for a month, wishing he'd come back. But this wasn't the boy who left. I didn't want the reminder that he'd changed.

My legs slipped out from under the covers, and my feet landed on the floor.

"Please stay," he begged, his anguished voice stabbing me straight in the heart. It hurt as much as the incredible sensation of Nathan's hand on my arm, holding me in place. I wanted to close my eyes, to sink into this fantasy, Nathan's hands on me, him saying a version of the words I'd dreamed too many times to count.

But he didn't mean it.

"You're drunk, Nathan."

He tugged me closer.

I didn't resist. Couldn't resist, not with the way his touch ignited my skin. He positioned me between his legs, his hands moving to my hips.

My heart pounded so loud, I heard it in my ears. It beat like this only for him.

But this isn't right. I shouldn't be here. He *shouldn't be touching me like this.*

"Nathan, we're not together anymore." My breathy voice poked holes in the resolve of the statement, already shaky at best.

"Just... pretend, Bren." The moonlight slanted into the room, illuminating his turquoise eyes, intense and locked on me. His fingers kneaded my hips.

I remained frozen to the spot, admiring him, marveling that we were this close again. That he was begging me to stay.

"Just tonight. I miss you. Please."

He pulled me into his lap, my legs bracketing his hips.

"This isn't..." I closed my eyes as Nathan dropped featherlight kisses along the column of my neck. I tried again. "Nathan, we shouldn't..."

Nathan whispered next to my ear, "It hurts how much I miss you. Just tonight, make it stop."

The torment in his tone, the desire in his gaze...

I leaned forward, placing my lips on his. Softly, so softly, as if at any moment, he could evaporate. But it was all the encouragement Nathan needed. His hands moved to my ass, pulling me to him as he lay back on the bed. He was hard, pressed against my leg. Knowing he still reacted that way to me... it felt *good.*

Nathan deepened the kiss, his lips moving fervently against mine. I missed the feel of him, the taste of him. Even the faint hint of beer lingering in his mouth didn't bother me. I wanted to drown in him.

The way he met each move of my lips, each swipe of my tongue, told me he felt the same.

Unable to resist, I let him pull me under.

When I opened my eyes the next morning, Nathan wasn't there. If his clothes hadn't littered the floor, I would've thought I dreamed him coming home and seducing me into the hottest make-out of my life. My eye caught the time on the clock on the nightstand next to me—six thirty a.m. *Shit.*

I flew out of bed to the window, heaving a sigh of relief to see my ladder still leaning against the house. Following the reverse path of last night, I was back in my room in less than ten minutes, hustling to dress for school. I had just enough time to splash water in my hair, brush my teeth, and apply a quick swipe of eyeshadow and lip gloss before I needed to be downstairs for family breakfast. A new tradition my mom instituted after Mr. Sharpe—Gordon, at his insistence—moved in, because she wanted to pretend we were one big happy family.

Initially, I didn't want to play along. To pretend my heart hadn't been torn open by what she'd done. What *they'd* done. But then Molly was born, the sibling I'd always wanted. She didn't deserve to live in a tension-filled house. Babies picked up on that. Their surroundings shaped them.

For her, I sucked it up. I played nice until it was no longer entirely pretend.

"Oh, good," my mother chirped, seeing me descend the last few steps. "We can have a full family breakfast for the first time."

My knees threatened to give out at the sight of Nathan Sharpe at our kitchen table. His frustratingly unreadable gaze met mine. Fireworks erupted in my belly. Those perfect lips had kissed me last night. I'd rested all my weight on him, savored his strength. Staring at him now, all I wanted was to do it again.

I am a terrible person.

"Isn't it great to have Nathan home?" Mom trilled with a smile.

Fake. All fake.

She didn't want Nathan here. I heard her tell Gordon it'd be best for him to stay with his mother, to give him time to cool down. Gordon had snapped back that Nathan was his son and bringing him back to Middlebury was his only shot at getting his forgiveness.

"Brenna, why are you just standing there?" She carried a plate of pancakes to the table. Her actions made me wonder if she'd been body snatched. "Take a seat."

"You look exhausted," Nathan chimed in, his blindingly beautiful grin stretching across his face. "Late night, Bren?"

I walked on unsteady legs to the head of the table, opposite Nathan. "Molls woke me up," I said, focusing my attention on moving pancakes to my plate.

"Good thing she's so damn cute," Gordon called from the stairs, Molly in his arms.

Nathan frowned before averting his eyes.

The doorbell rang. An anvil dropped in my stomach. I knew exactly who waited at the front door.

"Like clockwork," my mom muttered. I glared at her. "You're too young for a serious relationship, Brenna. I'm looking out for *you*."

Nathan shot up, his chair flying out from behind him, knocking into the wall. I helplessly chased him to the door. I grabbed his hand before he reached it, trying to pause time so I could talk to him before he invited my boyfriend into the house.

Nathan shook off my hand. His demeanor had transformed from the grinning boy at the table earlier. His nostrils flared, and his eyes were cold. "Don't you want me to meet him?"

The question stunned me silent while I battled being swallowed by my guilt.

"You're just like your mother."

I took a step back, clutching my chest like the words were a physical blow. My mouth parted, but no response came out. I kept staring at him, waiting for him to take it back, to apologize, to snap his fingers and break me out of this nightmare.

But he opened the door to Derek, dressed in a plain white T-shirt beneath a long-sleeved navy blue button-up. His megawatt smile faltered as he took in Nathan, then me.

Derek's eyebrows rose, but he snapped his fingers. "Nathan, right? Brenna didn't mention you'd be here."

"Brenna fails to mention lots of things," Nathan muttered under his breath.

In some far reach of my consciousness last night, I remembered I had a boyfriend, someone who had been nice when I was at my lowest. But Nathan consumed my every thought, and I betrayed the boy who approached me when I sat alone in the cafeteria.

I warned Derek he didn't want to sit with me, but he took a seat anyway, saying he'd make the judgment himself. I *liked* him. He was cute and smart, and we had fun together. I had to move on from Nathan, so why not him?

Nathan looked over his shoulder at me, where I stood cemented to the floor. "Aren't you going to introduce me to your boyfriend, *sis*?"

That ripped me out of my momentary trance. "I'm not your *sister*."

"No, but we share a sibling, and our parents are probably going to get married."

"I would be your *step*sister then."

Nathan shrugged, affecting nonchalance. Any walls that broke down last night were raised again. "Same difference."

"It's not."

Derek's head swiveled between Nathan and me as we volleyed retorts. In the quiet that followed, he stuck out his hand to Nathan. "I'm Derek."

Nathan wrenched his hateful gaze from me to take his hand.

"It's good to meet you," Derek said.

"Breakfast is getting cold," I said, pulling him toward the kitchen. I didn't look back at Nathan.

25

NATHAN

Now

Brenna hadn't worn her engagement ring in days.

Not since the night she returned to the house without her fiancé and he left town.

We hadn't talked about anything that happened that night. Not the moment we shared on the field. Not the revelation that I saw Brenna's marriage proposal. Not the sudden appearance and disappearance of her significant other.

There was either nothing for Brenna to tell me, or the absence of her ring had nothing to do with me. I didn't ask because I'd rather not have confirmation.

Withered fingers snapped in front of my face. "Your turn, Sharpe," Bertram barked. "Stop holding up our game. You think we have all the time in the world?"

The other two men guffawed. I'd never met people more amused by the prospect of their impending demise.

"Sorry," I mumbled, reacquainting myself with my cards. The regular group of seniors had beckoned me into this game thirty minutes ago during my break.

The front door chimed, stealing my attention. Gemma strode through, flanked by two women. A pretty woman, whose blue-dyed hair was piled on top of her head in a bun, sported a Palmer City Wolves sweatshirt. And on Gemma's other side... Deandra Collins.

"Nathan Sharpe," Deandra said, a thin smile breaking her cool expression.

Bertram sighed loudly. "We're in the middle of a game."

I tossed him a look, then dropped my cards on the table. "I fold."

It wasn't as if I had a shot at beating these guys. They only invited me to play to fatten their winnings and to annoy Allison, who'd been staring daggers at the rowdy group all morning.

Deandra and I met in the middle of the café, pulling each other into a hug.

"When Gemma told me you owned the place next door, I didn't believe it." She assessed me from my feet to my face. "You look the same as I remember."

I tilted my head to the side. She wore a long-sleeved white blouse tucked into a tight, knee-length gray skirt. Her black heels brought her close to my eye level. "And you look like you bust balls for a living."

The third woman in the group laughed. "Clearly he knows you."

Deandra gestured to her. "This is my friend, Kennedy. Kennedy, Nathan." She didn't explain how we knew each other. I wondered how much she'd already shared about our past.

"Good to meet you." I extended a hand to Kennedy. "How do y'all know each other?"

Deandra stared pointedly at Kennedy, as if she were communicating a message. "We used to work together for the Wolves."

"So…" I said to Gemma, elbowing the air toward Kennedy. "She's the best friend whose dad owns the team?"

Gemma grinned. "I told you I could get you tickets for a game any time you want. Just don't tell Bertram, or I'll never hear the end of it."

"Bertram already has season tickets," Kennedy said. "Right behind mine."

"Oh, he doesn't want tickets," Gemma replied with a sigh. "He wants to hang out with our men. Why do you think he and his gaggle of gamblers are here? It's been this way ever since he ran into Matt at the bakery. Bertram interrogated him. It took over an hour to pry him away."

Bertram and his friends were too busy arguing about their poker game to notice who walked into the café or to overhear the smack talk Gemma laid down. I didn't expect it to last, though.

"I thought you were on maternity leave. How's the baby?"

Deandra threw an arm around Gemma's shoulders and bumped their hips together. "This one can't stay away from her business, even though she can check in by camera at any time."

Gemma held up a finger. "Not true. I'm very happy at home with my little girl. Thanks for asking, Nathan. Matt needs some time alone with her too. And I miss getting dressed."

"And you *love* meddling," Kennedy added, to which Gemma *tsked*.

"Anyway, we're here to grab lunch," Deandra answered in earnest.

I gestured to a table on the opposite side of the café from Bertram and his band of happy gamblers. "You're in luck. We now serve breakfast."

Gemma laughed. "So it's still coming along?"

"We're working on it. Should have a lunch menu up and running next week."

"I'm surprised you kept Allison." Gemma raised an eyebrow.

I let out a deep sigh. "It wasn't entirely by choice, I'll say that, but I've enjoyed watching our regulars get under her skin."

We looked at Allison behind the counter, scowling at Bertram and his crew. They hadn't ordered anything in over an hour and took up the table in the window. Two strikes. Nothing she could do about it, though, since I made it clear they were welcome.

"So that's still going on, huh?" Deandra drawled. I followed her gaze to where Brenna stood watching us before she abruptly turned her attention to something on the tablet we used for checkout. She tucked her hair behind one ear, a classic self-conscious tell of hers.

"Don't," I warned. "She's engaged." Or *was* engaged? I had no fucking idea.

"Does she know it's not to you?"

"Nothing is happening between us." I gritted my teeth.

I wanted something to happen between us. Denying it hadn't made the feelings go away. And with that ring of hers no longer on display, it was hard to fight my thoughts about whether I could make the possibility real.

But then I remembered the agony of losing her, and it stopped me from doing anything rash. I didn't know if I could handle it again.

Deandra laughed, her dark pin-straight hair swaying as she nodded at Kennedy. "That's what this one used to say, and now she's at every game, wearing the guy's jersey."

"I'm going to love it when someone knocks you on your ass," Kennedy tossed back at her.

"Not likely, Kens." Deandra dropped her voice low. "Let's test your theory, Nathan."

She turned to Brenna and waved, a broad smile on her face. "Brenna!" she sang. "It's good to see you. This place looks great."

"Thank you." Brenna held up a flat hand, her mouth twisting with annoyance. I'd seen that look of simmering jealousy before, but not since high school.

Her gaze swung to me, disdain for Deandra remaining for a beat before her expression cleared. She pointed over her shoulder. "I've got to take care of something in the back." To Allison, she asked, "Do you have it covered?"

Brenna retreated before Allison could agree.

"Just as I thought." Deandra winked at me. "It's high school all over again, except this time, I won't be the pretty face you distract yourself with."

"Ooh." Gemma's voice rose a few octaves. "Please tell me this story."

"I'd rather not—" I started before Deandra swiftly cut me off.

She opened a mirror to reapply dark red lipstick. "Brenna caught us making out on the couch at her house. She was dating someone else at the time, and Nathan wanted to make her jealous." She smacked her lips before closing the compact. "Boy, did she want to kill me."

"I wasn't trying to make her jealous," I protested.

"Oh, please. We could have gone to your room. You wanted her to catch us."

I hadn't realized it then, at least not consciously. "Shit, I'm sorry, Deandra."

She flicked her hand at me. "It's fine. All of us knew the deal, Nathan. You didn't make promises."

I scratched the back of my neck, uncomfortable with this walk down memory lane. "All right. Well... I take your orders and get them into the kitchen."

Gemma smirked. "Do you usually take orders?"

Kennedy swatted her hand, understanding more about the dynamic here than I expected. When the food was ready, I carried it to the table so Brenna wouldn't have to. The three of them were eventually recognized by Bertram, who took a seat at their table after his friends left. Gemma grumbled before he came over, but she chatted happily with him.

Kennedy caught my arm as I was clearing their plates. She kept fiddling with something in her bag, which I realized was an excuse to hang back and talk to me alone. "Don't give up, yet." I thought she meant the café, but her eyes flicked to Brenna behind the counter. "Things tend to work out the way they should."

My heart swelled, desperate for any sign of hope for Brenna and me. Maybe Kennedy saw something in Brenna's expression that I didn't... or at least I couldn't trust that I did. Brenna and I used to communicate openly and honestly, but we weren't yet back to the place from before our parents fucked up our lives. One of us had to take the first step to repair us, to address our past, admit what simmered between us now.

She wouldn't. I knew Brenna to her core. She avoided hurting people, and bringing up our past would hurt me. I took a deep breath, rallying to ask if she wanted to grab lunch.

But the café door chimed, and Derek Ellis walked in, his eyes firmly on Brenna. "Ready to go?"

I slumped into the nearest chair and watched as Brenna left without a glance in my direction.

I needed to get the fuck out of Middlebury before I lost my damn mind.

26

BRENNA

Now

THE TEMPERATURE DROPPED FIFTY degrees in the last few days.

None of my clothes from California did anything to protect me from the cold. My heaviest winter clothes were still in my old roommate's storage locker in Chicago.

The HVAC didn't circulate as well as it should, and my room bore the brunt, always hotter or colder than the rest of the house. When I first got here, I basked in the extra heat, but now I was wearing leggings, sweatpants, a tank top, a T-shirt, and Nathan's sweatshirt that I never returned.

"You look like a snowman," Molly teased. She sat on the couch, eating cereal and watching cartoons, like we used to do when we lived together. We video chatted every Saturday morning since my temporary move to Middlebury, pretending we weren't thousands of miles apart.

"It's cold, Molls," I whined playfully, pulling the drawstring of my sweatshirt hood tighter.

She swallowed another bite. "It's warm here. I played outside yesterday in short sleeves."

"Oh yeah? Played what? Baseball?"

She giggled. "Hockey, of course."

I laughed with her. "Are you *sure*, Molls? Because I know how much you love baseball."

Thirty minutes later, after Molly and I finished watching another cartoon, Nathan bumped into my wedged-open door. "Christmas came early for someone," he announced.

He placed four cardboard boxes on the floor. Cappie and Bebe immediately moved from the bed to investigate.

"Hey Molly, I've gotta go. We'll talk on Thanksgiving, yeah?"

"Oh, I'm sorry, I didn't mean—" Nathan attempted to leave the room.

I held up a finger, telling him to wait.

She smiled. "Mom says we're going out to eat."

Huh. Not what I expected.

"That's okay," I told her. "I'll talk to her to figure out a time, all right? I love you, Molls."

"Love you, too," she sang before ending the call.

I turned my attention to Nathan. "Well, winter came early." I shifted underneath my mountain of blankets. "The weighted blanket you got me is a lifesaver, by the way."

"You said you missed yours, so..." Nathan cleared his throat. One hand scratched behind his neck. "Glad you like it."

Our conversations had been stilted since Jack came to town. Every word exchanged was pleasant—*too* pleasant, as if neither of us wanted to step one toe out of line. The topics Nathan and I avoided piled to the ceiling at this point. Nathan's eyes drifted to my ringless finger every day, usually when he thought I wasn't paying attention. But I was *always* aware of him.

"Did you confirm our appointment with the real estate agent?" I asked to end the suffocating silence.

Nathan's arms flexed as he propped them over his unconscionably fit chest and crossed one foot over the other, leaning into the doorframe. "Yeah, she'll be here Tuesday to do the walk-through."

All the rooms had been painted, except the two we slept in. We'd sold most of the furniture, aside from what we needed to live here. The appointment with the real estate agent would give us a sense of the listing price and ideas for other projects to tackle before putting it on the market. We didn't have the budget to pay anyone to do the work, so whatever projects we undertook had to be simple enough to do ourselves.

"What's that?" My eyes snagged on a large duffle bag in the hallway outside my door. Nathan shifted on his feet. "Are you... doing laundry?"

"Not exactly..."

"Wait, are you leaving?" I pushed myself to a sitting position. Mia growled at the sudden movement. "I'm sorry, baby," I sang to her in the soft, high-pitched lilting tone I reserved for the cats.

Nathan nodded.

"You didn't... why didn't you say anything?"

Nathan blew out a breath. "I didn't realize I needed to."

"I mean, it's common courtesy."

"Common courtesy," he repeated with a half laugh, though I wasn't sure what was funny. It wasn't like I didn't know if he'd come back. We were stuck together until our work in Middlebury was finished, but...

But I no longer wanted that to be the only reason he came back.

"Where are you going?" I asked, battling to escape layers of blankets. Once I kicked off the last one, I sprang to my feet.

Nathan stared at me with a bemused smile. "Home for a few days." Then he broke into laughter. "Bren, I can't take you seriously right now. You look like a snowman."

"I'm cold! And it's going to get colder with the storm— Wait! Nathan, you can't leave, not with the storm."

He waved a hand. "It's not going to be that bad."

"What about in Palmer City? Did you check?"

"My flight is on," he said firmly. "My car will be here in a few minutes."

"Do you have big plans or something?"

Nathan turned and picked up his bag from the floor. "No—"

"Then what's the big deal?" I tailed him as he walked down the steps. "You could reschedule for another time. You're going to fly back during peak Thanksgiving travel."

Thanksgiving was less than a week away. We'd been preparing at the café, hoping to have an influx of families buying coffee and eating breakfast that weekend. We even made an agreement with Gemma to sell some of her baked goods.

Nathan spun to face me, immediately halting my descent. "The big deal, Brenna, is I need to be somewhere else. I need a weekend to myself."

The words burned like a slap. "You need a weekend away from me, you mean."

"I need... a break."

"I thought we were getting along?"

"We were... we are..."

"Is this because I went to lunch with Derek?" I blurted out, desperate to keep him talking, worried if he left before we got to the bottom of this, we might never talk about it again.

"What?"

"It's not... like that... if that's what you're worried about," I sputtered, tracing circles in the carpet with one socked foot.

An emotion flickered over his face before his expression quickly slipped back to frustrating blankness. "I'm not flying home because you had lunch with Ellis, Brenna."

"Then, what is it?" I flung my arms out wide, frustration seeping into every bone.

He stared, his head tilted, waiting for me to finish my thought.

"What is your reason for pushing me away?"

"I'm not—"

"You are," I insisted, trying to fight the sting in my eyes. "You know you are. Just tell me why."

A car horn sounded outside. Nathan pulled his phone from his pocket and unlocked it, his eyes scanning the screen. "I've gotta go." He turned, taking the last few steps to the front door.

"Nathan!" I called, stopping on the bottom step.

He stood in the open doorway. A crease formed between his brows. "What happened to your engagement ring, Brenna?"

He stepped toward me until we were so close, we breathed the same air. My fingers twitched at my side, longing to reach out to him, to wrap my arms around his neck, to pull his mouth to mine.

I could. I wasn't promised to anyone.

My lips parted, readying to answer, to say something, anything. But no words came.

"I'll see you in a few days, Quinn," he whispered before he walked out of the house, leaving me behind.

My hands rustled through the nightstand drawer before I could stop myself. I never opened the letter Gordon left for me. I didn't want to see his last words. I held onto people, experiences, feelings for far longer than other people. Endings were never easy for me.

As soon as Nathan closed the front door of the house, all I wanted to know was *why* Gordon did this to me. He knew I was highly sensitive. He knew I'd always loved his son, agonized over his loss. Gordon also knew the depth of Nathan's stubbornness and pride. What made him think we'd get it right this time?

I took a deep breath before slipping the paper out of its once-sealed envelope and unfolding it.

My dearest Brenna, the letter started. A choked laugh spilled from my mouth at the formal greeting. This from the man who used to scream from the dugout to get my ass in gear.

I imagine you're reading this letter pissed off because of my heavy-handed attempt to intervene in your life. My parents were strict when I was growing up, and I promised myself I'd never be like them. I'd give my kid the chance to choose his own path in life, not force one on him. I'd support his dreams without trying to live through him. Instead of cleaning up his messes, I'd let him make mistakes so he'd learn.

But I'm cleaning up my own mess now.

It's my fault it took death and a legal document to get you and Nathan in the same room. You blamed your mother, but it was just as much on me. I made a mistake that cost me my wife and the respect of my son. It brought me Molly, and it gave me an official title in your life, so I can't completely regret my actions, but I regret that I caused a lot of harm.

Growing up, we think adults have it all figured out, but we're flawed. I'm sure you see this now—how easy it is to make a mistake that affects your entire life, and there's not an undo button to fix it.

I deserved to live with the repercussions of my decisions, but you and Nathan didn't. You don't, Brenna. Be mad at me for putting you in this situation, but don't waste the opportunity. You won't get another chance to fix my mistake. To get back the person who belongs in your life.

I'm sorry it falls to you. I know it's not in your nature to push, or to go after what you want. So do it for Nathan. You are what he wants. You are who he's always wanted.

I can't think of anyone I'd rather have loving my son.
I've included a letter to Molly. I leave it to you to decide if and
when to give it to her.

Be happy, Brenna. That is my only wish for you.

Love,
Gordon

I read the letter again and again, hearing his voice speak the words in my mind. Waiting for the ache in my chest to subside. But it didn't.

I *missed* him. The way he listened to me. His offbeat stories.

I wished Nathan hadn't left. He was the only person in the world who could understand, who I wanted to share Gordon's words with.

Nathan was who I always wanted too.

27

NATHAN

My rideshare was pulling up to the sidewalk at the airport when I received a text telling me my flight had been canceled.

The winter storm hadn't reached Palmer City, but it would in an hour or two. Unlike lightning storms when airlines kept passengers waiting, delaying the flight over and over again, the airport would shut down for winter storms. Just like the entire city. Even though we'd only get an inch or two of snow and ice.

I'd lived in North Carolina long enough to expect this, but I had to leave that house. So I left, hoping my flight could sneak out before everyone hunkered down.

"My flight just got canceled," I said to my driver. "Can you take me back home?"

"Seriously, man?" the young guy groaned.

"I'll give you fifty dollars on top of the trip cost." I held up my wad of travel cash.

Snowflakes were falling by the time I got back. I assumed the dark house meant Brenna and the cats were congregated in her bedroom, which had no windows facing the front. But when I opened the door, there was no light anywhere.

Did she leave?

"Brenna?" I called.

No answer.

"Bren?" I repeated louder.

I took the steps two at a time, adrenaline thrumming beneath my skin. She wasn't in her bed.

Did she go to Derek's the moment I left the house? Did I lose her again before I'd even won her back?

I hustled to my room to drop my bag, to ready myself to drive to his place—

My body sagged in relief to find Brenna snuggled beneath the covers of my bed, surrounded by our four cats. She fucking *belongs* here, and I couldn't keep pretending I didn't think so. I wanted to wake up beside her, to touch her soft skin, to breathe in her sweetness, to listen to every word she had to say.

I'd *always* wanted that, and the feeling would never change.

The cats' heads perked up, and they tracked my movements. As quietly as possible, I shuffled into the room, deposited my bag beside the bed, and sank onto the chair in the corner.

Waiting for her to wake.

❖

Brenna yawned a couple of hours later, stretching her arms over her head. Her gaze immediately landed on me, presumably drawn by the light of my phone. I'd polished off a movie and started a second, my body surprisingly calm despite the anticipation of talking to her when she opened her eyes.

"You came home."

I heard the same relief in her voice that had surged through me when I found her in my bed. She chewed her lower lip and pulled a blanket around her shoulders. The movement revealed she was wearing *my* sweatshirt.

"My flight was canceled."

My eyes flicked to the window, where I could see the earlier snowflakes had turned to freezing rain, sure to ravage our roads with ice. Brenna stared at the storm raging outside, her expression distant. I wanted to keep her with me, to repair the rift between us. Being stuck inside the house with her down the hall was a torment I could no longer endure, not when it might not have to be that way. If only we could remove the armor we'd encased ourselves in eight years ago.

One of us had to begin to remove pieces.

"You have no idea how hard it was to come back and live in the same house as you." My soft voice sounded loud in the quiet atmosphere of the storm.

"I think I know *exactly* what it was like, Nathan."

I leaned forward and rested my elbows on my knees. "With one big difference."

Brenna's gaze locked with mine. "What's that?"

"You were in love with someone else. You were happy with someone else. I was *dying* inside, having to watch it." I let out a sigh, raking a hand through my hair.

After the custody arrangement was finalized, I returned to Middle-bury angry but desperate to see her. The universe delivered when I found her in my bed, just like tonight. I lost it, damning any consequences, because I needed her close. Finding her there had to mean some part of her missed me.

I still remembered the soft moan she let out when I hauled her against me as we kissed. By some miracle, she still wanted me. I rode that high until the next morning when her boyfriend rang the doorbell. Eight months apart, and all I could think about was *her*. She'd already found another guy.

Brenna broke through my thoughts, her tone filled with as much pain as mine.

"How many girls did I have to see you with?"

"Come on, Quinn." I shook my head. "You knew they all meant nothing."

She clutched the blanket tighter around herself, knuckles going white. "No, *Sharpe*, I didn't. *I* felt like nothing more than a speck of dirt under your shoe when you pretended the night in your room hadn't happened. You made me question whether I dreamed it. You made me feel *delusional*."

"What did you want me to do? You had a boyfriend."

"But you knew—"

"No." I stood, pointing a finger at her. "I *didn't* know. And I hated you for making me a party to cheating. An affair tore my family apart, Brenna."

"I know!" Her face landed in her open palms. "I know," she repeated, her defeated voice barely audible through her hands.

She took a deep breath, then dropped her mask. "This pull between us"—she motioned in the air—"I've never been able to resist it."

I chanced a step forward, then settled on the edge of the bed and took her hands in my own. With that barest of contact, my heart rate throttled. "Me either. I realized the only way to get through living in the same house with you while not being with you was to make you hate me. I made it easier for you. You got to hate me—"

Brenna released my hands as if they'd burned her. "Fuck you, Nathan, for thinking you did me a favor by throwing your women in my face." She ripped off the covers and scrambled out of the bed, away from me. "For all those nasty one-liners. You, more than anyone, knew how well they would land, how deep they would cut. Hating you was misery for me. Don't you dare rewrite history."

One moment Brenna and I were staring at each other with eight years of pent-up emotions between us.

The next, the house was plunged into total darkness.

"Fuck," I muttered, knowing what this meant even before walking to the window to verify every house and the streetlights were dark. "Power's out."

"The backup generator is in the basement, but we have no gas to power it," I said.

Brenna stood in the kitchen beside a collection of flashlights, batteries, candles, and matches. Between my recent grocery run and the gas stove, we'd be able to cook and eat for several days.

We had light and food, but heat was an issue. As if punctuating the point, Brenna shivered, running her hands up and down her arms.

"We need to go up to my room," I said.

"What? Why?"

"It's small, so we can trap the heat in. And it's naturally warmer than your room."

Brenna looked at her feet and murmured, "I'd rather be in my room."

She wanted to hide from me and the emotions our conversation had unearthed. If the electricity hadn't gone out, I had no doubt she would've bolted. But I would have followed her... maybe not right away, but eventually. It was time to break this pattern.

"The cats will follow you, Bren. They're smaller than us—"

She narrowed her eyes. "Are you actually concerned about the cats or is this a ploy?"

Can't it be both? I wanted to say, but the words halted on my tongue at her stern expression. "It might be days before we can turn the heat back on," I said instead.

I would walk miles in the snow to the nearest gas station before I let her suffer in the cold.

She put up a hand. "Fine, fine. I get it."

Maybe using the cats to convince her was a low blow, but I'd do anything to protect her.

We also couldn't repair our relationship if we were on opposite sides of the house.

28

BRENNA

Now

NATHAN AND I WORDLESSLY climbed the stairs to my room, gathered a cache of blankets, and took them to his.

I didn't want to be in the same room with him after our argument. I'd rather hide and try to forget the words we'd hurled at each other. He had no right to cast himself as a hero for giving me reasons to hate him. Implying he suffered more than I did. Acting like he'd done me a favor.

There was no way I could sleep beside him, even for warmth. I'd rather shiver for days than put myself in that agonizing situation.

But then I watched the cats jump onto Nathan's bed without an ounce of the apprehension brewing in my belly. The rest of the house would soon feel like ice, including my room. I wouldn't let them suffer because of my sensitivity.

I slipped under the covers, settling on my side of the bed and pulling up an e-book on my phone. Maybe not the smartest thing to do when the electricity was out, but I couldn't read an actual book without lying on my back, which would put Nathan distractingly into my periphery. It was bad enough his bed offered no reprieve from him, especially with four cats there with us.

At least I wouldn't be cold.

His footsteps echoed moments before he slid into bed beside me. I refused to stir, to turn, to look at him. This bed, this man... memories overwhelmed me.

"I don't know how you sleep like this." Nathan tossed some blankets, pushing more fabric onto me. I didn't mind one bit. "I feel like I'm suffocating in cotton."

"No one is making you stay."

He sighed and I detected pain in it. My heart squeezed. I hated hurting Nathan, but I'd learned that setting boundaries was critical to protect myself. Lying beside him would dredge up a well of emotions that would slowly drown me. Maybe I could get him to leave.

But I couldn't forget his words. *You were in love with someone else. You were happy with someone else. I was* dying *inside, having to watch it.*

Once again, his pain was mine. Every time he brought around a girl, a hand would reach through my chest and tear off another piece of my heart.

"Brenna. I don't want to fight with you."

His breath hit the back of my neck, and I suppressed a shiver.

The exhaustion due to running from my past, from him, from every ugly feeling I still harbored threatened to undo me. We'd both run from our problems for years.

"Convenient." I placed my phone on the nightstand, and rolled over to face him, even though I risked losing my train of thought by looking into those turquoise eyes. "You said everything you needed to say."

"Not even close, Bren."

Keeping him at a distance was *too hard*. But I couldn't get close to him again until we'd dealt with the shit piled between us. Maybe we *needed* to fight, even if it made me uncomfortable.

"Well, I can't lay next to you and keep pretending."

"In what way are you pretending, darlin'?"

Goosebumps spread over my arms. Our closeness, the suggestive question. Nathan's damn southern lilt.

I closed my eyes, trying to keep my breathing even. From beneath the behemoth of blankets, I still couldn't shield my rapidly moving chest.

"Stop doing that," I whispered.

"Doing what?"

I blew out a breath, then opened my eyes to level him with a look. The heat in his eyes made me ache between my legs. "We either talk, Nathan, or you leave."

"This is *my* room." His lips twitched.

"Don't think I don't have ways to force you out."

He tucked a strand of hair behind my ear. "I think I might like those ways of yours, Bren."

I batted his hand away. "If you stay in here, there are rules."

His eyebrows rose. "Rules?"

"Yes."

"Ever a good girl."

Nathan's smirk sent a bolt of longing low into my gut.

"As if you're *so* dangerous."

Except he was—and always had been—lethal to me.

"No touching," I said before he could respond, needing to stop the flirtation.

He laughed, flopping onto his back. His head swiveled toward me. "That's your rule?"

My cheeks heated. I was so transparent, I might as well have been freshly cleaned glass. Hastily, I added, "I said there are *rules*. No lying. We each get two time-outs to use when we need a break."

His smile stretched to a full-on grin. "How do you plan to enforce this no-lying rule?"

"You have a tell."

Nathan had never lied to me before, so I didn't know if this was true, but it sounded convincing.

"You do too."

I rolled my eyes. "I'm well aware. So is everyone who has ever met me."

"Just in case..." Nathan said, rolling to his other side to pick up something from the floor. He thrust a bottle onto the bed between us. "Any sign of bullshit, and it's a shot of whiskey."

"Where the heck did that come from?"

He snorted. "Did you think we'd survive this blackout *without* alcohol?"

"Can't we drink something other than whiskey? I hate it."

"Better tell the truth then, Quinn."

"Fine. But you need to do shots of almond milk." Nathan fake-gagged at my suggestion. One side of my mouth lifted before I could smother the reaction. "It's only fair. You like whiskey."

He grumbled but retrieved the almond milk from the fridge. He plopped it, along with two shot glasses, next to the whiskey bottle. "And because you made me leave this room, I'll kick us off. What happened to your engagement ring?"

He voiced the question I'd seen in his eyes for weeks. I wasn't ready to tell him the story, to tear down the protective wall my engagement had raised around me. Nathan would never make a move on anyone in a relationship. If he knew I was no longer in one, I didn't know what he'd do. Attraction simmered between us, and we were stuck in the same bed. If he acted, I wouldn't be able to resist, even though my heart would shatter when we went our separate ways again.

Or maybe it would give us closure, and we could finally move on from each other. People banged to get it out of their systems all the time... didn't they?

I met his stare. "I returned the ring to its owner."

Nathan narrowed his eyes. "Descriptive." He shook the whiskey bottle, but I didn't budge. He wasn't getting more information, even with the distractingly soft look in his eyes. "Suit yourself."

He poured a healthy shot and held it out to me. My fingers grazed his as he handed me the glass, and a well of want churned in my gut. Each time I thought I'd reached its depths, Nathan reminded me just how deep my desire for him went.

I wrenched my gaze from him to focus on the task at hand, tossing back the amber liquid, feeling it burn a path down my throat. I sputtered at the harsh taste and tears stung my eyes. Nathan covered his mouth, at least *trying* to suppress the laugh.

"What did the note from your dad say?" I asked after the burn subsided.

I thought about asking about his shoulder. It'd serve him right for hurling a fastball with his first question, but I *needed* this to work. Besides, I did wonder what the note Nathan crumbled and tossed angrily into the trash had said. Despite my curiosity, I'd resisted the urge to fish it out and violate his privacy.

"A piss-poor excuse for his actions," he answered.

Without my prodding, Nathan took a shot of almond milk. He chased it with a swig directly from the whiskey bottle. "That's fucking disgusting," he muttered.

"Not as bad as regular milk."

"Says the woman who considers cardboard a snack." He fired his next question before I could defend rice cakes—one of my main food groups. "Why are you seeing Ellis?"

"We're friends," I retorted.

Nathan shook the whiskey bottle back and forth, pushing it in my direction.

I swallowed, preparing to share something no one else in my life understood. I didn't expect him to be any different. "Derek is giving me legal advice. I'm trying to get custody of Molly. Kathy's not fit to raise her."

His head jerked back. "Not what I expected."

"But you're relieved?"

He took another swig of whiskey. "That you're not fucking the smug prick? Yeah, Bren, I'm relieved."

"You know he's not a bad guy. What's the real reason you don't like him?"

Nathan blinked. "I told you."

"He got the moments with me that you wanted?" I repeated his words from over a month ago in a mocking undertone, too cowardly to say them any other way. "Come on. You didn't want anything to do with me back then. At least not when you were sober."

Nathan shook his head. "That's not true, Brenna."

"I thought we said no lying, Nathan."

"I'm not."

"Prove it."

Nathan gripped the almond milk carton, readying to pour a shot before abruptly shoving it back on the bed. "You know what? No. You want the truth, Bren? The night I found you in my bed? I was plastered because I was losing my shit over seeing you again. I worried you wouldn't want anything to do with me. I was still in love with you. I wanted you back. I was prepared to do *anything* to make it happen. Then I found you here, in my bed... and you kissed me. It wasn't what I'd planned, but *God...*"

Nathan let out a sexy groan that had me squeezing my legs together for relief. I watched his perfect mouth form the words, utterly captivated, unable to look away.

"It felt fucking *good* to have you in my arms again."

His eyes bored into mine, sending my stomach into a tizzy.

"I stopped us before anything went too far because I needed to know you were in this *with* me. I was miserable without you, but if we took that step, I didn't know if I'd recover. I couldn't unknow what it felt like to be inside you, how you tasted. You would have ruined me."

I could barely think of anything beyond the incessant pounding between my legs.

I *wanted* Nathan Sharpe to ruin me.

"Nathan?" I hadn't ever heard my voice sound like this, desperate and needy. "I need..."

He turned toward me, his gaze focused on my parted lips. "Yeah?"

I licked my lips, relishing the way his eyes followed the movement. He'd kiss me if I let him. I wanted him to overwhelm me, so I couldn't think beyond his lips, his body, his attention.

And oh the ways I knew he'd make me feel. My body vibrated with anticipation, every single cell craving his touch.

Except one.

I couldn't ignore the voice in the back of my mind—not this time. I'd grown since I was that stupid in-love kid, desperate for any scrap he'd give me.

I'd only accept *all* of him now.

"I need a time-out," I sputtered, scrambling from the bed to the bathroom.

29

NATHAN

Now

BRENNA SHUT THE DOOR of the bathroom and clicked the lock.

I'd been mere seconds away from breaking her no-touching rule by kissing her so senselessly, she'd forget all about it. I closed my eyes, listening to the running water, hoping it would calm *all* of me. Thank God for flexible waistbands. The last thing Brenna needed was to see the physical manifestation of how much I wanted her after she asked for distance.

The door inched open, and she stepped through, staring at the floor as she tiptoed back to bed. She gave me a small smile after laying on her back beneath the covers.

I was flooded with gratitude for this snowstorm trapping us here. Alone with her was where I wanted to be, more than anywhere else in the world.

I'd been a coward to book the flight to Houston this weekend. Especially when what I needed was to tell her *everything,* to play all my cards and hope it'd be enough to bring her back to me. However long it took, I'd be patient. She was worth the wait.

"Are you okay?" I asked.

"Yeah," she said, tucking hair behind her right ear. "I, uh, just needed a second."

"I'm sorry I got carried away." I shoved my hand into the pocket of my sweatpants to keep from reaching for her. "I want you to feel comfortable. I can go to your room—"

She grabbed for my hand, and her lunge pressed her body to my side.

"You're breaking your own rules," I whispered.

"You make me want to break them."

I studied her face—the freckle on her cheek, those hot-chocolate eyes, her button nose. *So beautiful it hurt.*

"I don't know if that's a good thing or a bad thing."

"It's like gravity. Not good, not bad. It just is." She released my hand and fell onto her back. Her gaze darted to me while she took a steadying breath. "When you found me here... back in high school... I thought I was dreaming. It wouldn't have been the first time I dreamed you came home. No one told me you were coming back."

The wind from the storm provided the only backdrop of noise.

"I remember." Alcohol hadn't let me forget my actions from that night. A deserving punishment.

"I knew it was wrong to kiss you," she continued, "that I was betraying someone. There's no excuse... but having you here, begging me to stop your pain... I felt it deep." Her hand landed on her chest, right over the stencil of my team name on my sweatshirt. "Because your pain was my pain. And I needed it to stop."

My fingers smoothed a tear blazing down her cheek. "I don't think knowing about Derek would've stopped me, Bren. Kissing you was the first time I'd felt anything other than hatred and anger since I found out about our parents' affair."

"I was going to break up with Derek," she confessed. "The next day. But then you acted like nothing happened."

"I wanted to punch a hole in the wall when I found out you had a boyfriend."

No other moment in my life had ever made me *that* jealous, aside from witnessing her accept a proposal to marry another man. Not even watching my friends make the big leagues before me.

"I missed you so much it hurt. All I wanted was to make things right. In my mind, it hadn't been that long since I left, but you'd moved on?"

"I liked Derek," she said, and I winced. Another man's name on her lips didn't belong in this moment. "I was tired of feeling sad. Mostly, he was a distraction. I know that makes me an asshole."

"It doesn't." I huffed a laugh. "If it does, I'm one too. Because I did the same thing."

Brenna bit her lip, toying with a seam on the blanket. "I didn't want to tell you my engagement ended."

I heaved a sigh of relief. The answer to the question that had ricocheted around my mind on repeat. *She's single.*

"Your missing engagement ring was kind of a giveaway." I chuckled, basking in the nervous laugh Brenna granted me. My tone turned serious again. "Why didn't you want me to know?"

She swallowed hard, her eyes downcast. "It kept me away from you."

My fingers gripped her chin, lifting it until she met my gaze. "Why did you want to stay away from me, Bren?"

My other hand connected with Brenna's. I threaded our fingers to give her comfort, but also because she was my fucking addiction. After holding back for so long, touching her was intoxicating.

A ragged breath escaped her lips. "I've been fighting this since I fell off the damn treadmill. I broke when you left, Nathan. I've avoided putting myself in situations that could hurt me like that again, but..."

I traced patterns on the back of Brenna's hand. "But?"

"Lying here next to you, not kissing you, it's killing me. I feel on fire, Nathan."

I trailed a finger over Brenna's plump bottom lip, basking in the way she trembled at my touch. "I love when you get flushed, but we can't have you combusting... at least not yet."

———◆———

I reached for the hem of the sweatshirt Brenna had turned into hers these last couple of months. I'd wanted to rip it off her for weeks, but never thought I'd get the chance. Even after the ring disappeared from her finger, I didn't think she would offer herself to me.

But she was now.

I feel on fire, Nathan.

It would get hotter for her in the foreseeable future because I was going to take my time with Brenna Quinn.

Even if it damn near killed me.

"You've been driving me wild wearing this," I growled, pushing the fabric up her body. "Lift your arms for me, darlin'."

She obeyed without saying a word. I loved our push and pull, but her willingness to follow my instructions made my cock stiffen. "Good girl."

I flung the sweatshirt across the room, the sound of a cat landing on the floor followed.

"I might need that if I get cold!" Her eyes sparked with mischief.

I tossed a leg over her hip, straddling her body. The bed bore most of my weight until I dropped my hips down, enough for my cock to press into her stomach. "Better?"

Brenna whimpered. "Nathan…"

"That might be the best way you've ever said my name." I smirked, reaching for her next layer of clothing, an Owls T-shirt. "I'm betting that will change."

This time, I didn't need to ask her to lift her arms. Her T-shirt soon joined my sweatshirt on the floor, leaving Brenna in only a white tank top.

I cursed, seeing her hard nipples poke through the fabric. She wasn't wearing a bra. How the fuck could I go slow? The anticipation had been building for *years*.

"I told you I might get cold." She grinned, clearly enjoying the way I'd reacted to her body.

I leaned forward, taking one of her nipples in my mouth through the fabric. Brenna's hands sank into my hair as she gasped. With her breathy moans urging me on, my hands moved beneath her tank top to the smooth skin of her stomach. She shivered when my hands moved north, taking her last layer with them. I lifted my lips long enough to slip the tank top over her breasts, then dipped back down to suck the nipple again before releasing it with a loud smack.

Brenna lifted herself, taking my face in her hands and placing her mouth on mine. The faint taste of whiskey lingered on her lips, but I savored a sweetness that was distinctly Brenna. My tongue pushed her lips, needing more. She parted for me, deepening our kiss.

Our tongues collided, each stroke ratcheting up the flood of desire. My cock strained, craving relief.

As if reading my thoughts, she reached for my ass, gripping me through my sweatpants, pulling me closer. She slid back toward the headboard until our bodies aligned, the friction of my dick against her core a delicious torture.

She kept moving me against her, her grip on my ass getting tighter the longer we kissed. When she sucked my tongue, my vision blackened at the edges.

"I don't know how long I'll last if you keep doing that," I grunted.

"Then stop teasing me," she said, pawing at the band of my sweatpants, trying, unsuccessfully, to pull them down.

I laughed, my forehead falling to rest on hers.

"Are you going to help? Or have you had enough?"

Hot-and-bothered Brenna exceeded all my fantasies. I never imagined she'd be so assertive. I liked that her need for me brought it out of her.

I rolled my hips against her. "Does it *feel* like I've had enough, Bren?"

The exhale of her moan brushed my cheek. "I need your clothes off, Nathan."

"If you insist." I leaned back and gripped the hems of my sweatshirt and T-shirt, pulling them over my head in one slow motion, gradually revealing my bare skin to her.

She swallowed, eyes roaming my body before a trembling hand landed on my stomach. I didn't have rippling abs and ridges of muscles, but my time in the gym kept me toned. Being an athlete came with certain expectations, and I worried about falling short of what she'd imagined.

"Dammit, Nathan," she muttered, her fingers running along my obliques. "Do you even eat bread?"

I huffed a relieved laugh. "I can eat more if I'm not to your liking."

"Oh, shut up." She nodded to indicate my pants. "Don't stop."

My laughing continued as I shifted onto my knees to drag my sweatpants down my legs. I didn't know sex could be like this, funny *and* hot. With other women, my focus had been on getting to the end goal. I didn't want to lose the spark or slow the momentum.

It wasn't a worry with Brenna. I wanted to relieve the throbbing tension between us—fucking *needed* to, or Brenna wouldn't be the only one dying tonight.

But I didn't have any desire to rush to the inevitable outcome.

I wanted to revel in her, in the blush of her cheeks, her dilated pupils, how her breath stuttered for me.

I wanted to stay in this moment with this woman, who I had never stopped loving. And I never would.

30

BRENNA

Now

My whole world narrowed to Nathan pushing his sweatpants down his legs.

I'd dreamed of this moment for weeks, subject to him sauntering around the house in gray sweatpants, as if he had any right to look *that* good. I fought my attraction to him with all I had, knowing what I truly wanted was to fail.

This wasn't smart, being with him before we finished sorting our emotional baggage. But like so many times before, logic stood no chance against the depth of my feelings for Nathan Sharpe. I had no idea what would happen after tonight. I wanted him regardless of the consequences.

Nathan smothered me with his now naked body, bringing his lips back to mine. I couldn't remember the last time I'd kissed someone this long, felt this satisfied enjoyment on my lips. His mouth devoured mine, like I offered a lifesaving elixir and he was moments from death.

Nathan's desperation could fuel me for a lifetime.

I could exist on only this.

My body was nerve endings, sparks becoming flame again and again at his touch. The tips of my nipples rubbed the hard planes of his chest, lightly dusted with dark hair. My legs, wrapped around his waist, squeezed us closer together.

It wasn't enough.

He pulled back from my mouth, his teeth grazing my bottom lip, sending a bolt of electricity between my legs.

This was torture I never wanted to end.

"Nathan," I breathed, bucking my hips toward him, demanding more friction.

"I know," he groaned, the words reverberating against my skin.

He kissed my neck the way he'd plundered my mouth, dragging his lips to my collarbone in sloppy movements. I ignited at each place he lingered and leisurely sucked my skin.

"But we're not rushing this, Brenna. I want the time we missed."

"Death, Nathan," I groaned into his ear while his attention was focused on the crook of my neck. "Or did you not hear me befor—"

My words cut off when Nathan hauled me to him, hooking his arms around my body. He flipped us over, dragging me on top of him, his hands on my lower back to steady me. One of my legs landed between his, the other outside his hip. My center pressed his thigh when I leaned toward his lips, needing to reconnect.

I let out a low moan at the throbbing ache between my legs, amplified by his tongue splitting my lips and finding a slow rhythm with mine.

"Yes, Brenna, use me," Nathan murmured against my skin.

My hips hadn't stopped grinding on his thigh. My soaked panties left wetness on his skin as I shamelessly writhed against him.

We kept kissing, a delicious sliding of lips, like fingers intertwining and tracing each other, not wanting to separate. I could feel the familiar zip of tension, signaling I was oh-so-close to coming apart. My hips moved faster with no real rhythm, only animalistic need as I barreled toward a release years in the making.

Nathan took my earlobe in his mouth, his hot breath whispering against my ear. "Fuck, Brenna, I've never been this hard in my life."

The strain in his voice brought on my orgasm, a match finally exploding in a fire spreading through my body. I continued bucking, my movements becoming slower and shakier until I collapsed on him, panting, spent.

My inner walls clenched around nothing, emphasizing what I still needed from him.

Nathan tipped my chin back with a finger. His other hand smoothed away the flyaway hairs matted to my forehead, dotted in sweat. "And you were worried about being cold."

I shoved him, letting out a sound I thought was a laugh, but my body still hadn't normalized. I didn't want it to.

"I need you inside of me. Right now," I said as soon as I caught my breath. Beneath me, Nathan's dick jerked. "Seems like you need it too."

His laugh reverberated along my body. His fingers moved back and forth on my cheek. "I'm sorry to break it to you, Bren, but we don't have any condoms unless you brought them."

"You're joking?" I damn near growled the words. My body wasn't even close to sated. How exactly was I supposed to lay beside Nathan, in this bed, controlling myself until the electricity returned? Until the storm cleared and we could go to a store?

I had an IUD and hadn't had sex since my last gyno appointment three months ago. I wanted Nathan so badly, I almost volunteered the information, but my heart couldn't take hearing him stumble through an explanation of his sexual history.

"Why are you smiling?"

I gripped him through his boxer briefs, my hand moving slowly from the tip of his cock to its base. The motion sent Nathan tipping his head back, the smile knocked straight off his face as he let out a guttural groan. His hips involuntarily thrusted into my fist, seeking more friction.

I said, "Yeah, exactly how I feel."

"There are other things we can do, Bren."

His roguish grin sent a zip of anticipation through me. Nathan's hips pushed his cock back and forth through the grip of my hand. He beckoned me to him with a flick of his wrist.

"Take your panties off and come here."

My body was already alight again, primed for Nathan, even after coming harder than I ever had only moments ago. That bossy tone of voice did something to me.

I eagerly shimmied out of my panties, discarding them on the floor with the other clothes. But I didn't move toward Nathan's face, beelining instead to remove his boxer briefs until they were nothing more than another piece of unneeded fabric.

His eyes darkened, watching me lick my palm before stroking his considerable length.

"Bren," he choked out, "wrong... direction..."

"I said I needed you *inside* me," I said over my shoulder.

"If that's what you need. Now... get. Over. Here."

Ugh, *that* tone.

I scrambled toward him, positioning myself over his face, legs bracketing his head, back to the headboard. Nerves crept in, threatening to extinguish the warm feelings of need. I'd never been good at receiving oral sex, too focused on the other person's opinion of me, whether I tasted good, or something I'd forgotten to do earlier in the day. It was never long before my body tensed defensively, and my partner chose to abandon his efforts.

"My *God*, Brenna," Nathan said between kisses on the sensitive skin of my inner thighs. "You are fucking perfection."

His words shoved every thought out of my mind.

"I'm so glad your flight got canceled," I said through panted breaths. "And we lost power."

His tongue surged through my core as his fingers applied pressure to my swollen clit. I let out a moan, relishing the feel of his mouth on me before dropping my mouth to the head of his cock. His body jerked at the first contact of my tongue swirling the tip before running along the length of him.

I gave everything, taking him deep each time I slid my mouth down his shaft, letting him hit the back of my throat. My eyes watered, but I couldn't stop—*wouldn't* stop. I wanted to make him lose control, to feel as good as he made me feel. So good, he'd never be able to forget.

Nathan expertly wielded his tongue, discovering a spot that had me squirming against him. His hands clamped on my hips, keeping me in place as he applied more and more pressure, until I thought I might break apart from the inside.

I pulled my lips into my mouth, allowing my teeth to grip his cock tighter. His legs began spasming against my hands resting there, urging me on, and I knew he was close.

The two fingers Nathan pushed inside me sent me careening over the edge I'd been teetering on these last few minutes while I focused on his pleasure. I cried out against his dick but continued moving, my tongue pressing his skin while I moved up and down, savoring the way his body jerked in response to my touch.

Nathan let out a groan, from deep in his throat, against my core which he hadn't stopped teasing. "Bren, I'm going to—"

I moved quickly down to the base, taking the hot liquid into my throat. I swallowed the evidence of how good I'd made Nathan feel.

He gently lifted me off him and moved me to my back. "Fucking hell, Brenna," he said, before his lips landed on mine, both of us tasting ourselves in this kiss. "I'm never going to survive you."

A weight pressed on my chest, filled with years of feelings for Nathan. I'd avoided this moment, when the valve would loosen and these feelings would consume me. But the way my body vibrated with need for him, from my lit-up brain to the rapid rise and fall of my chest to my curling toes, I couldn't remember why.

"Good," I whispered. "I don't want you to."

31

NATHAN

Now

SOMETHING PRESSED INTO MY face.

I tried to swat it away, not ready to rouse from sleep. The poking continued until I finally opened my eyes. Bebe sat above my head, on my pillow, trying to wake me. The cats usually stayed with Brenna, but I was the one who dropped food into their bowls before working out in the morning.

The clock on the nightstand wasn't back on yet. Brenna slept soundly beside me, the other three cats curled around her. The sun shone through the window, illuminating her caramel blond hair spread across the sheets.

No part of me wanted to leave her alone in this bed, not after how long it took to get her here. I didn't want to come back and find it empty.

I banished the thought, quietly sliding out of bed, tiptoeing to the door, and soundlessly opening it. The cats made more noise than me, happily getting up for breakfast. Brenna didn't stir. A stupid surge of pride hit me at how thoroughly I'd exhausted her last night. Memories surfaced—the sweet taste of her soft lips, the sound of her breathy moans as my tongue sank between her legs...

Dammit. As if I wasn't painfully hard already.

When I came back into the room ten minutes later, Brenna mumbled, "You weren't here when I woke up." She eyed my crotch as I walked to the bed. Her fingertips trailed over her naked breasts, and she sucked her bottom lip into her mouth. "I would have woken up earlier if I knew you were walking through the house like that."

"My eyes are up here, Quinn."

She beamed, her radiant smile stabbing me through the chest. I wanted the life we were robbed of. Letting her get away had killed something inside me, and it never grew back. I wondered if that was what stirred in my chest now, the lost piece coming back to life.

"They are nice eyes, Nathan." She fluttered her lashes. "Are you staying? Or do you need to do your morning workout?"

I planted a knee on the bed. "How do you expect me to focus on a workout when I know you're up here, looking like *this*?"

She rolled onto her side as I settled into the bed and pulled her warm body against mine. My mouth immediately found hers.

Brenna tilted her head, giving me access to kiss her neck while my hand palmed her breast.

"Why are there no condoms in this house?" she bemoaned.

I hadn't been with anyone since my end-of-season physical, so I knew I didn't need a condom. Brenna was the one who had been in a long-term relationship, but I had no interest in asking about their sex life. Which meant I couldn't sink my cock into her until the streets were cleared from the storm and I could go to the store.

With her need for me straining her voice, it was fucking misery.

We hadn't talked about our past or our feelings, so I had no idea what sex with me would even mean to her. A temporary hookup? Working me out of her system?

If it was either of those, I didn't know if I would ever recover. Having her once, exploring her body inside out, was not enough for me.

I pushed the thought out of my mind, refocusing on Brenna's want for me.

"Damn, Bren," I groaned, my fingers slipping inside her pussy. "Someone's turned-on this morning."

"That feels so good, Nathan," she murmured into my ear.

I moved two fingers in and out, pressing my palm firmly against her clit.

"Right... there..."

I'd never forget this image of her getting exactly what she needed from me—her head thrown back, lips parted, breath leaving her in pants. I dropped my mouth to her breast, careful not to stop the rhythm of my hand. My lips wrapped around her nipple, my tongue teasing.

"Nathan." She exhaled the sexiest moan.

That was now my favorite way she'd ever said my name.

Her eyes opened and found mine, like she wanted to see me watching her come undone. She shuddered around my fingers, her hand fisting the sheets, her muscles tensing, limbs tightening until she erupted.

Fuck, I can't wait to feel her finish around my cock.

I surged forward, kissing the edge of her mouth. "You are beautiful when you come," I whispered before kissing the other corner.

She was still trying to catch her breath but shifted so my lips landed on hers, teasing me with her tongue. Then she was moving away, bouncing onto her knees.

"Wait—where are you going?"

Seconds ago, her eyes were clouded with sleep, but she had renewed energy as her hand gripped my dick, sliding slowly up and down in a fucking torturous rhythm.

"To take care of you. The way I want to."

She hit me with a look of pure heat, her dark pupils blown out, overtaking her light brown irises. Her tongue swirled around the tip of my cock.

"If it's okay with you, of course."

This woman will be the end of me.

With the heat of her mouth around me, I didn't last long. Brenna climbed up my body, curling against me, her back to my front. My arms wrapped around her, my head resting in the crook of her neck.

"The power's not back on yet. Should we resume our game?"

Her laugh reverberated against me. "You want to play a drinking game before noon? Is there something I should know?"

I shook off the laughter, not wanting to lose my chance. "I want to keep talking, Bren."

She angled her head to look at me. "We don't need a game to talk, Nate. Ask me something. I'll answer."

"Why did you end your engagement?" I regretted the question when she stiffened. Maybe it made me a bastard to bring up her ruined relationship right now, to talk to her about another man while we were in bed together, basking in each other post-orgasm. But I needed to know. I couldn't go forward with her, bare more of myself to her until I did.

"It wasn't right." The room descended into an extended silence. I thought that was all she would share until she started talking again. "He was a good guy, but I don't think he understood me. Something was missing, and when I moved, the distance highlighted it. I was *fine* without him, but I shouldn't have been, you know? I dragged it out too long... well, you know how I am."

I nodded. Brenna despised confrontation. It was partially how the two of us had managed to live in a house together for more than seven weeks without addressing our issues or the blazing attraction between us.

"Wait... I thought you were living in Chicago. You're not?"

"Oh. No. I've been living with my mom and Molly in California for three months."

"What happened to PT school?"

"How did you know I was studying physical therapy?"

I shrugged. "My dad must have mentioned it."

Her hand snaked between us, tickling the side of my stomach, drawing an embarrassingly high-pitched choking laugh from me.

"Okay, okay. I *might* have checked in on you sometimes."

"I read your box scores every now and again," she admitted quietly. "I couldn't watch, but... I liked checking in on you too." I had one moment to bask in her revelation before she turned the conversation to the topic I least wanted to discuss. "That's how I know your shoulder isn't what it used to be, Nathan."

"It's fine," I said stiffly. "I'm taking care of it."

The room fell quiet again. Not even Brenna could get me to talk about my shoulder.

Baseball was my true north. No matter what else was fucked-up in my life, I always had the game. I couldn't face the possibility of needing shoulder surgery, of losing the game forever. I knew the stats on players who had my likely injury. Only about a third returned at the level they were before, and the recovery was even worse for my position. I was nothing if I couldn't pitch.

A loud, angry gurgle interrupted my thoughts.

"Was that your stomach?" I asked, relieved to have something else to focus on.

"Yes," she replied sheepishly, then turned in my arms to face me. "*Someone* hasn't fed me yet."

I shook my head, my nose rubbing against hers. "*Unforgivable.*"

"I'll let you make it up to me." She grinned. "Guess how?"

"Chocolate chip pancakes," I said without hesitation. "I still speak your love language, Bren."

I kissed her forehead, letting my lips linger before reluctantly dragging myself from the bed and throwing on a pair of sweatpants so I could feed my girl.

◆○◆

Our realtor arrived a day later for a walk-through after the power returned, but not alone. I looked at Brenna as she quickly descended the steps to our *two* guests.

"I didn't realize we were expecting more than one person. I would have baked more cookies."

My jaw clenched to the point of pain. The last thing I wanted was her ex-boyfriend here, ruining our bubble of bliss, interrupting as we figured out what we meant to each other.

History was repeating, except I had nothing to worry about when it came to the two of them. Bren said they were friends, and I believed her. Though I wondered if Derek got that memo.

Brenna's lips parted to say something, but they snapped shut when Ellis announced, "I'm here to support Brenna."

"Aw, you hear that, Bren?" I replied in a lilting voice. "He's here to *support* you."

Brenna rolled her eyes. She didn't need to speak; she wanted me to knock it off.

She shook hands with the agent, who still stood in the doorway, a bemused smile on her face. At least we entertained her. "Hi, Ms. Marin, I'm Brenna Quinn. Come on in."

"Shelly, please." She had about twenty years on us, wore her hair short, and had on a heavy coat that rivaled Brenna's. "And you must be Nathan Sharpe? I'm so sorry about your father."

I nodded, still unsure how to respond when I heard this refrain. "It's good to meet you."

Shelly followed Brenna to the kitchen. Brenna playfully grabbed my side as she passed. Derek's gaze ping-ponged between us, absorbing the interaction.

I smirked. "After you, Ellis."

I should've been beyond the petty high school bullshit, but the memories of spending two weekends a month across the hall from Brenna, pretending to feel nothing for her, weren't something I'd ever forget. I had to watch Ellis and Brenna giggle like damn schoolgirls, sharing glances and beaming at each other over the breakfast table.

He got moments that should have been mine—walking her to school senior year, holding her hand in the hall between classes, escorting her to prom. I played hundreds of baseball games without her on the field or in the stands. Not sharing baseball with her had dulled the fun of the game.

I had no idea what her life had been like these last six years, other than what she posted online. So many aspects still unknown to me. Who was her best friend? What classes did she struggle with in college? Did she live in a dorm, an apartment, with roommates? When she was low, how did she cheer herself up? What did she wish for her future?

So many seconds, minutes, hours, weeks, months, years wasted without her because of my stupid pride. Because I was afraid to call her, convinced I was better off not reopening that old hurt. Sure she wouldn't want anything to do with me.

But nothing hurt more than knowing she'd existed in this world without me. I could never get that time back.

"Nathan?" Brenna spoke.

"Hmm?" The three faces staring at me came into focus.

Brenna's brow furrowed. "Shelly was asking if you'd thought about a minimum amount you're willing to accept for the house."

No, Shelly, I've been too busy thinking about how to convince the woman who owns this house with me to become mine for the rest of our lives.

"No," I said. "Have you?"

Bren shook her head.

Shelly typed something into her phone. "You should discuss it. It'll be an important data point when considering the list price."

"Have you called the financial adviser?" Ellis asked Brenna.

She glanced at me before turning to him. "No... um, not yet. Nathan's been working on the books at the café. My mind's been... elsewhere."

"We can call this week," I assured her. "We'll figure it out."

I hoped Ellis would take the fucking hint. Brenna said he was in a relationship, so maybe he was only trying to be supportive as he claimed. But he needed to back the fuck off and let me take care of her now.

Shelly stood from the table. "All right, shall we go through the house?"

Brenna grabbed a chocolate chip cookie. She covered her mouth as she chewed, but I knew a smile graced her lips. I took one as well, savoring it almost as much as her smile.

I couldn't wait until we were alone again.

32

BRENNA

Now

THE NEXT FEW WEEKS flew by in a blur as Nathan and I focused on getting the house ready to sell.

There had been meetings with the financial adviser and phone calls with Shelly, who worked to schedule an open house. When we weren't at the café, we tackled a long list of projects we agreed to complete after her walk-through—installing new faucets, putting dimmers in the family room and bedrooms, staining kitchen cabinets, power-washing the driveway and patio. We also painted the final two rooms, the ones we'd been sleeping in. It was easier once we shared a bed. We moved into my old room for a few nights while the paint in his room dried.

"This place looks so cute." An older woman complimented the decorations in the café as she approached the counter.

"Thank you." I nodded at Allison at the other end of the counter, packing baked goods for another customer. "It was all her."

As Nathan and I focused on the house, Allison brought Christmas to the Courtside Café with a Christmas tree in a window and several wreaths hanging outside. Somehow, she'd made the windows look snowy. Inside, string lights hung from the ceiling and garland looped above the chalkboard behind the counter. It reminded me of Christmases here as a kid. Nathan's mom always decked the place out right after Thanksgiving, and it immediately put me in a holiday mood.

Nathan and I hadn't discussed holiday plans. I hoped we'd spend it together.

"Someone's in a good mood today."

The words sounded like an accusation rather than an observation. I had to remind myself not to let Allison's tone get to me; she usually didn't mean anything bad. "You and the boy finally pull your heads out of your asses?"

My eyes trailed to Nathan, sitting with Bertram and his crew in their usual spot. He leaned back in his chair, laughing at something Bertram said, reminding me of *my* Nathan, from before our families complicated our lives. I liked seeing this ease in his demeanor and thinking maybe I had something to do with it.

It took effort to keep rosiness from entering my cheeks. "Maybe I just appreciate all you've done to help us."

She shrugged. "It's what you're paying me to do."

It was more than that. We weren't paying her enough to take this much pride in her work.

"You love this place, don't you?"

"Contrary to what the prodigal son thinks, I loved Gordon. And Gordon loved this place."

I wondered if she suspected Gordon's love for the Courtside Café had to do with his first wife, the one who got away. He'd held onto the house and business he'd shared with her, which was too much of a coincidence to mean anything else. But if she suspected, Allison didn't care. It made me trust her motivations.

"He talked about you and Nathan a lot," she went on. "Especially toward the end. All he wanted was Nathan's forgiveness. I think that's why he wrote you into his will. He knew Nathan needed you, even if he wouldn't admit it. I told Gordon it was ridiculous to think some girl could help his son move forward."

Allison nodded toward Nathan, who held Bertram and his crew's attention captive with a story, his arms flying through the air, a wide smile on his face. "He doesn't look like the same person who showed up on my doorstep earlier this year. He doesn't even look like the punk who tried to lay down the law with me in October."

"I can't take credit for that."

"Well, it sure as shit wasn't the café. I bet that arrogant know-it-all is looking down and laughing at us."

Cheers echoed from Bertram and Nathan's table as the old man waved some cards in Nathan's face. He swatted playfully at his hand, the other two men watching with wide eyes. Allison shook her head and headed to the back, where she could pretend they weren't gambling. She'd given up trying to stop them.

Bertram cleared his throat to get my attention, his coffee cup in the air. We didn't do refills or table service, except for this particular table.

"You beckoned?"

"Oh, don't you complain," Bertram huffed, smacking his cards onto the table. "I've won enough money off your man here, you're in for a good tip today."

My man. My heart beat against the wall of my chest, a hard knock reminding me of its presence.

Bertram lowered his cup to the table, and I poured coffee to the brim. "You mean my co-owner," I said, feeling Nathan's eyes on me.

Bertram waved his hand. "Oh, pishposh hogwash. I'm old, not blind."

Nathan's gaze held mine steady, sending a rollercoaster through my stomach.

He shrugged. "He's very perceptive. It's why he keeps beating me."

"I keep beating you, boy, because you're always looking at her."

Nathan scoffed. "She's easier on the eyes than your ugly mug."

Bertram flipped him off, which sent Nathan into a fit of laughter. Merriment filled his gorgeous eyes. No sight had ever made me happier.

"I'm about to side with Allison over your little gambling club," I said, motioning to the table.

"Idle threats," Bertram said. "Aside from my *very* generous tips, I've got an ace up my sleeve."

He gestured to Nathan who flashed me his most decadent smile, one that adorably crinkled his eyes. I wanted to see it every day for the rest of my life.

I fought to keep my face impassive. "*That* has *no* effect on me."

Bertram slowly shook his head and placed a hand on my forearm. "Kid, you would be awful at poker."

33

NATHAN

Now

I PULLED BRENNA TO me as soon as the front door to our house closed, signifying the end of a successful open house.

"Nathan!" she yelped, momentarily leaving her feet while her body pressed solidly against mine.

I grinned at her, unable to keep my lips from settling into a once unfamiliar shape.

"Okay, now that that's done"—I twirled a strand of her hair around my finger—"it's time for Christmas."

"Uh, Christmas is in two weeks, Nate."

No one else called me that. I'd never liked the nickname, but *all* words sounded good from her lips.

"I know. And we're not ready. At all." The barren house stood in stark contrast to the café and every other spot in Middlebury. We didn't have plans to show the house again until the new year, so we had weeks to do as we wished. "Go get ready, because we're about to change that."

A slow smile crossed her face. "What are we doing?"

"It's called a date, Quinn." I dropped a kiss on her forehead. "We've got a lot on the docket, so stop dawdling."

For weeks I'd thought about this—Brenna and I enjoying a day to ourselves, not worrying about the house or the café. Middlebury had no shortage of magic at the holidays, and I wanted to share it all with her.

Brenna wore a black peacoat, a thick scarf, and a beanie with a pom-pom on top, even in this mild weather. It was hard to believe she'd survived the Chicago cold for years. My lips twitched as I studied her winter attire, but I didn't say anything, instead enjoying how adorable she looked in it. She clutched my hand as we left the house and headed to my father's car.

It took ten minutes to get to the Christmas tree farm on the outskirts of Palmer City. We navigated the busy parking lot, apparently not the only people who had waited until the last minute to buy a tree. I hoped to find something decent of a manageable size to carry into the house.

I rubbed my bare hands together to bring some warmth. "First order of business is picking the perfect tree."

"Does this mean we're spending Christmas together?"

A couple of minutes in the cold, and Brenna's cheeks had already turned crimson. That flush of hers nearly had me hauling her back to the car and showing her exactly how much I liked the color on her.

"I was hoping..." I started. "I didn't know if you'd be staying."

"Flights are so expensive, and it's not like I could leave for long. Molly and I have plans to open presents together on a video call, then watch *Home Alone*, our favorite Christmas movie."

"You disappointed?"

She shook her head slightly. "Not entirely, as long as you stick around."

I took her gloved hand in mine. "The only way I'm celebrating this holiday is with you, darlin'."

God, I'd do anything to keep that beaming smile on her face.

"We have a lot of work to make this the best Christmas yet."

I pulled Brenna to my side as we walked down the first aisle of trees. "What else do you have in mind?"

She rattled off some favorite traditions from when we were kids—singing Christmas music while decorating the house, baking cookies and drinking eggnog, eating puppy chow during a Christmas movie marathon, ice-skating and drinking hot chocolate in downtown Palmer City, making each other gifts, which she said now included the cats.

"Sorry, I'm getting carried away." She stopped at the end of the first row of trees. "You already had a plan?"

My fingers danced across her bottom lip. "You and me, darlin'. That's all I need."

She shoved me. "Come on, Nathan. There's got to be *something* you want for our perfect holiday."

I stared up and to the left in mock-thought. "Well, I wouldn't mind seeing you *dress up*."

She stopped walking, her reply breathless. "Yeah?"

I nodded, my hands finding her hips.

"What were you thinking?"

An image sprung into my mind. Thank fuck I had a jacket on to conceal the way those thoughts had blood surging to my groin. At a fucking Christmas tree farm.

This woman. My *woman.*

"Don't tease," I told her, trying to move us along.

Brenna resisted, rooted to the spot. "I want to be whatever you want, Nathan."

"You're already everything I want, Bren."

She leaned in close, rising to her toes to whisper in my ear. "Tell. Me. What. You. Imagine. Me. Wearing, Nathan."

The command in her voice... *fuck.*

"Knee-high socks." My voice was guttural. "Short skirt. Lace bra. Christmas hat."

"Interesting." She kissed my cheek, then walked ahead of me. "Thank you."

I blew out a breath, trying to cool myself down. "What about me? What should I wear?"

"Oh, I'm easy." She spun back around, a teasing smile on her face. "*Nothing.*"

I laughed, rushing toward her as she zipped around the corner to another row of trees. Brenna stopped abruptly, and I bumped into her back. I steadied her by her shoulders before she could fall forward.

"This is the one." She pointed to a tall tree, which I suspected would reach the ceiling of our house.

"Of course you want the biggest tree on the lot."

She hip-checked me. "I thought you wanted Christmas to be perfect."

Brenna still didn't get that we could sit in an empty house, no decorations, eating four-day-old spaghetti, and it would have been perfect for me. Being with *her* is what mattered. I would do anything to make the holiday what she wanted.

"Let's load it up!" I waved my hand in a circle above my head.

Brenna cheered, briefly throwing her arms around my neck before darting off to find an employee. It took three people to strap the tree to the car, hopefully securing it tight enough to travel home. Brenna and I would have one hell of a time getting it into our house.

She eyed the tree jutting out over the windshield. "Was this a bad idea?"

I shifted the car into gear. "Don't tell me you've given up on our mission for a perfect holiday already?"

She bit her lip. "How are we going to decorate this thing? We don't have money to throw around right now."

"It's good I didn't listen to *someone* who told me to clear out all the boxes in the basement." I winked at her. "I kept the Christmas stuff hidden for just this occasion, along with a few other things you might be interested in."

She snorted. "To decorate the big ass tree I demanded?"

"*Demand* is such a strong word."

Brenna shook her head, lip ensnared in her teeth. "Who even *are* you? Two months ago, there was a permanent scowl on your face." She, poorly, imitated my expression, brows bunched together, eyes comically squinted into slits, lips pinched into a pout.

I sputtered. "I have never made that face in my life."

"You're right, it's more like this," she said, contorting her face into something that resembled constipation.

"Bren, are you trying to get me to crash the car?"

"Of course not." She shifted in her seat until she faced forward again, but I could hear a smile in her voice.

We drove slowly along back roads for a few minutes, the faint sound of Christmas music playing in the background.

"Nathan." Her serious voice.

"Yeah?"

"What's going to happen after we get an offer?"

This was the question neither of us voiced these last few weeks. I spent most of the time hoping no one would want to buy our house so we could exist here a bit longer. Stay together for as long as we needed to figure out what this last month meant.

I wasn't in a rush to get back for the upcoming baseball season, not with my shoulder bothering me. I still hadn't heard whether the Blitz were inviting me to spring training for a shot at the major league team, or if they'd keep me with my current team, the Triple-A Sharks. I didn't yet know if they'd bring me back at all. The end of the season hadn't been my strongest, not with my arm troubles. If I hadn't been sharing a bed with Brenna, the thought would've kept me awake at night.

"I don't know, Bren," I answered honestly.

"Shouldn't we figure it out?"

"Yeah, we should. But not today. Unless you want to miss out on what I have planned next."

She perked up. "There's a *next*?"

"This would be a terrible date if there weren't."

"No," she said quietly, reaching for my hand. "That's not true."

I clasped her hand in my palm, so fucking grateful for this day with her. I'd stretch out this date as long as possible, for our entire lives if I could.

34

BRENNA

Now

I IMAGINED THIS WAS how zero gravity felt.

Every pang of worry these past six months left my body, holding me suspended in the feeling of free fall. Stomach dropping. Limbs light. Brain lit up. Happy.

I wished we could hide on this date forever.

Nathan grabbed my hand as we left the rink downtown after hours of skating. He easily glided across the ice while I clung to him for dear life. It had been years since I'd ice-skated—not since I was last at this rink with him—and it hadn't come back to me at all, which brought Nathan immense joy. He liked imitating the way I flailed my arms unsteadily. He laughed when I nearly face-planted trying to chase him, but I ended up safe in his arms.

I didn't mind the last one.

"You're doing pretty good with this whole date thing." I swung our arms between us as we walked to the parking deck.

"It sounds like you doubted me?"

I let out an exaggerated gasp. "I would never."

"It's not over yet."

"You don't want to quit while you're ahead?" My mouth hurt from grinning, an ache I never, ever wanted to go away.

"I'm pretty confident you'll like where this night is headed, Bren."

The nickname that had once felt like shattered glass on my skin now warmed me from the inside out.

My heart pounded harder every time Nathan snuck a glance my way during the drive to our next destination. Wild smiles broke across our faces whenever our gazes collided. We each knew neither of us could keep our eyes from the other for too long.

I knew this feeling, had felt it before with the boy next door. But never since, not like this.

There was something about first love that couldn't be recreated. It was like reading a book for the first time, the anticipation of what would happen when the page turned. Equal parts joy and dread, because it could unfold in wonderful or devastating ways. People chased that high, the dopamine rush of falling in love.

I understood it, of course, but there was something different about what I was experiencing now, falling for Nathan Sharpe a second time. Like I knew how it would feel when I was too far gone, and though I couldn't wait to get there, I wouldn't rush it. I wanted to enjoy this journey.

"I think you oversold our next activity." I flashed him a playful smile.

The Christmas tree I picked out waited in the garage. Nathan gripped the end of the tree that would require him to walk backward into the house, while I took the opposite end.

"You're about to talk yourself out of it, Quinn."

Nathan turned left, easing the tree into the family room. After I cleared the mudroom, he increased his pace. He glanced over his shoulder, tracking his proximity to the corner wall. "I'll ease it into the stand and hold it while you secure the screws, okay?"

"Yessir," I sang, to which Nathan sighed, full of pretend exasperation.

It took all of five minutes before our tree stood on its own, already improving the atmosphere in the empty house. But the good feeling bled from me when Nathan winced while getting to his feet. We weren't on the baseball field now, but I was attuned to him just as closely. I didn't want to ruin the night, but I couldn't not ask.

"Are you all right?"

Nathan cocked an eyebrow. "Do you need me to show you how *all right* I am, Brenna?"

"Is that what's next?" My blood buzzed beneath my skin.

"So impatient," he chided, tapping the tip of my nose with a finger as he passed me on his way out of the room.

I was unashamed of exactly how impatient I was to have him between my legs again, but I was embarrassed at how quickly he distracted me.

When he came back moments later, he plunked down a brown box with the words *Xmas decorations* written on the side in his mom's handwriting. No wince this time.

I battled my instincts. He continued doing physical therapy exercises every morning. If his shoulder was fine, he wouldn't need them, at least not that frequently. But he didn't want to admit to injury. I couldn't figure out why.

Was it *me*? Did he not trust me?

Nathan rolled up the sleeves of his gray ribbed sweater, revealing those tattoos I savored, then dropped to his knees. I nearly toppled over at the sight. *Hot fucking damn.* Was he doing this on purpose to distract me? He focused on unpacking the box, not peeking to catch my reaction, so probably not. Still worked like a charm though.

"Ooh, I remember this," I said, plucking a circular glass ornament Nathan made in middle school from his hands.

The glittery ornament was filled with picture cutouts of his favorite things from that year—a bat and baseball, us on the field together, Nathan with his parents in front of the Owls stadium, a video game controller, an album cover. The ornament I'd made that year was probably long gone, chucked in my mother's cross-country move.

"I think you missed your calling by not pursuing this whole art thing."

Nathan rolled his eyes. "Hilarious. I guess you don't want to see what else I found in the basement then?"

I leaned over him, trying to see what he concealed. He held me back with one hand while the other covered his discovery.

"Stop holding out on me," I whined.

"Good things come to those who wait." His tone was lilting, and he sported a shit-eating grin.

I stopped struggling and pushed back on my heels. "You know, Nate, that's sound advice. I'll be sure to remind you of that when *you* get impatient."

Recognition of my threat flashed in his eyes. He immediately held a box out to me. I laughed loudly, drunk with power.

"No need to go nuclear on me."

Inside, I found a half dozen VHS tapes and a couple of photo albums. "Oh my God. Y'all kept these?"

I seized the small album on top, decorated with a sunflower and a baseball bat. Until now, I would've avoided a trip down memory lane because it would remind me of what I'd lost. But today, all I could think about was what I had found again. I wanted to replace the hurt I associated with our past with joy.

And there was joy. It poured out of every page as I flipped through this album.

"If you couldn't tell, my father saved everything that ever entered this house."

These photos were from our freshman year in high school. Nathan with his parents at the table in front of a birthday cake, probably rolling his eyes at me for taking the photo. Next came a panoramic view of the Owls stadium from behind the dugout on the first base side of the field, our preferred place to sit. Nathan, Ax, Stark, and Freeze stuffing their faces with pizza in this very room.

Most of the pictures didn't include me because I took them. I ran my fingers over one of the two of us in our baseball uniforms, cheeks sunburned beneath our caps, his arm slung around my shoulders. I looked at him with such love in my eyes while he grinned at the camera.

The image speared my chest.

"You went through that whole photography phase, remember?" Nathan was studying my expression.

I cleared my throat, closing the album. "I think I used it as an excuse to take photos of you."

"I've been told I *am* a perfect subject." He tossed me a smug smile. "Seriously, you were good, Bren. You didn't want to study it?"

I set the album aside and snatched a couple of ornaments from the box. "Photography? No."

"We need to do lights first," he said, stopping me from hanging an ornament.

He squatted and began zig-zagging a string of lights across the bottom of the tree, unspooling them from an empty wrapping paper tube where they'd been stored. Once he got higher, we worked in tandem.

"What did you study in school?" Nathan asked. It hit me how strange it was for someone to know so much about me but not simple details about my life.

"Kinesiology."

He paused, hanging onto the lights, forcing me to look at him. "And you like studying physical therapy?"

I shrugged. "Some of the classes made me queasy, but it's been worth it."

"Too much blood?"

"Yeah." I chose not to tell him how many times I thought about quitting because of it. I persisted, knowing it wouldn't be part of my day-to-day work with patients. "I like putting things back together. And I always wanted a career in sports."

He turned his focus back to the lights, passing them to me again. "I don't know if I like the idea of you putting *other* athletes back together."

I half grinned. "Want to keep me all to yourself, huh?"

"That's never been a secret, Quinn."

I handed the lights back to him and headed to the box of decorations, my cheeks heating, unsure how to respond.

Well, I *wanted* to throw myself at him, but he'd made it clear decorating came first. I was grabbing an ornament when the box of memories snagged my attention again.

"What do you think is on these tapes?" Each video was labeled with a month and year, but nothing else.

Nathan ducked down beside me, flicking some of my hair over my shoulder. "I'll give you one guess." He snatched a box of ornaments and headed to the tree. "Put one on, if you want."

"Your dad kept a VCR?" I hadn't seen the ancient technology in at least ten years.

"Of course he did. Bottom of the box, Bren."

Nathan paused the tree decorating to help me hook up the video player. I popped a tape in and stared, transfixed, at the screen, where twelve-year-old Nathan stood beside home plate, looking down the third base line to his dad, waiting for the batting sign. He stepped into the box, his cleats scuffing the dirt before he settled in. The pitcher was starting his windup when Nathan pointed his bat toward the left-field wall, signaling where he planned to send the ball.

And then the fucker bunted, catching everyone off guard as he sprinted to first base.

I burst out laughing. "Talk about phases. Remember when you wouldn't stop calling your shot?"

On-screen, Gordon threw his hat to the ground, shaking his head and glaring at his son.

"Oh yeah," Nathan said through a laugh. "My dad lectured me about playing with more humility, so I started to do it at least once a game. Then he *grounded* me!"

Nathan and I full-on wheezed from how hard we laughed.

On-screen Nathan ignored his father, instead focusing on me as I walked to the plate. He clapped his hands and cheered me on, capturing my attention. And there was that smile on my face again, full of undiluted joy. His dad whistled to pull my attention from his son.

"Yeah," I replied, "but you kept doing it anyway."

His hand snagged mine, bringing me to my feet. "It made you laugh."

I wrapped my arms around his shoulders. "That's not why you did it."

"It is. You've always underestimated how much you mean to me, Bren." He squeezed my hand. "Maybe stop doing that?"

I surged to my tiptoes, silencing his teasing with a kiss. I didn't need to see my face to know Nathan brought out the smile full of joy.

The smile reserved for him.

35

BRENNA

Now

"YOUR EYES BETTER BE closed," Nathan said as I waited in the kitchen for the big reveal.

After I begged for food, Nathan paused our first Christmas movie of the season and untangled our limbs—his leg unhooking from my ankle, his hand pulling back from mine, fingertips skimming my palm, leaving a tingle in their wake. He eased me off his chest, and I groaned at the lost contact, then he took my hand, guiding me into the kitchen.

"They are, but you only have a minute before I open them." I jolted when his hand connected with my hip.

"Open your mouth." Nathan's words settled deep in my gut. Oh, how I adored the ache now that he could relieve it.

Nathan's fingers briefly brushed my bottom lip before the taste of chocolate hit my tongue. Silky smooth and creamy. I moaned, my senses overwhelmed by the decadent dessert and Nathan's hands on me. I opened my eyes to find him watching me, rapt.

"When did you get this?"

The dessert—chocolate chess pie—was my favorite from a restaurant in Palmer City. They decked out the place in lights and decorations every Christmas, and our families had eaten there once a year to take in its ambiance and eat the incredible pie.

"Yesterday." He let out a sigh when my hands eased under his sweater, exploring his taut skin. "I want this Christmas to be everything you want, Brenna."

My hands skimmed his abdomen, all toned strength beneath my fingers. Nathan took a step forward, easing me backward to the edge of the counter.

"Why?"

He gripped my hips, his gaze dipping to my lips before rebounding to my eyes. "I need you to remember..."

"Remember what?"

"How good we are together." Nathan leaned forward until his forehead rested on mine.

My hands settled on his face, guiding his lips to mine. I kissed him briefly, pulling back to whisper, "You don't need to remind me. I know, Nathan."

He surged forward, his lips taking mine, desperation undergirding each movement. He lifted me onto the counter. My legs hooked around his waist without my conscious thought, tugging him close, until I could feel the heat of his body pressing into my core.

I pulled back to find his pupils wide. "I want you now." My breath blew out of me in short pants, but I forced out the rest of my words. "I'm tired of waiting."

We bought condoms as soon as the streets cleared from the storm, but we hadn't yet used them. Nathan said he wanted to make our first time special, to wait for the right moment. He promised the anticipation would make it hotter. We'd hardly been hands-off, so I got enough of Nathan to keep my craving at bay. But I wanted *all* of him. Now.

Nathan grinned, pointing behind him. "You don't want the rest of your pie?"

"Later," I whispered before wrapping my arms around his neck and recapturing his mouth. I put everything I had into the kiss. I wanted Nathan to feel my desire for him. Need for him. Love for him.

The pounding between my legs increased with every slide of our lips, every tangle of our tongues.

Closer, closer, closer chanted in my mind. I wouldn't be satisfied until Nathan pushed inside of me.

I fumbled with his belt, the clanging metal driving me wild.

"Brenna," Nathan hissed between kisses.

Neither of us wanted to separate, every movement between us happened with eyes closed, mouths occupied.

I yanked his shirt up to his shoulders, then unzipped his pants, my hand grazing his cock. I'd never get over the first feel of his hardness, his reaction to me. Nathan made incoherent sounds when my hand slid into his boxer briefs, a finger tracing him from base to head, teasing his sensitive skin.

I loved knowing how I affected him, how simple movements could make him lose his mind.

Nathan's hands clawed at the band of my leggings, and he broke our kiss to focus on getting me naked.

I took him in my palm, moving slowly, up and down.

He swallowed hard. "*Fuck.* Can you... can you give me a minute to focus?"

My lips sucked on the sensitive skin where his neck met his shoulder. "No. You're far too hot like this."

He growled. "I can't wait to make you scream for me."

I sucked in a breath, so turned-on by this new side of Nathan. Flustered. Foul-mouthed. Frenzied.

"Hips. Up. Now."

My hips immediately lifted into the air. Nathan shimmied my leggings down until the fabric pooled on the floor. He removed my sweater in one swift movement, then stepped out of reach. His eyes roamed my body, covered only by bra and panties.

"You're so fucking beautiful, Brenna." Nathan's gaze simmered. His attention was sunshine on my skin in the dead of winter.

I crooked my finger, beckoning him to me. I yanked at the hem of his sweater, and he smirked, allowing me to pull it the rest of the way off.

"Much better," I drawled. "Now are you going to give me my surprise?"

Nathan laughed softly. "You know the surprise was pie, Quinn."

"But it's not what I *really* want."

His hands slid over the small of my back. "Tell me what you want then."

"I want you to fuck me, Nathan. Right here."

He inhaled sharply, clearly just as taken with my foul mouth as I was with his.

"There's something I need to do first." He took one smooth step forward, hooked an arm around my waist, and tugged me to the edge of the counter. He yanked my panties aside, his eyes flashing with heat. His thumb teased the source of the incessant pounding, the pressure almost too much.

Nathan dropped to his knees and pressed his mouth to my center. I moaned, my head falling back against a cabinet.

His skilled tongue was demanding and desperate, ramping up the tension in my limbs. Two of his fingers slid in and out of me, a steady rhythm on the spot that never failed to shatter me.

My heels dug into the cabinet handles below.

"I need you inside me. Now."

"Not yet, darlin'."

I whimpered at the brush of his perfect lips forming words against me. Nathan slid his hand up my body to flick my nipple. A breathy moan escaped, which spurred his tongue to slide deeper.

My hands gripped the back of Nathan's head, keeping him in place. Legs shaking, I wouldn't last long...

"That's it, Bren," he panted. "Fall apart for me."

My hips worked against his face, taking what I needed until the tension inside me splintered, spreading heat through my body.

I released my death grip in his hair, and slumped my useless, ragged limbs to the counter.

"That was so good," I mumbled through labored breath. "*So,* so good."

Nathan's head was still between my legs, a wicked smile on his lips. "I think you're ready now."

He pulled a condom from his wallet. I watched spellbound as his boxer briefs dropped and he rolled it on.

I ached for him again, even as warm feelings from my orgasm swam through my blood.

Nathan rose to his full height, brow furrowed. "Are you ready, Bren?"

His question wasn't about having him buried inside of me. He wanted to know if I was ready for the way this would change our relationship, for the deep emotions that would overwhelm me after we connected this way. Every cell in my body responded to the question with a resounding *yes*.

Because I loved Nathan Sharpe.

Holding myself back from him physically wouldn't stop me from falling again. I thought allowing these feelings for him to come roaring back would be the end of me, because I never thought he'd return them.

But there Nathan stood, regarding me with more longing and concern for my feelings than anyone else in my life. He'd proven his feelings by planning this entire day, by recreating the magic of Christmases past. Every time he left me a full pot of coffee. Kissed my forehead before leaving the bed when he thought I was still asleep. Buying a weighted blanket to help with my anxiety.

He chose to stay in Middlebury when he didn't need to. Because he knew I did.

My heart pounded faster, thinking of all the reasons I loved this man.

Close enough didn't exist, not with him, but I'd take as much as I could.

"Now, Nathan."

He didn't break eye contact as he lined his cock up with my entrance and eased inside, slowly. I gasped, reveling in the way he filled me, the stretch as my body made room for him.

His jaw clenched while sweat beaded his brow. I knew I wasn't alone with this indescribable feeling, both torture and bliss.

I already dreaded the moment we'd disentangle.

"Nathan..." I murmured. He thrust his hips toward me, my hands white-knuckling the edge of the counter. My legs gripped him tighter.

I wanted nothing to exist between us, not even an inch of air. "You feel *so good*."

He pushed my hair over my shoulder. "Nothing in my life has ever felt this right."

He moved faster, and I pushed back with everything he gave me. My hands moved to his shoulders, clutching him for this give-and-take. Only one thought broke through the haze of pleasure consuming me—*more*. My legs shook, my body desperate to release the coiled tension.

Nathan found my lips again, aware of what I needed. His teasing tongue in my mouth echoed the desire in my core, where we were also connected, pounding into each other.

It was too much, being physically, mentally, emotionally overwhelmed by Nathan. It wasn't long before I burst into blinding euphoria that had me shouting his name before again collapsing to the counter. He kept moving, wringing every bit of pleasure my body had to give.

"Fuck, Brenna," Nathan mumbled against my forehead. That strain in his voice sent a zap between my legs, even as my inner walls contracted around him. His movements became choppy, thrusts without pattern. He looped his arms around my shoulders, his grip tightening.

He was so close, and I needed to watch him crumble because of me. I leaned forward, tracing my tongue up the column of his neck until I sucked his earlobe into my mouth.

"*Bren.*"

I'd never liked my name more than in Nathan's sexy groan.

"Come for me, Nate."

Nathan seized my mouth with a bruising kiss. I hoped it would leave a mark, proof this perfect night had really happened. He released my lips as he found his release, grunting my name in one long drawn-out syllable.

Nathan slumped over the counter, his weight falling onto me, his breath coating my skin.

I wrapped my arms around his neck. My heart felt like a balloon filling with air, expanding beyond what I thought was possible.

How could I ever go back to a life without him, knowing we made each other feel this good? It wasn't only this moment, Nathan still inside me, clinging to each other. It was Nathan's gaze catching mine across the café. Our hands threaded together while we walked to the car, trading stories about the day. The mischief in his eyes when we bantered.

Exchanging the first and last words of my day with him.

"That was perfect," I breathed.

36

NATHAN

Now

BRENNA AND I EVENTUALLY disentangled from each other.

I'd been right; I couldn't survive without her, especially not after experiencing the feeling of completeness when I was inside her.

It wasn't only the heavenly way her body wrapped around my cock, but everything that accompanied it. Brenna moaning my name while her body spasmed. Her wild eyes connecting with mine, desire blowing out her pupils. The floral scent of her hair in my nostrils. Her hands digging into my back, desperate to fuse us. Laughing together as we came down from our highs, happy to be in each other's company.

The promise of more time.

I climbed the stairs, carrying the pie and a bottle of wine. As I approached my room, I heard the shower. The idea of studying Brenna in the bright light of the bathroom was highly appealing. These past few weeks, I'd become intimately familiar with her naked body, but mostly in the dark, sometimes with pale morning light from the windows. Tonight, there'd been little chance to drink each other in, to explore and play. We'd needed each other so badly, we barely got our clothes off.

I had just dropped my pants when I heard Brenna's piercing voice, low like she was trying to keep quiet.

"Can she hear you right now?" Unmistakable anger underlined her words.

I yanked my pants up and took a step back before curiosity rooted me to the spot. Eavesdropping wasn't my intention, but I could hear her from the bed.

A few beats later, Brenna said, "She's not a bag of groceries you can drop whenever."

Her next response came quicker. "No, I am... of course I want to spend the holiday with her."

She let out a deep sigh.

I waited a minute to be sure her phone call was finished, then rapped my knuckles on the door. "Bren?"

"Yeah?"

I eased the door open. She sat on the lip of the bathtub, chin in her hands. "Are you okay?"

Only one person in Brenna's life reduced her to this sullen shell of herself. The same person who had ruined my family. The first domino in a long string of events forcing Brenna and me apart, living separate lives across the country from each other.

My pulse accelerated, the sound filling my ears. My teenage temper was also to blame for our distance, but I'd worked on controlling my emotions in situations like this. I took a deep breath in through my nose, and quietly let it out through my mouth over several seconds. The ball of anger in my chest unfurled, easing enough for me to speak calmly.

"You can talk to me." I leaned on the sink across from her, unsure if she wanted me closer or not.

Her lips parted but no sound came out. She kept staring at the floor.

"That was your mom?"

Brenna's eyes found mine. I nodded at the phone in her lap.

"Were you eavesdropping?"

I crossed my arms over my chest. "Not on purpose."

"But you were," she accused, her voice as sharp as it had been minutes earlier on the phone.

"Bren, I'm not the one you're mad at." Her shoulder drooped an inch—a good sign. I pressed on, my tone gentle. "Tell me what's going on."

"You want to know what's going on?" She thrust a hand through her hair, pushing some to the other side of her head. "My mom was invited by her *married* ex-boyfriend to take a trip over Christmas. Without Molly. She's excited that he might want her back. But this *always* happens. He's probably in a fight with his wife and will use my mom to make himself feel better. And she'll choose those crumbs over her daughter."

I thought about how many times Brenna stayed at my house when we were kids because her mom needed to travel for "work." It wasn't until we were in high school that I realized it wasn't work. Brenna once told me she loved staying at my house, being around a real family, but I suspected she'd also been upset about being left behind. It hurt her when her mother chose someone else over her, again and again, even if she wouldn't admit it.

I wanted to hug her, make sure she knew I loved her, that I would choose her over everything else.

But this wasn't about me.

"She plans to dump Molly here while she jets off to the Bahamas with this douchebag. Molly's old enough to understand what's happening, and I hate it for her. *This* is why I want custody. I'd never fall apart and neglect to take care of her. I'd never leave her on Christmas for some *guy*."

The room descended into silence, a stark contrast to the loud pitch of her voice. Brenna's breaths labored under the weight of her emotions. I wondered how long she'd kept these feelings inside. Did she have anyone to talk to about her relationship with her mom?

"You deserved better."

Brenna's head snapped up. "This isn't about me."

I raised an eyebrow. "Isn't it? History is repeating. You know how Molly feels because *you* felt it every time your mom left you at my house."

Brenna swiped at a tear on her cheek, quickly, as if she wanted to pretend it never fell. "It doesn't matter, Nathan. My concern now is for Molly."

I pushed away from the sink, then took a seat beside her. "Bren, it's fine." I ran my fingers through the silken strands of her hair, still soft and perfect, even after our workout downstairs. "We'll have to reconfigure some plans. No more fucking in the kitchen for one."

She punched me in my nonpitching arm, shockingly hard.

I grinned. "Too soon?"

Brenna rolled her eyes. "Be serious."

"I am."

She paused again, mulling her words. "I know you don't want her here, Nathan. I can rent a place."

An anvil dropped on my chest at the thought of her not being here for the holiday. "You want to spend Christmas apart?"

"No," Brenna replied hurriedly, turning to face me. "No, of course not. But I don't want it to be uncomfortable for Molly." She sighed, reaching to shut off the water. "Do we have to talk about this now?"

Brenna stood abruptly and left the room, punctuating that she didn't want to talk about it.

But I couldn't end this conversation with her thinking I was another problem in her life.

Molly had been a point of contention in our past, one we never discussed. Shame burned through me when I thought about how I'd behaved as a kid. I didn't even know how to begin to apologize for it. I didn't want to ruin today, but I couldn't run from our past, shuffling the baggage between us even further from sight.

We had no chance if we kept doing that, and I needed us to have a fighting chance.

I trailed Brenna out of the bathroom. She'd already flopped on the bed, sprawled horizontally, arms flailed wide, hair around her head like a halo. She was so beautiful, this woman I'd loved for half my life. I wanted to devour her all over again.

"I want to have Christmas here, with you *and* Molly," I announced.

Brenna pushed herself onto her elbows, lifting her head to meet my gaze, her eyes wide.

"We don't have to talk about everything right now, but I need you to know I want to have this holiday here with you and your sister. You've seen how well I can plan. Let me do this."

She gave a slight shake of her head. "I don't want you to feel obligated—"

"Obligated?" The word came out with a choked laugh. "That's what you think? Brenna, I'm fucking *grateful* to be with you. That you're giving me a second chance."

"But Nathan—"

"I'm the guy for you, Brenna Quinn," I interrupted. "I want to be everything you need, and you need a partner who will make Molly a priority. Let me show you, all right?"

Her pink-stained face lifted, a slight smile forming.

"Besides," I added, "not celebrating Christmas with you would be misery."

One finger danced along her bottom lip. "So we're doing Christmas here then?" she asked. "Our own little family?"

A stab of happiness pierced my chest. *Our own little family.*

"We're doing this," I confirmed.

Brenna's smile stretched to a full-on grin. "I'm ready for pie and wine now."

I flopped beside her in bed, gathering her to my body. "Is that *all* that you're ready for?" She giggled as my lips trailed down her neck. I wanted to bottle that sound, the evidence of the joy I gave her.

"I'm never going to get my pie, am I?" she teased, already breathless from this little bit of contact.

"Eventually," I said, then seized her mouth.

37

NATHAN

Seven years ago

My car eased up to the curb outside my father's new home where I'd stay this weekend.

The court forced me to come here two weekends each month. I followed their orders because I didn't want my actions to blow back on my mom. She'd already been through enough.

This was the fourth month enduring the torture, counting the minutes until I could leave my complicated past behind. And because it was December, I would have to be *here,* in this house, the entire weekend. No escaping to a baseball game, which usually gave me a reprieve from the newly formed family I wanted nothing to do with.

I trudged up the driveway, duffle bag on one shoulder, baseball bag on the other. I let out a sigh of relief to see the dark and empty house. They reserved Friday nights for family dinner, and with me arriving later than usual, I thought maybe they'd gone out to eat. I turned my key in the lock and pushed open the door.

"Hello?" I called, praying no one answered.

When there was no response, I dropped my bags in the doorway and headed to the kitchen. My dad's six-pack of beer stared at me when I opened the fridge. *What the hell?* He was too in the doghouse to say shit to me, and I wanted something to help me survive the weekend.

I climbed the steps to the guest room. *This is your room, Nathan,* my father told me my first weekend here. He'd given me a tour, as if I hadn't been in this house thousands of times with Brenna. I knew exactly where the guest room was—right across the hall from her bedroom.

I would never consider it my room.

Brenna's door flung open. Her hands rapidly smoothed her hair as she stepped into the hallway. No matter how many times I ordered my brain not to react to her, there was always a swooping in my gut at first glance. My eyes hungrily took her in, starting at her feet, covered in thick fluffy blue socks, then the leggings molded to her toned legs, to the Owls sweatshirt two sizes too large for her.

My fucking sweatshirt.

Did she forget it was mine? Or had she kept it because she missed me?

The sound of a belt stole my attention, and my eyes fell to who stood behind her. My ribs squeezed tight. I wanted them to break, to give me something to focus on other than the walloping pain in my chest.

"Nathan," Brenna breathed. She subtly tried to close the door behind her, to shield Derek, but she couldn't hide what I'd already seen. "What are you doing here?"

I glowered at her. "Third Friday of the month, *sis.*"

Her eyes shot daggers at me. She hated the nickname. Our parents weren't even married, but it seemed inevitable now that they lived together and had a kid. Maybe if she hadn't moved on from me so quickly, we'd be navigating how to date while our parents married. People in this stupid small town would talk. It would've tested us, but maybe we could've found a way to deal with it.

We'd never know.

Derek stepped out beside Brenna, who remained frozen in the doorway. He looped his arms through hers.

"Mom and Dad know you have a boy in your room?" I smirked, slipping on a mask of indifference. I hoped the longer I wore it, the more natural it would feel.

"Lay off, man." Derek's bad impression of a guy with an ounce of toughness did nothing to deter me. He'd gone through a growth spurt since I last saw him, his body shooting up before the rest of him caught up.

I didn't even deign to respond to him and directed my attention to Brenna. "I'll take your silence as a no."

She crossed her arms over her chest. The movement forced Derek's arm to slip from hers. It shouldn't have given me a feeling of victory, especially when I knew they'd been doing more behind her bedroom door, but I took the small win. "We're babysitting Molly while they're on a date."

I glanced around, pretending to look for her. "You're doing a bang-up job."

"She's napping." Brenna took a small step toward me and lowered her voice. "And we need to wake her up or she won't sleep tonight. You can do the honors."

"Pass."

"She doesn't even know who you are. How are you *okay* with that?"

I made a circular motion with my finger, gesturing around the house. "I have no interest in being part of this fucked-up family you've all created. Maybe you can overlook that your mom banged her married neighbor and got knocked up to trap him, but it's too bitter a pill for me to swallow."

Brenna scoffed. "You think she did all of this on purpose?"

"Well, she didn't trip into my dad's bed. And it wasn't just one time. She *chose* to betray her best friend—and *you*—over and over again. I'd say it was pretty purposeful."

Her gaze fell to the floor. The truth fucking hurt.

By staying here and living in their little fantasy world, Brenna got to ignore the real consequences of what her mother had done. Some of us didn't have the luxury.

Derek stepped forward, putting his hand up as a stop sign. "Haven't you hurt Brenna enough?"

I jabbed a finger in his chest. "You don't know what the hell you're talking about."

He slapped my hand away but only managed to move it to the opposite side of his body. "Might want to rethink that. *I'm* the one with Brenna every day."

Not every day. The devil on my shoulder dared me to tell Derek about how his girlfriend had been in my bed only four months ago, more than willing to give herself to me. This annoyingly forthright guy would dump her if he found out. And I wanted to knock the arrogance out of him.

"Back. Off." My nostrils flared, a lick of anger winding up my spine.

Brenna folded in on herself. Because of the part of me that would always love her, I deflated every ounce of anger, wanting to put her out of her misery. As if she could sense me watching, her head lifted, and her watery eyes met mine.

"How is any of this *her* fault?" Brenna pointed down the hallway to Molly's room. "She's innocent."

I stepped back until I reached the guest room door. "So am I."

I opened the door and snapped it shut behind me.

"She's your sister too," Brenna called.

I slipped my headphones on, blocking out the world around me. I chugged the rest of my beer, hoping it would relieve me of the emotions raging inside me.

No such luck.

38

BRENNA

Now

I BOUNCED ON MY feet, waiting near the luggage carousel for Molly's flight.

My mother arranged the unaccompanied minor service with the airline before I could object to my seven-year-old sister flying cross-country alone. At least on the way home, my mother and her married companion had booked a connecting flight through Palmer City. Otherwise, I might not let Molly leave.

Molly's Palmer City Wolves baseball cap caught my attention first—the black cap stark over her braided blond pigtails. She released the hand of the airport staff once she spotted me and sprinted straight into my arms.

"Molls," I said into her hair. "I've missed you so much."

The airline assistant held out Molly's baseball cap which had flown off her head during her run. "Thank you," I said, accepting the hat and securing it back on my sister's head. "For everything."

"You've been gone longer than two days," Molly whined.

I held out my hand to her, and although she was miffed, she took it.

"I know. But you remember what I told you I was doing?"

We turned toward the carousel, keeping an eye out for her suitcase. The crowd had thinned, so it wouldn't take long to spot with fewer bags in circulation.

Molly huffed. "Fixing a house."

"And I own a café now too, remember?"

Her eyes grew wide. "Does that mean I get free food?"

I put on a mock-serious look. "Within reason."

"Mom said I'm on vacation."

I held in a sigh. My sister hadn't seen enough of the world to know how messed up her home life was. Until I got custody of Molly, I didn't *want* her to realize that she missed out, so I kept commentary about our mother to myself.

I snagged Molly's luggage before it skated by us. "She's right." The words were like marbles in my mouth. "We have a ton of fun stuff planned."

"Who's we?"

I led her by the hand toward the airport exit, rolling her backpack behind us with my other hand. "My... business partner. Nathan owns the house and the café with me. He'll spend the weekend with us."

"Is he your *boyfriend*? Mom said you got rid of Jack."

Got rid of Jack. Like I had him murdered. *Thanks a lot, Kathy.* I assumed Jack told her about the end of our relationship. I certainly didn't.

We crossed the street to the parking deck, and I used the time to write and rewrite my response. "Jack and I are no longer together, but it was a mutual decision." *Sort of.* I wouldn't get into the details with her. "And that's a great question, Molls. Why don't you ask Nathan?"

Nathan and I spent each day of our last week consumed in each other. I'd barely slept and worked through the exhaustion. But as soon as we got home and shut out the world, energy zinged through me and I came back to life.

So did Nathan. I looked forward to seeing the unmistakably happy smile when it became only us. I didn't want to bring up questions of the future and cause his smile to slip. I did wonder whether we would continue whatever we were doing after the house and business sold, and how exactly we'd make it work, living hundreds of miles away from each other.

Maybe Molly's curiosity would get me some insight into Nathan's thought process.

Molly gasped when she realized the house all lit up for Christmas was ours. My heart leaped at the awe on my little sister's face… and also because Nathan knew the importance of this first impression with her. He strode out of the house as soon as we arrived, probably waiting at the window for our return. He told me he'd prove he could be the partner I needed, and he was off to a great start.

"Hey," I greeted, a little breathless from the emotions swelling in me.

Molly and I stopped in front of Nathan at the end of the walkway. We hadn't been apart long, but I still fought an instinct to run into his arms.

He glanced over my shoulder. "You don't need help bringing stuff in?"

"Nope," I said, popping the P. "We're good. Molly, this is Nathan. Nathan, this is my sister, Molly."

Nathan squatted until they were eye level. He stuck his hand out and shook hers gingerly. "Very nice to meet you, Molly. Brenna has told me all about you."

"What has she said?" Suspicion underlined her words.

He tapped the brim of her baseball cap. "That you're the biggest Palmer City Wolves fan out there."

"They're the best." Molly bobbed her head in agreement. "Do *you* play hockey?"

"Afraid not," Nathan answered, his voice apologetic.

Dammit if it didn't make my insides glow, knowing he was trying to make a good impression on her. It was more than I could have hoped for.

"I play baseball."

"Like Brenna." Her hand tugged on mine. "I think baseball is boring."

Nathan straightened to his full height. "I'll try not to hold it against you."

"That's what Brenna says too!" Her voice rose, looking accusatory, like maybe we'd coordinated our answers. "My sister wants to know if you're her boyfriend."

Oh, Molly, you little snot.

"I'd like to be." His eyes found mine, and a hurricane brewed in my stomach. Nathan said to Molls, "Maybe before you leave, you can tell me whether you think it would be okay."

I was so gone for this man. Far past the point of no return.

I slipped into bed beside Nathan, curling my body around his and allowing his warmth to seep into my skin. His fresh laundry and bubble gum scent surrounded me. *Home.* The word clanged around in my mind as my body relaxed against him.

Nathan's head twisted over his shoulder to look at me. Hazy-eyed, he mumbled, "Brenna?"

"Expecting another woman?"

His laugh rumbled through me.

"Never. I didn't think I'd see you tonight." He turned toward me, pulling me to his naked skin. His hand slipped between my legs and up my shorts. When he discovered no additional barrier to his fingers, he made a satisfied grumble. "Do you need me, Quinn?"

"We shouldn't." I placed my hand on his, stilling him. "We might wake her."

"We can be quiet... can't we, darlin'?"

Nathan's rough words against my ear sent a zap of pleasure to my belly.

My head nodded of its own volition, my body already lost to his touch and silky voice. My head fell to his shoulder, while my hips moved slowly against his fingers.

"That's it, Bren." His teeth grazed the shell of my ear. "I love you like this. Flushed. Desperate for me."

I bit down hard on my lip to stop a moan. I was hot all over, burning for Nathan, *needing* him.

His fingers kept moving leisurely in and out, each stroke winding me tighter. I reached toward his boxer briefs, wanting to give him a taste of his own medicine.

His hand clamped on mine, plastering it to his stomach. "Uh-uh, Bren. You're the greedy one, not able to go even one night without my cock."

"Nathan," I whimpered.

"Tell me what you need."

Nathan pulled his hand back, drawing a groan from deep within me. My eyes popped open to find him smirking. Damn him.

"I need you inside me. Right. Now." I panted. "You're the *only* person who can give me what I need."

Nathan seized my lips, his tongue teasing mine before he pulled back again. "You're the only person I want to be with, Brenna. Now come here, back to me."

I granted his request, turning and scooting until the hard planes of his body pressed into my back. He slipped my sweatshirt over my head, leaving me in a thin white tank top. One arm reached around my body to my breast, fingers playing with a peaked nipple.

"I love feeling you through this."

I clenched my legs together, barely holding on as the rasp of his voice teased me. It was too much. I couldn't take it.

"Nathan..." He'd reduced me to a begging, shaking mess. "I *need* to come."

"Oh, you will, Bren." His teeth grazed my earlobe. "So fucking hard."

I'd never heard a more beautiful sound than the rip of the foil wrapper. Nathan and I both groaned as he pushed into me. I'd never get tired of these first moments, the pleasurable sensation of his cock stretching me.

He waited for me to adjust—attuned to my needs as always—and then he thrust into me. One of his hands teased my breasts, the other gripped my shoulder for leverage. I nudged against him each time he thrust, finding a rhythm.

This was new for us, this slowness, this leisurely way Nathan moved in me, like we had all the time in the world. And time did seem to slow as I always wished it would when we were tangled up in each other.

"Touch yourself, darlin'."

My fingers obeyed, teasing at the apex of my thighs.

"Good girl… just like that."

I worked myself harder, spurred on by his approval. His thrusts quickened, becoming erratic when his hand landed on top of mine, the added pressure from his fingers sending my body over the top. My orgasm slammed into me, making me clench around him while I moaned into a pillow.

"I fucking *love* that sound."

Nathan thrust one last time and sent himself over the edge, biting my shoulder to stay quiet. The spark of pain, the way Nathan worked to even out his staggered breath, the evidence of what *I* did to him. Happiness bloomed in my chest, bright and warm and so strong, it could burst straight through my skin. I turned in his arms until we faced each other, then kissed him with every good feeling that existed inside me.

"Just so you know, this isn't why I came in here."

Nathan smoothed a wayward hair behind my ear. My smile must've been as ridiculously big as his.

"Good to know you don't think of me as a piece of meat."

I shoved him, and both of us huffed out laughs.

"That was a first." I pulled back to stare at his ridiculously handsome face, into those turquoise eyes. He arched an eyebrow. "The… talking."

One side of his lip lifted. "I like seeing how many ways I can make you come undone."

"Aren't you going to ask if I liked it?"

"No need."

He snagged me around my waist and pulled me to him, as close as possible. He found my lips again, and I *melted*.

"I *felt* how much you liked it, Brenna."

He kissed my forehead once, then rolled off the bed to dispose of the condom. My eyes hungrily took him in—his strong thighs, the toned planes of his abdomen, his haughty, hot expression.

"So did I," I said, as if this were an argument over who enjoyed our sex more.

Nathan leaned over the bed, a cocky smile still on his lips, and winked. "Hell yeah, you did."

After both of us cleaned up, we found each other again beneath the sheets, our bodies pressed together. His heart pounded steadily, a soothing rhythm that would put me to sleep if I wasn't careful.

"Thank you for everything you did tonight." My finger traced shapes on his chest.

He ran his fingers through my hair, the light touch of his fingertips on my scalp sending tingles down my spine.

"She seems great, Bren."

"She is," I agreed. I even enjoyed her when the precocious little kid called me out.

"If I could take everything back, I would."

He didn't need to elaborate for me to know what he meant. Ignoring Molly when she was a toddler. Acting like the girl we once thought was his half sister was a stranger.

I nodded, my cheek rubbing his skin. "I know, Nate."

He held me tighter. "I love that I get to celebrate Christmas with both of you."

The ball of happiness near my heart expanded against the confines of my chest again. Everything could go wrong this Christmas, and still, it would be the best one I'd ever had.

39

BRENNA

Now

"I think Nathan is your boyfriend."

Molly's legs swung against her chair, her feet hitting the counter at the café. She took another bite of Gemma's addictive cinnamon roll.

Not that I'd ever tell Gemma, but the quality of her baked goods had declined when she was on maternity leave. She'd returned to baking last week, which meant several specialty menu items became available again. Cinnamon rolls on Saturday morning were one, a special once-per-week event. People often stopped here for coffee after picking some up before heading back home in their PJs.

I wiped down the counter in front of the coffee machines with a rag. "Why do you say that?"

"Boyfriends and girlfriends sleep in the same room."

The beating of Nathan's heart *had* lulled me to sleep—well, that and other things. When the sun streaming through the curtains finally roused me, I bolted back to Molly's room to pretend I'd been beside her all night.

No such luck. I found her downstairs eating cereal in front of cartoons.

I hummed noncommittally.

"And they stare at each other a lot, like Bugs Bunny and Lola Bunny."

Well, shit. How could I argue with that? I was the one who introduced her to the old-school cartoons I'd watched as a kid. And there were a million photos of me through the years with that lovesick expression. Even my baby sister, who'd been here for less than twenty-four hours, could see my love for Nathan reflected in my face.

"It sounds like you know a lot about this, Molls." I stared at her pointedly. "Do *you* have a boyfriend?"

She stuck her tongue out, white icing still coating it. "Ew. No. Boys are gross."

I'd thought so too until I moved next door to Nathan Sharpe when I was three years older than she was now. "They very well can be," I agreed, smiling broadly at my sister.

I loved having her here, being silly with her over breakfast. We used to do this every morning before I walked her to the bus for school.

"Now, who is this?" Bertram's booming voice echoed through the mostly empty room.

Our early morning rush had tapered hours ago. I suspected many people were traveling for the holiday two days from now. We would close the Courtside Café this afternoon and not reopen until the day after Christmas.

I gestured across the counter. "This is my sister, Molly. Molly, meet Bertram. He's one of our best customers."

He let out a low whistle. "Good sales tactic, Miss Brenna." He took a seat beside Molly, who regarded him with apprehension. "I am *the best* customer, Miss Golly-Oh-Molly."

"My name is Molly," she huffed before returning her attention to her half-devoured cinnamon roll.

"Now I see where you get your attitude from," Bertram said to me.

I glared at him, and though it was playful—like our dynamic—it proved his point.

"Is your other half here?"

"In his office. I'll get him for you."

"No funny business back there," Bertram called as I disappeared behind the curtain.

I heard my sister ask "What's funny business?" and prayed to God Bertram handled the question with the care and discretion it required.

I knocked once on the office door before letting myself in. Nathan seized my hand, pulled me into his lap, and wrapped his arms around my waist. I squealed before relaxing into him.

"You've been summoned." I swatted at his arm.

He lifted me as he stood, holding on until my feet hit the ground. "You're no fun."

"I will be later," I crooned, heading back out front.

Nathan followed me, tickling my side as I swatted at him again. I gave him a stern look to stop before we emerged from the back.

"Your tickets have arrived," Bertram announced, holding them out to Nathan.

Molly perked up. "Tickets?" She shifted to her knees in her chair to peer over the counter.

Nathan fanned the tickets, waving them back and forth, but it was Bertram who answered.

"Three tickets to the Palmer City Wolves game tonight. The first home game I'll miss in years... after being *hustled*."

Molly screamed, high-pitched and soul-shaking. Every head snapped in our direction. I tried to hush her.

"I'm so sorry! My sister's just excited for a game tonight," I told the rest of the café.

Molly climbed off her chair and rushed behind the counter to Nathan, wrapping her arms around his legs. "It's okay if you want to be Brenna's boyfriend."

Unfortunately, her whisper was loud enough for Bertram to hear. He raised an eyebrow, his mouth open to, no doubt, say something inappropriate for seven-year-old ears.

I jumped in. "Thank you for the tickets, Bertram."

"It isn't a gift," he grumbled. "The kid won them off us in our last poker game."

"Maybe that will teach you not to gamble."

He pointed at me and busted out another laugh. "Good one, missy. The day I stop gambling will be my last day on this earth."

Tears pooled in Molly's eyes as she returned to her seat.

"I take it you're a Wolves fan." Bertram made another attempt at conversation with her.

Molly's glare screamed *duh*.

"All right, kiddo. Let's see how well you know the team."

She inhaled the last piece of her cinnamon roll before shifting to face him. I rolled my eyes at the two of them before retreating to the other end of the counter to take a customer's order. In the background, I tracked their conversation.

"Who's the captain?"

"Easy," Molly answered. "Matt Harris."

"Highest goal scorer?"

"Alexei Volkov." Molly stuck out her tongue in triumph.

"How about the youngest player on the team?"

"Zach Briggs."

I tuned them out when Nathan's hands found my hips. "Did you hear I got approval to be your boyfriend?" He rested his chin on my shoulder. "Someone told me you wondered if we are in a relationship."

I elbowed him in the chest. He stumbled before returning to the same position.

"That's not how the conversation went at all," I countered.

"No?" He pressed a quick kiss to my neck. "So you aren't wondering if I'm your boyfriend?"

I shook my head. "You're the worst."

"That's not what you said last night," he whispered into my hair. His hands tightened on my hips, as if the memory brought the same flood of lust to him as it did to me. "I want to be in a relationship with you, Brenna."

My breath caught. I wanted a relationship with Nathan Sharpe, badly and against all logic and reason. Regardless of our circumstances, not one part of me wanted to hesitate or think about this for longer than a millisecond.

I shrugged, feigning nonchalance. "Okay, sure. Why not?"

"You'll pay for that later, Quinn," Nathan said directly in my ear.

I couldn't wait.

40

BRENNA

Now

NATHAN AND I HELD Molly's hands while she skipped toward Cole Coliseum.

Molly's wide eyes took in everything, from dozens of tailgaters to individuals walking to the arena decked out in Palmer City Wolves gear to the mammoth arena getting larger with each step.

Molly insisted we all wear something to show our support for the team, so we stopped at the merch store, cleverly named The Den, before going to our seats. Nathan bought a sweatshirt for himself and a winter hat with a pom-pom for me. Since Molly already had a jersey and hat, she chose a half-green half-black triangle flag that read Wolves with their logo of a wolf howling.

"I love it here." Molly tracked the players zipping around the ice.

I clutched her hand as we descended the steep cement stairs to our seats. Balancing the merch, popcorn, and drinks without falling was a feat.

Nathan and I hadn't talked about it, but we ended up sitting as I'd hoped with Molly sandwiched between us. I liked that he understood how important it was for me to have time with her and for the two of them to build a relationship. Only a man who invited my sister into his life deserved to be in mine.

"Nathan?" The woman in front of us spun, her short dark hair flipping with the movement. "I didn't know you'd be here."

My heartbeat quickened as I watched Deandra Collins place her hand on Nathan's forearm and throw her head back, laughing at whatever he said. I couldn't hear it over the white noise filling my ears. My mind recounted the time in high school when I found Nathan on the couch on top of Deandra. His shirt was off. Her sweater buttons were half undone, revealing the laciest bra I'd seen in person. I'd stopped breathing. *Of course* he moved on to someone like her. Hot, popular, not a tomboy.

In the present, Nathan and I were desperate for each other. We owned a house and business together. He'd asked me to be his girlfriend. And yet, that helpless, heartbroken, wrecked girl lived on inside me, deciding to appear at the worst possible times. I didn't know if I would ever shed her.

I cleared my throat. "What was that?"

Nathan's forehead creased. "I asked if you wanted to tell them about how we got these tickets."

NATHAN

Now

Brenna's body language morphed from loose and carefree to tense.

"You're the one who won the tickets." She carelessly waved a hand, unbothered. "It's your story."

She could pretend all she wanted, but the change had everything to do with Deandra's presence. For such an ordinarily forgiving person, she couldn't let this go. I should've been flattered—and part of me was—but I hated that she didn't have confidence in us, that a meaningless hookup from high school was even on her radar.

It was my mission to change that.

"Are you a hockey fan?" Kennedy asked from beside Deandra. She sported a black Wolves jersey with the name Volkov in green across her back. "I'm Kennedy, by the way."

Bren gave her a small smile. "I'm Brenna. And not really, no. But this one here"—she embraced Molly around the shoulders—"has loved hockey ever since she was a little kid. So Nathan got us tickets."

"I *won* us tickets," I clarified, launching into the story of how Bertram and his friends gambled in our café every day and coaxed me into joining them. My earlier losses became worth it when the guys wagered one game of their season tickets, a three-pair. If it hadn't been for the two people beside me, I wouldn't have called in the payment.

"Bertram will hold it against you forever," Kennedy said with a laugh. Her attention shifted to Molly. "So, who's your favorite player?"

With the way her eyes were glued to the ice, I didn't think she was listening. But then the buzzer went off, calling the players to the locker rooms so the crew could prep the ice. Molly swallowed her popcorn. "Briggsy. He's the fastest and funniest player."

"Everybody loves that kid," Deandra said. "He's social media gold."

"I will not be telling him that," Kennedy said.

Molly gasped. "You *know* him?"

Deandra leaned toward Molly. "Kennedy is dating Alexei Volkov, and Zach's her roommate."

Kennedy added, "You'd find him less funny if you lived with him. Trust me."

"Wait... you're Kennedy *Cole*?"

She nodded, cheeks turning pink.

"You own the team."

"My *dad* owns the team."

Molly slumped back in her seat. "Wow."

"I think you broke her," I said.

Deandra shrugged. "Not the first time it's happened. So, Brenna, what happened to that ring of yours? I thought you were engaged."

The abrupt change in topic gave me whiplash.

"Don't mind her," Kennedy said apologetically. "She's in the early stages of soda withdrawal. It's never pretty."

Deandra's longing stare at Molly's drink earlier now made sense. She ignored my glare, her gaze fixed on Brenna. At the café, she'd stirred things up to make a point to me, but I had no clue what her goal was tonight. I prayed silently this conversation wouldn't sink our entire night.

"Oh, she got rid of Jack," Molly chipped in, repeating Kathy Quinn's characterization. It baffled me how Molly and Brenna were this well-adjusted, given Kathy's brand of dysfunction.

Deandra arched an eyebrow, one side of her lip tugging up. "Is that so?"

"Molls," Brenna warned.

Molly continued, unaware of how she'd captured the attention of every adult around her. She happily chowed down on popcorn while watching the big screen over center ice showing a reel of highlights. "And now Nathan is her boyfriend. I like him better."

I suppressed a laugh at the expression on Brenna's face, a cross between shock and annoyance. She liked her privacy. Having our dirty laundry aired for all of Middlebury had been hell. But she also enjoyed this side of her little sister, when she playfully pressed her buttons. She feigned annoyance when I did it too.

Deandra poked Molly in the arm. "You, little wolf, are my new best friend. You're invited to any game."

Molly gave Brenna a massive smile, stretching the width of her face. "Did you hear that? We can come to *any* game!"

I gazed over at Brenna, enjoying the way her cheeks reddened.

"It's about time you two figured it out," Deandra said in a warm tone. Her gaze shifted from me to Bren. "I'm happy for you. Seriously."

"Thank you," Brenna said, clearly taken aback. She hadn't known Deandra like I did though. Deandra showed everyone pretty and popular, so they assumed her life was a breeze. But she had a lot going on behind the scenes. She was smarter and more generous than people recognized. A good friend.

I reached behind our seats to rest a hand on Brenna's shoulder, reveling in her devastating grin back at me. I kept my hand there for the rest of the first period. Molly danced with Deandra and Kennedy when the Wolves scored a goal, making it onto the big screen. She also screamed, far louder than someone so small should be able to.

Our own little family. It had been so long since I had family, and I missed it. I'd forgo any other wish for the rest of my life as long as I got to keep them.

Brenna took Molly to the bathroom at the end of the period, leaving me an opening with Deandra. "Hey," I blurted as she stood. "Can I ask you something?"

"I've already arranged to take her to the locker room after the game."

"You did? Wow, thank you."

She waved a hand. "Don't mention it."

"But that's not actually my question." I scratched the back of my neck. "I've been having trouble with my shoulder. Is there any way you can get me an appointment with the team doctor? I need someone at the top of the field."

Deandra's brow furrowed. "Why are you being secretive about it?"

"I don't want my team—"

She cut me off. "No, with Brenna."

"Bren knows. She's the one who made me realize I need to face this." The one who made me realize I could handle anything that came of it. "But she worries. I'd rather go to her with all the facts."

Kennedy jumped in. "We can get you an appointment as soon as you need."

"Thank you." I dipped my head. "You have no idea what this means."

Kennedy held up her thumb and pointer finger, leaving only a smidge of space between them. "I *might* have an idea, seeing how I'm dating a stubborn athlete and all. I'm glad you didn't give up, by the way. Brenna seems great, even if she does hate my best friend."

Deandra poked Kennedy in the shoulder. "As if you'd be any better if you ran into a woman who had slept with Alexei." Kennedy's lips fell into a thin line, which sent Deandra into hysterical laughter. "See! Just the thought has you tied up in knots."

"You'll understand one day, D," I said, rescuing Kennedy from having to respond. Her eyes were doing this scary, intense thing. I wondered if my expression mirrored hers when Brenna's ex-fiancé came to town. "When you meet the right person."

Deandra huffed. "I'm too busy taking on the world to train some boy how to be a man."

Kennedy and I exchanged a glance, two people who had been bull-dozed when the right person came along. In the best way possible.

It was adorable how Deandra thought she'd be immune or able to fight the feelings. She, like everyone else, would never stand a chance.

41

BRENNA

Now

"WELL, *GOOD MORNING*," I crooned when I saw Nathan cooking in the kitchen on Christmas morning.

His sleeves were rolled to his elbows, showing off his strength. I admired what I could see of his tattoos—vines, flowers, and leaves, all dark and sexy. With the red Santa hat on his head, it created quite the mindfuck. I might never be able to think of Christmas without remembering this moment.

The scent of pancakes had beckoned me downstairs, and I followed it to the real prize.

Nathan turned to me, giving me a view of his bare chest through his half-zipped hoodie. *Merry Christmas to me.*

"How do you expect to make this a wholesome family holiday when you look like *that*?"

He grinned, then tugged the zipper to the top, covering his chest. "Better?"

"Barely. And it's too late. That image is permanently burned in my mind."

Nathan turned off the stove after flipping the last round of pancakes. He brought a plate to the kitchen table and took a seat at the head. "Come eat some breakfast, Bren. I made your favorite."

I made a mock-serious face at him. "Don't think you can distract me with chocolate chip pancakes."

He forked one of the cakes and waved it back and forth in the air. "I know you want them," he said, his voice lilting.

Cappie jumped onto the table and lunged at Nathan's arm. He lifted it higher before Cappie could snag our breakfast. "Down," he ordered the cat, who immediately flopped to the ground, staring up at Nathan with an adorably innocent expression.

"Real smooth, Sharpe," I said through my laughter.

"At least someone wants the breakfast I made," Nathan muttered.

I walked to him, sliding into his lap, one leg draped outside his legs. One of Nathan's hands landed on my hip, fingers splayed wide. He lowered his other arm, dripping a strand of syrup onto my chest before the bite of pancake reached my mouth.

I grinned at him. "This is what happens when you mess around, Nathan."

He leaned forward, his head dipping to bring his mouth to my chest, his tongue darting out to lick up the syrup, all while he locked eyes with me. I suppressed a moan each time his lips pressed another part of my skin. He continued moving until his insistent lips landed on mine, deliciously sweet. It took effort to pull back, but I didn't want Molly's Christmas tainted by the sight of me devouring Nathan.

"*On Christmas?*" I said in the cadence of an innocent southern woman saying *I do declare.*

He laughed into my skin. "The day doesn't make a difference, Quinn."

"Ooh, I can't wait for Flag Day."

Nathan tapped my ass as I stood. I yelped, moving quickly to the opposite side of the table.

"Seriously, Nathan, thank you. For breakfast. For not giving up on me. For loving me as I am."

Nathan reached across the table to clasp my hand, playfully bumping my leg with his foot. "Merry Christmas, Bren."

I nudged him back. "Merry Christmas, Nate."

Molly stampeded down the stairs, feet loudly hitting each one to announce her presence. "It's Christmas!" she cheered, "It's Christmas." Her feet halted when the lit-up Christmas tree with two piles of wrapped presents came into view. "Wow. Can I open them? Can I open them?"

She bounced on her feet, bursting with more energy than I would muster in a week.

"Go ahead," I said, following her into the family room.

Molly plopped down in front of the tree and began rifling through presents. Hands landed on my shoulder, and I looked up to see Nathan grinning down at me. I tugged on his hand until he dropped down beside me, his arm snaking around my waist, pulling me to his side. We watched Molly tear into her first present, squealing when she found a bobblehead of her favorite hockey player. She threw her arms around me before hugging Nathan, then flopped back to the ground to choose another gift.

Later, the three of us cooked lasagna and an assortment of appetizers. Molly and I baked, and then ate, way too many sweets. We marathoned

Christmas movies while snuggled under blankets on the couch in front of the fireplace, the glow of Christmas tree lights brightening the room.

I'd never been happier.

NATHAN

Now

The day after Christmas, everything went to shit. Molly was collecting rent from me for landing on Park Place when the doorbell rang. Then we heard the click of the doorknob before the door swung open.

I launched out of my seat, snagging a kitchen knife. I wouldn't take any chances with the two people here with me.

When I turned the corner, I stopped dead in my tracks.

No one was robbing us, though part of me would've preferred that.

The woman who stood in the foyer of my family home was the same person who had wrecked it.

Kathy Quinn's villain aura remained, but she had more wrinkles and blonder hair. She wore a short-sleeved low-cut dress and sandals, despite the cool weather. Heavy makeup. Necklaces, bracelets, long dangly earrings. All of it screamed *Look at me!*

She swiveled her head, taking in decorations adorning every inch of the house. "Well, isn't this cozy? The two of you shacking up like you're teenagers again."

Brenna appeared a heartbeat later, arms crossed over her chest. "What are you doing here, Kathy?"

She opened her arms wide, beckoning Molly. "Come here, munchkin."

Molly stood behind Brenna, not moving. The sight broke my heart.

"Ah. I see. You've been telling her stories about me."

"Why are you here?" Brenna repeated. "We weren't expecting you for three days."

Kathy fussed with her hair. "Plans changed. Richard needed to go home."

"You mean he made up with his wife."

The dynamic between Brenna and Kathy had changed since childhood. Brenna used to allow her mother to steamroll her, never saying a word against her. I didn't think Bren even realized it, living on an emotional rollercoaster her entire life, willing to do anything for a steady road. Now Brenna did what I'd always wished she'd do back then; she didn't let the bitch push her around.

Kathy scoffed. "How's Jack, Brenna? Seen him lately?"

"We broke up."

Something she damn well knew.

Kathy gestured to me. "Before or after you jumped back into his bed?"

"Seriously?" Brenna shrieked, covering Molly's ears, as if she could remove the words from her brain.

"You're out of line." I pointed to the door. "Get. Out."

Kathy remained rooted to the spot. "You're one to talk, Nathan. Giving her hope you won't break her heart again. Did she tell you how she fell apart last time? Every single day, sobbing over the boy who wouldn't return her calls. *I* was the one here with her—"

Brenna stepped to my side. "Congratulations on fulfilling the most basic function of parenting. Yes, you were here, but you made me feel like a complete failure. I was suffering, and you chided me for not getting over it when I wasn't *capable* of it, at—"

Kathy blew out a long, exasperated breath. "Here we go again, you prattling on about your harebrained diagnosis."

Diagnosis? Brenna had never said anything about a condition.

"I don't care whether you believe it's real," she snapped.

Kathy took a step toward Brenna. Instinctively, I moved in front of her, my hand resting on her forearm.

Kathy rolled her eyes. "If I'm *so* bad," she said, "why did I take you in when you needed me?"

"Needed you?" Brenna roared. She paused to let out a cold cackle that sounded nothing like the kind woman I loved. "I never *needed* you. I told you that so you'd let me live with you. Molly needed *me* because you stopped taking care of her."

Once the words burst from her, Brenna remembered herself, that she stood in front of the sister she wanted to protect. Molly didn't need shielding from this message though. She was growing up with Kathy Quinn, and faster as a result, just like her sister. Molly's eyes shone with gratitude at Brenna for having her back.

"You have no idea what you're talking about," Kathy said smoothly, not missing a beat. "I don't need to explain myself to you."

Brenna's lips parted, and I knew the words *You'll need to explain to a court* were readied there, but she swiftly shut her mouth. She didn't want to tip Kathy off to her plan to sue for custody.

Kathy shook her head, conveying judgment with this smallest of movements. "He'll do it again, Brenna. They always do." She turned on her heel and walked to the door. Before she stepped through, she looked at us over her shoulder. "Molly and I have a flight in two hours. I expect her to be ready to go in fifteen minutes."

The door clicked shut. Brenna let out an audible breath, but her body was still tense thanks to the cyclone Kathy Quinn's arrival blew into our house.

Molly clung to Brenna's legs. "Please don't make me go. *Please.*"

A flurry of tears fell from Bren's eyes, rushing down her cheeks.

I wrapped my arms around them both, wishing I could fix this, could stop their hearts from breaking. But all I could do was make things as easy as possible.

I left them alone in the foyer and slipped upstairs to pack Molly's belongings.

⸻◦○◦⸻

My phone vibrated on the table moments after Brenna's stopped. I reached for it, seeing it was our realtor. Calling us on New Year's Eve.

"Hey, Shelly, I'm surprised to hear from you today."

I paused the movie. Brenna stirred in bed next to me. She'd drifted off to sleep an hour ago. She was sleeping more than usual after Kathy Quinn crashed our holiday. Had withdrawn into herself too. I kept waiting for her to talk to me, *really* talk to me. When she didn't, I spent most of my time looking for signs she might be ready for me to bring it up.

It hadn't happened yet.

"Realty stops for no one," Shelly replied over the background noise of kids' voices. "I'm calling with good news. Hot off the presses. I didn't want to wait to tell you."

I sat up in bed. "What is it?"

"I've received an all-cash offer on the house. Asking price."

After several lowball offers we didn't consider, here was serious interest. This news *should* have been exactly what I wanted to hear. It was the culmination of months of work, but it sent a pit to the bottom of my stomach.

The house would no longer belong to us, at least not after the sale processed three months from now. Our realtor had made the terms of the will known to all potential buyers—no final sales until April.

I was terrified our relationship could only survive here, that once we left the house, we'd return to our separate lives, like these past few months were a dream, a vacation from real life.

"Nathan, what's wrong?" A crease formed between Brenna's eyes.

"Nathan? You still there?" Shelly asked.

"Ye-ah." I cleared emotion from my throat. "Yes, that's great news."

I could hear the smile in her voice. "I knew you'd think so."

"Let me talk to Brenna, and we'll get back to you."

I agreed to let her know tomorrow after she warned the buyers would move on if we didn't answer soon.

"Talk to me about what?" Brenna asked.

I repeated what Shelly told me.

"Seriously?" Brenna beamed, her excitement appropriate for good news.

She didn't ask why I wasn't equally over the moon, but she could tell I didn't share her enthusiasm. And because I'd known her most of my life, I recognized it wasn't her not caring. She knew this could open the pandora's box of topics we avoided. The ones I desperately needed to talk with her about before my heart broke like a glass hit with a sledgehammer.

My father's voice filled my head. *Don't repeat my mistakes.*

He'd let the love of his life walk away without a fight. By the time he realized his fuckup, my mom had moved on with someone else. No one had died and left everything to my parents to force them back together. Not for the first time, gratitude for my father washed over me. He'd known what my stubborn ass refused to admit. My life would not be full without Brenna Quinn in it.

"We need to take this offer." She pushed into a sitting position, facing me. "I need to go back. I can't leave Molly alone to deal with *her*."

Finally. The words Brenna refused to voice. This relationship would never work if we didn't tell each other the truth.

I smoothed her hair back from her face. "All right," I said, even though my lips rebelled against the words. "Book your flight. I'll wrap up everything here."

Her head jerked back. "Really?"

"Really," I repeated. "I'd never keep you from her." I reached for Brenna's hand, wrapping it in mine. "Give me tonight. And I get to pick what we do."

Brenna sighed dramatically. "I don't want to go to that Wolves party."

Gemma had invited us to a New Year's Eve party Kennedy was hosting in Alexei Volkov's new house. She'd explained she usually hosted but decided not to this year because of the baby. Though that wouldn't stop her from "tearing it up at Kennedy's future place."

I tipped Brenna's chin to me. "I'm not sharing you with anyone on our last night here, darlin'."

"Then what do you want to do?"

"Talk."

She stilled. I took a deep breath, readying myself for her to retreat further from me.

She surprised me by squeezing my hand. "Okay, Nathan, but you're going to need to feed me."

I squeezed her hand back. "Pizza is already on the way."

42

BRENNA

Six years ago

TODAY I GRADUATED FROM Middlebury High School, putting four years behind me that I'd rather forget.

I'd spent most of this year distracting myself from what I'd lost. Working in the trainer's room, gaining experience I could put on my resume when I pursued physical therapy. Bonding with my baby sister. Spending time with Derek, going to dinner and school events.

Never baseball games.

Nathan's dad made him come to my graduation. Gordon often ignored the strain between Nathan and me, forcing us together like nothing had changed. The ever-present reminder that it *had* changed was torture. So was the depth of my feelings for Nathan, which made me feel guilty for continuing to date Derek.

But I needed to move on from Nathan. If I lost Derek, I'd be all alone. And alone hadn't been good for me.

But now I needed to end our relationship. It wouldn't go anywhere long-term, though I suspected Derek wouldn't agree. At least he hadn't applied to the same schools as me or made his college decision based on mine. I wouldn't have been able to bear affecting his future like that.

Tomorrow. I'd tell him tomorrow. After we celebrated graduation tonight.

I maneuvered through the crowd of graduates and their families until I found my own, still seated in the stands at our football field. Mom and Gordon stood upon seeing me, offering congratulations and hugs. I wasn't used to seeing them so well dressed—my mom in a formfitting summer dress and Gordon in navy pants and a jacket. I'd become accustomed to their loungewear as they cared for Molly, who currently slept peacefully in her stroller.

"Bet it feels good to be out of here," Nathan murmured from his seat in the bleachers.

I hadn't expected him to acknowledge me. "You could say that." I turned away from him and used my hand to shield my eyes from the sun. "Have you seen Derek?" I asked my mom and Gordon.

Nathan scoffed.

"No, I—" Mom started, but Molly stirred, drawing her and Gordon's attention.

With their focus elsewhere, Nathan and I were alone, the last thing I wanted. Especially today. More graduations lay in my future, but this one still meant something. It was a rite of passage. I'd survived two of the toughest years of my life.

Nathan leaned forward, elbows on his knees. "I don't know why you don't do it already."

"What?" The word came quickly. I hated that I still craved his attention, even when his next words would likely upset me.

"Dump Ellis. You're not into him."

My mouth fell open. The *audacity*.

"You're only here two weekends a month. You have no idea what you're talking about."

Except he does the voice in the back of my mind taunted. As much as I loved spending time with Derek, my romantic feelings had faded. Derek was such a great guy—caring, kind, smart—and he loved me. He didn't deserve to have his heart broken.

Nathan's lip quirked. "I'm uniquely qualified to make that judgment, Quinn."

Quinn. I used to melt when he called me by my last name. But now the word came with venom, a weapon to shatter my every defense and crack my heart in two.

"Why are you even *here*?"

"My dad—"

"As if you listen to your dad," I cut him off. "You didn't have to come."

Nathan's balance teetered when he shot to his feet. I'd missed the sheen in his eyes, each corner bloodshot. His voice had been loud, but given the unrelenting noise from the crowd of graduates, their families, and the marching band, I hadn't thought anything of it. Until now.

He dropped a hand on my shoulder. "And miss *Brenna Quinn's* graduation? We'll never see each other after today, you know? Figured I should say goodbye."

Against all logic, I watched as his eyes dipped to my mouth.

My heart pounded. I couldn't tear my gaze from the hunger in his expression. My tongue licked my lips of its own volition. Logical thoughts need not apply.

"Brenna, we did it!"

Derek's excited voice broke the spell, and my head whirled toward him like whiplash. Shame sank like a weight into the pit of my stomach. I worried he could read the complicated feelings for Nathan on my face.

Derek stopped abruptly, his smile vanishing when he saw Nathan beside me, his hand still on my shoulder. I stepped away from Nathan, not caring if he keeled over without me there to steady him. I held my hand up to Derek for a high-five, a universal sign of friendship if there ever was one. He frowned but still slapped my hand.

"You two are so wholesome. *Absolutely* adorable," Nathan wise-cracked.

Derek tossed an arm around my shoulders, pressing me to his side. "Your jealousy is showing again, Sharpe."

Confrontation happened every time Nathan came for the weekend, but Nathan wasn't usually drunk. It made him bolder.

"Jealousy?" He scoffed, wobbling to his feet. "At least I'm not a simpering fool in love with a girl who hooked up with me the first chance she got."

My overheated skin drained of its warmth, even in the North Carolina June weather. I blinked, hoping this was a nightmare.

But no, when my eyes opened, Nathan watched me, not the least bit chagrined for revealing the secret both of us had silently promised to keep.

It had been a huge mistake. I thought he kept quiet as a favor to me, but maybe he'd only been biding his time, waiting to drop it at the moment of maximum impact.

Tears stung my eyes. I bit the inside of my cheek, desperately trying to keep them at bay. Derek's arm dropped away from my shoulder as he backed away from me, the center of the blast radius.

"You're welcome," Nathan mumbled, patting my shoulder as he passed. "Now you don't have to do it yourself."

White hot hatred burned in my chest. He thought he did me a *favor* by telling my boyfriend about the night I cheated? The guilt from which still made it difficult to breathe. I chased Nathan, catching him easily beside the bleacher steps. I shoved him, not hard, but he stumbled from his inebriation before steadying himself with one of the bleacher slats.

"What is your problem?" I shouted, stepping toward him. "How can you not *care*—"

"Don't pretend to understand how I feel," Nathan snapped, pushing off the bleacher. "Talk to me when *your* family falls apart, when your best friend lies to you, when your *girlfriend*—" He stopped abruptly and turned away from me. "Leave me alone, Brenna. You've done enough."

"Me?" I roared, ignoring stares from people around us. "I'm not the one who ignores an innocent baby sister. *I'm* not making a scene at graduation. Do you have any idea what you just did to Derek?"

Nathan laughed hollowly. "You're the one who led him on, Quinn. Own it."

He started to stumble away from me without apologizing. I shouldn't have been surprised after our interactions this year, but some naive part of me hoped that somewhere deep down, he still loved me and it would win out over his hurt and anger. I clutched a hand to my chest, at the incessant pain, the physical manifestation of the realization our friendship would never recover.

"I fucking hate you, you miserable jerk!" I screamed at his retreating form. "I will never forgive you for what you've done. For how you've treated Molly."

He didn't even pause, only held one hand over his head in a wave goodbye. "Don't worry, Bren. You'll never have to see me again."

The words filled me with relief and dread in equal measure.

<h1 style="text-align:center">43</h1>

BRENNA

Now

NATHAN BROUGHT THE PIZZA to the screened-in porch, pleasantly warm thanks to a space heater in the corner.

"Wanna come in?" I lifted one end of the blanket draped over me.

Nathan didn't hesitate, then held up a finger. "But we're talking, Bren, so don't get any ideas."

"I'll do my best," I answered with a laugh, then tilted my head to the side. "Maybe you should have that conversation with yourself."

As Nathan settled beneath the blanket, pressing into my side with his warmth and strength, I thought about how I'd like tough conversations more if they all happened with him, skin to skin. A reminder that he cared. I could take tough truths if they came with a promise he wouldn't leave.

He handed me a paper plate with one slice of pizza. I inhaled deeply, savoring the cheesy aroma and the steam warming my cheeks. "When did you even have time to order this?"

"When I went downstairs to make hot chocolate."

I shook my head. "You're the best."

"I never get tired of hearing you say anything good about me. Every time, it erases a bit more of the words you shouted at me after graduation."

I paused, returning my pizza to my plate. "Nathan—"

"I deserved it, Bren. Every word. It's a miracle you can stand to be with me after everything I did to you." Nathan's fingers tipped my chin to him. "I made you cry for months when I left." He swallowed, his fingertips moving to stroke my cheek. "And then I came back, and I was, as you so eloquently pointed out, a *miserable jerk*."

Everything that had happened seemed like a lifetime ago, and those emotions paled in comparison to the bright, all-consuming feelings I had for him now. Even though I didn't think we needed to dissect the past, maybe Nathan wasn't wrong. As kids, we didn't have the emotional intelligence to wade through the muck of our lives, of what our parents did to us, of what we, in turn, did to each other. Now we could deal with it once and for all and move forward.

"What did Kathy mean about your diagnosis? Are you sick?"

"Not sick," I said quickly, unable to tolerate the way Nathan's body tensed against mine. "I struggled… after everything. I couldn't move on, and no one understood, you know? I thought it would get better when I moved away. I was in college. I was supposed to be having the time of my life. I thought something was wrong with me."

Needing to feel closer, I wrapped my fluffy-cotton-covered foot around his ankle.

"I got a bad grade, and I nearly cried in class. I made it back to my dorm before sobbing, feeling worthless and alone and weak. Other people brushed things off, but I never could. It wasn't new, but… I don't know. Maybe I thought I'd outgrow it? Anyway, I called your dad."

Nathan's eyebrows rose. "My dad?"

"Yeah, I… I had no one else. It helped to talk to him about how I was feeling about school… and you. He recommended I see a therapist. Offered to pay for it."

"Did you?"

"Yeah." I snuck in a bite of pizza. "My therapist told me I'm a Highly Sensitive Person. HSP for short. It's a trait. She told me there wasn't anything wrong with me. I experience the world differently, and I wasn't the only one. It helped to know there were other people like me."

I took a staggering breath. "It used to make me feel weak, but I'm trying to see it as a superpower, feeling more deeply than other people do."

Nathan pressed a kiss to the top of my head. "I never saw you as weak, Bren."

My laugh was watery. "Even if I cried when we lost? There's no crying in baseball, remember?"

"It showed you cared. I love that about you."

Nathan had protected me from ridicule, heading it off before anyone could think that mocking the lone girl on the team for being emotional was a good idea. I loved that about *him*.

He reached for my hand. "You choose to see the best in everyone, even when they don't deserve it. You're there for people when they need someone, even if they won't admit it. To listen to their problems. Bren, you went to physical therapy with me twice a week the summer I hurt my shoulder, then did my physical therapy exercises with me to make sure they got done. There were a million other things you could've been doing, but you chose to be there for me."

I averted my gaze. "Well, that was because I loved you."

Nathan guided my face back to him until we breathed the same air. "I felt it every day. When we stopped being friends, I could see you still loved me. It endured, even after I hurt you."

"Trust me, I know." I turned away to give myself a moment to gather my thoughts. Nathan's attention—his recognition of who I was at my core and *never* thinking it meant anything other than that I was strong—overwhelmed me.

"I've never known someone as loyal as you, Quinn. Remember how small I was when you moved to Middlebury? How I had trouble pronouncing my Rs? You held it against every kid who laughed at me. *For years.*"

I shrugged. "Of course I did. You would do the same."

"And when Coach pulled me from a playoff game sophomore year?"

"You were pitching well," I contended. "The outfielders lollygagging after pop flies wasn't your fault. You deserved the opportunity."

He laughed. "I always pitched well, according to you."

I nudged him in the arm. "Because you *did*."

"Not always. But I loved that you thought so, that you always had my back." Nathan tugged me into his lap, my legs resting horizontally against his thighs, his chin on my shoulder. "So tell me more about being an HSP."

I looked at him. "You want to know?"

"I want to know *you*."

"Okay." I swallowed hard, taking a moment to gain control of my emotions. "Well, I need time to decompress when I go through emotionally draining experiences, even when it's good things. I usually do that by lying under my weighted blanket in a quiet room. Loud sounds can be a lot for me to handle, unless they're *my* sounds. Explains how I love rock music but can't stand when the TV volume jumps during commercials."

"Oh, this explains a lot," Nathan murmured. "Molly's crying."

"Yup. It's why I had to escape to your house so often. Oh, and I can't stand strong smells, like meat cooking." I shivered. "I usually need to light a candle or open a window to get through it."

"Sounds like you've learned how to care for yourself."

"Mostly. The gut-wrenching feeling of disappointing someone isn't something I've been able to handle yet, but I'm working on it." I rolled my eyes and flashed him a self-conscious smile. "Setting boundaries and all that."

He absentmindedly played with the ends of my hair. "Thank you for telling me."

I fought the burn in my eyes. "Thank you for accepting me, for not thinking that being sensitive is a bad thing. Or that it's not *real.*"

"It's who you are, Brenna. How could it be a bad thing?"

44

NATHAN

Now

BRENNA IN MY LAP, her cheeks adorably flushed, was an absolute dream. My strong, sensitive woman.

I eased her off my lap to sit in front of me. Her question about what I was doing cut off as soon as I caged her, one thigh beside each hip, securing her in place. My hand wound itself into her hair, and I savored the silkiness in my fingers.

"I thought we were *talking*," she said.

The teasing smile fell off her face when I was close enough to kiss her. "It's called a reward for good behavior. It's motivating."

"For me? Or you?"

"For both of us," I murmured before dropping a kiss to one side of her mouth, then the other. She turned her head so the second kiss landed squarely on her lips.

She sighed contentedly, echoing my relief at getting to do this whenever we wanted. We kissed and kissed, sliding lips, teasing tongues, exploring hands, until Brenna hooked her legs around my waist and I pulled back.

I was tempted to forget about the tough questions we needed to discuss, but we only had hours until she left for California. "We haven't finished our conversation, Bren."

She pouted. "But what about my reward?"

"What do you think this was?"

"I call that getting started."

I pressed my lips to her forehead before pushing back to a sitting position. I cleared my throat. There were so many things I wanted to tell her, needed her to know, but in that moment, one flashed like a neon sign in my mind.

"You weren't there on my draft day, Bren," I said.

She blinked, immediately working to get herself vertical again. "What?"

"It was both the happiest and saddest day of my life."

Brenna frowned. "Your dad and I watched together. Both of us wished we were by your side." Her leg pressed harder into mine, a comfort. "I hated how good you looked."

"Can we be serious?"

"I mean… I was serious, but I'll stop." Brenna saluted me, then inched her way to the other end of the couch. It created a modicum of space between us, enough that we were no longer touching.

"I never want you missing another pivotal moment in my life. And I want to be there for every one of yours. I'm afraid if you leave tomorrow, that's it for us. We'll go our separate ways."

"I don't want that, Nate." Her brows furrowed, a dent forming between her eyes. "Are you going back to Texas?"

I sank further into the couch. "I don't know. My contract ended this past season. My agent's been working on it. I thought I would hear something by now…" I dragged a hand over my face and took a deep breath. "I should know soon whether I'm getting re-signed. I'll be off to Arizona for spring training next month if I do. If not… I don't fucking know."

Kennedy and Deandra got me an appointment with the Wolves' doctor for tomorrow, despite the holidays. Brenna didn't know about it. I didn't want to worry her or go to her without a plan.

If I couldn't play baseball, what the hell could I offer? I'd ignored my father's warning that I'd want a college degree if anything went south. I barely earned any money playing in the minor leagues, something I'd supplemented with side gigs during the offseason. Brenna might've looked at me like I'd hung the moon when we were kids, but she had different priorities now. Chemistry mattered only so much when building a life. And she was doing it not only for herself, but also for her sister.

"I'm sure you'll hear soon," she said.

"Are you going back to school?"

"No. I, uh, took a leave of absence when Molly needed me."

I shook my head. "Of course you did. You let Kathy ruin everything for you."

"I'm not doing it for her."

Her defensive tone nearly scared me off. I didn't want to fight before she left, but Kathy was another topic we couldn't avoid. She directly affected our future.

"But you're still bailing her out. She has you bankrolling their lives. How long will you keep doing it?"

"Until I get custody."

"And if you don't get custody?"

Brenna didn't reply, which was answer enough.

"You'll put your life on hold as long as it takes."

"Nathan, I can't..." She stopped to take a steadying breath. "Molly deserves better—"

"Than you got?"

She stayed silent for a few moments before changing gears back to me. "We don't have to sell the house. If you need to stay here."

I shook my head, one violent swing. "You need the money to fight for Molly. It won't be easy."

Neither of us wanted to say the words, but we were both thinking them. *How the hell can we make this relationship work with all the barriers between us?*

"Nathan," Brenna whispered.

I met her gaze, my heart launching into my throat, seeing anguish mirrored back at me. "I know, but I'm not letting you go. I'm *not*."

I didn't know which one of us moved first. Maybe we both did, needing to squash the desperation and sadness gripping us. When our lips connected, it was messy.

Brenna slid back into my lap, maneuvering her legs until she straddled my waist, her feet hooked around my back. Neither of us broke contact—each kiss leading to the next, the force of our movements enough to bruise our lips. I tugged at the waistband of her sweatpants. Brenna lifted her hips so I could push the fabric to her knees. She gasped as my hands grabbed her ass, my fingers kneading her skin.

She broke our kiss to yank my basketball shorts and boxer briefs down. Her hand roughly palmed my cock, sliding up and down.

I let out a hiss.

"I don't have a condom down here." I forced the words out, my voice coated with agonizing pleasure.

"You don't need it. I mean, I don't. I have an IUD and haven't been—"

"I don't need it either." I cut her off, not wanting to hear about the last time she'd been with another man. On top of everything else, my heart might wither and die in my chest. She'd never put me at risk. And I'd rather die than hurt her again. "You sure?"

She nodded vigorously. I yanked her panties to the side, lifted her with one arm wrapped around her body, and eased her onto my cock.

The feel of her without a barrier between us... fucking indescribable. A first for me. If she hadn't already wrecked me for anyone else, this would've been the moment.

The sound of her satisfied moan at the feel of me inside her nearly made me combust. I took a deep breath, thinking of anything but the way Brenna was rocking her hips against mine. There was a joke in there, thinking about baseball, but my brain was too scrambled to formulate it.

Brenna found my lips again, her arms wrapping around my neck. We clung to each other, to this moment, to this perfect thing we'd found a second time against all odds. I wanted to tell her I loved her. It was all I could think, over and over, while we moved together, her moans mixing with my grunts, our eyes locked.

But saying it now felt like goodbye, resignation that this night was it for us. That this sex was our last. That I would never get to watch her eyes flutter closed, consumed by the pleasure I gave her. That tonight would be the last night we nestled into each other in bed, drifting to sleep, completely content.

I couldn't bear to lose her again.

"You're it for me, Bren."

She let out the sexiest moan, sending a bolt of longing to my cock. I wouldn't last much longer. Not when I could feel her inner walls contracting around me.

Her lips landed on mine, and my release barreled into me, hot blinding pleasure shooting through my blood. Brenna kept moving as she careened over the edge, stretching the moment for as long as she could. Then her body slumped against mine, her head resting in the crook of my neck while she greedily inhaled oxygen to her depleted lungs. I smoothed a hand over her damp hair, my touch featherlight, easing her down from her high.

She pressed a kiss to my pulse point, then looked at me through her lashes. "I never stood a chance after I saw you from my bedroom window when I was a kid. You've always been it for me, Nathan."

I was it for her too? I couldn't believe it. Not after our history and the obstacles in our way. Fate couldn't be so cruel to bring her back into my life, for me to win her back, only to have distance force us apart again.

Fuck. My instincts screamed to stop her from leaving, to keep her here with me.

I didn't want to believe tonight was the end.

"I'm not giving up on us, Brenna, all right?"

Those hot-chocolate eyes held mine. "I'm not either."

45

NATHAN

Now

THE HOUSE LOST ALL its magic without Brenna.

The Christmas decorations taunted me, a cruel reminder of the days with her and Molly. I could still see Brenna curled on the couch, soaking up warmth from the fireplace. She'd beckon me, lifting one end of her blanket and wriggling her eyebrows. And when I took my place beside her, she fit snugly against me, head on my chest, hand tracing my abdomen, as if she'd been molded for this purpose.

I thought we had more time for nights like that.

Even the cats meowed angrily at me this morning because I was still here while their favorite person wasn't. *I know the fucking feeling.*

She loomed over every inch of this house, a place that used to bring only pain. As I moved through it now, a film of memories of *us* played. The kitchen where we bantered, pretending we didn't want each other.

The guest room where we fought with paint—it had been the first moment since we'd reunited that I thought trying to win her back might not be a lost cause. She stared at me with watery eyes from the steps, begging me to stay and not fly to Houston. Her relief at seeing me when she woke in my bed hours later. The fucking kitchen counter. And my bed...

I refused to let my mind wander there. Being turned-on while sad was too weird of a combination. But I had plenty of favorite memories to choose from in that particular setting.

Brenna was in the air, flying approximately two thousand six hundred miles away from me. I might've checked the exact distance while I sat in my car outside the airport after watching her disappear behind the automatic doors. She'd turned and waved, knowing I'd still be there. Even from fifteen feet away, I could tell her eyes were full of unshed tears.

In the four hours since I'd dropped her at the airport, my heart had splintered apart.

Time was not on our side.

My appointment with the surgeon wasn't for several more hours, so I climbed back into bed like the miserable asshole I was. Her honey-peach scent clung to everything—the sheets beneath me, the pillowcase beside me, the fucking air particles I breathed. A stab of pain burst in my chest. I settled into it, letting it flow through me and pull me into the memories of us here.

The next thing I heard was the doorbell ringing, incessantly, pulling me from sleep. I blinked through the sunlight, checking to see if Brenna stirred before I remembered she wasn't here. All that greeted me were Mia's wide eyes in Bren's spot. The other three cats watched me from their places on the bed. We'd congregated to mourn her loss.

The doorbell rang again, twice. *Shit.*

I stumbled out of bed, stepped into a pair of sweatpants, and hurried down the hallway. The pounding on the door started as I hit the stairs, followed by a voice I knew all too well.

"Nathan Sharpe, I know you're in there! Wake your pretty ass up, Sleeping Beauty!"

Oh, please. If either of us were a pretty boy, it would be blue-eyed, blond-haired Leo McGinnis. He hadn't earned the nickname *DiCaprio* for nothing.

I unlocked the door and swung it open, tossing him an unimpressed look. I didn't try to get a word in, knowing he'd barrel right over me, but my expression must've conveyed it.

He studied me, starting with my bare feet, quickly working his way up the rest of my body until he met my gaze. "I can see you've been enjoying yourself these last few months."

"Shut up, man." I rolled my eyes. Brenna never complained about my body, so I wouldn't let his insults penetrate.

"I gave you to the new year, but now it's time to get serious, Sharpe." Leo tossed his bag over his shoulder and pushed past me into the foyer. He slipped off his hat, revealing his fluffy hair. "All right. Where's this woman who trapped you here? It's about time we met."

I sucked in a breath like I'd absorbed a physical blow.

"Brenna, Brenna, Brenna," Leo sang with the musical grace of a spoon in the garbage disposal.

"She's not here, jackass." I slammed the door closed and headed to the kitchen to make coffee.

"So you're here alone?"

I closed the fridge door after grabbing milk, cringing at how loudly it shut. Seeing her disgusting almond milk felt like a shiv in my side. "I am now."

Leo tipped his head back and gazed at the ceiling. "Shit, man. You lost her *again*?"

"I didn't lose her," I growled.

Leo's energy wasn't the kind I needed now, not as my world dimmed lower than it had in a long time. Even lower than when I first got here. That version of me didn't yet know how incredible it was to live the future of his dreams. A glimpse, that was all I got, and now nothing would compare.

Since the night we first kissed during the blackout, I'd thought constantly about how to make this relationship work. And I hadn't figured out how to keep us in the same location, not with Brenna caring for Molly and me pursuing a baseball career.

Optimism was as much a part of her DNA as her pretty brown eyes, but deep down, she had to recognize the uphill battle to gain custody. Unless her mother signed away her parental rights, it would take Brenna months—years—to prove her mother was unfit. If she even could.

All the while, Bren would fund her mother's good-for-nothing life. Give up her dreams of becoming a physical therapist to protect her little sister. Deprioritize her own needs for as long as it took.

I didn't make enough money to provide the kind of lifestyle her mother sought, or to pay for the legal services Brenna needed. She might've consulted Ellis for advice, but he wasn't a child custody specialist. She needed the best lawyer money could buy.

Leo draped a hand on my nonpitching shoulder. "You okay, man? You're wound tighter than a nun. I thought I'd at least find you well-laid."

I shoved him off me. He wasn't prepared, so he stumbled back into the kitchen counter. He only laughed.

"What are you doing here, Leo?"

"It's January. Go time! We report in six weeks."

Leo and I used to count down the days until pitchers and catchers were required to arrive at spring training. Last year, we were both invited to the major league team's training camp for the first time in our careers. He'd get another one for sure, but my future was uncertain.

I shook my head. "No contract for me yet. You'll be reporting by yourself, DiCaprio. Coffee?"

"*No* contract? What the hell, Nathan?" He didn't wait for me to respond and kept ranting. "This is why you gotta get back to Houston and talk to management, *prove* to them you want to be there, that you're more than ready for the seaso—"

"I'm seeing an orthopedic surgeon today," I cut in.

Leo's jaw went slack.

I never expected my shoulder pain to go away, only hoped I could stave off the worst of it. But no amount of ice, heat, physical therapy exercises, or CBD halted the slow decline of my shoulder after years of throwing thousands of pitches. Every season, it got a little bit worse until it started to bother me outside of baseball. When I reached for a plate on a high shelf. Typing on my computer. Anything that involved a stretch of the muscle or lengthy activation.

Fooling around with Brenna hadn't flagged the pain, but I suspected I was too distracted to notice.

"You think it's necessary?"

I nodded. "It's time."

"Shit." Leo snagged a bottle of whiskey from the counter and took a swig. "I'm coming with you."

46

BRENNA

Now

THREE MONTHS AGO, I'D assumed coming back to California would bring me a sense of relief.

But now as my flight taxied to the gate, my low-level anxiety turned to full-on dread. Since I'd opened my eyes this morning, a rock had sat in my stomach at the idea of leaving Nathan. Our holiday together—hell, these last three months together—had been the best of my adult life.

Middlebury was the first town I ever called home and meant it. My mom had moved us around, following guy after guy, and I never had time to settle into any place we lived. Not until a divorce netted her enough money to buy a house in a small town, next to a baseball-playing boy and his family. I still remembered seeing Nathan Sharpe tossing a ball high into the air and catching it, how when he spotted me in my window, he beckoned me outside.

The rest was history.

Despite the promises we'd made, I worried that getting on this plane had made our second chance history too.

I pulled out my phone to text Nathan.

> **Brenna**
>
> Just landed. I miss you and our home.

I deleted *and our home* and clicked send. We'd already accepted an offer on Nathan's childhood house, so it wouldn't belong to us much longer.

The rideshare from the airport to my mother's townhome took thirty minutes. Nathan didn't respond to my message, or even read it. We weren't in the same time zone, though, so I'd have to get used to it.

"Brenna!" The front door of the house swung open before I reached the porch. Molly sprinted toward me, then wrapped herself around my legs.

I prayed for a sibling for years, craving this feeling, this unconditional love. Something my mother had no idea how to offer.

Molly didn't only need me. I needed *her.*

My mother appeared in the doorway, disdain lining her features as she watched our hug. "Look who finally tired of playing house and decided to come home to her family."

She'd put effort into her appearance today, like she had in Middlebury, which was unusual after a breakup.

When I was younger, I'd wondered why my mother didn't offer me the kind of love Nathan received from his parents. I thought it was because of me, my lack of anything in common with the woman who gave birth to me, my sensitivity which disappointed her.

Thanks to therapy, I now recognized the problematic interactions that made my skin crawl for what they were—abuse.

I bent down to Molly's level, ignoring my mother. "Hey, Molls. How was your flight home?"

"It took forever," she mumbled, throwing her arms around my shoulders. I wrapped my arms around her, wishing I could shield this wonderful girl from every hurt flung her way.

My mother sighed dramatically. "She cried the entire way to the airport. She takes after you more than me."

Big fucking sigh of relief there. I'd never forgive myself if I let Kathy Quinn mold my sweet sister into a bitter bitch who thrived on making others feel small.

"How disappointing for you," I muttered, rising to my feet. I walked Molly into the house, past Kathy, who didn't step aside. "I brought you something."

Molly bounced on her feet. "What is it? What is it?"

I slipped the Palmer City Wolves calendar from my carry-on bag. As soon as I laid eyes on it in an airport bookstore, I had to have it for Molly. She flopped onto the floor, flipping through the pages and naming each player, her voice filled with excitement.

Kathy closed the door behind us, leaned back, and crossed her arms. "So did you finally sell the house?"

"Yep." I climbed the stairs, carrying my suitcase and carry-on.

Her feet clunked on the steps behind me. "Took you long enough. Probably weren't trying *all* that hard, if what I stumbled on was any sign."

I didn't respond. She wanted to put me in my place, to remind me who reigned supreme in this house, especially after learning I didn't need to live here. That I was doing it because she failed to take care of Molly.

"How much money are we getting?" she asked, on my heels as I strode down the hall to my room.

She hadn't stated it outright before I left for Middlebury, but I suspected she hadn't given me a hard time about leaving my jobs because she anticipated Gordon's money. All of her income came from me, aside from some government assistance, something she'd never admit. She'd been ashamed to receive it when I was young too. I never understood why. There was no shame in accessing help.

I spun toward her. "*You* are not getting any money. Gordon named *me* in his will, not you."

"I *earned* that money." Her shrill tone nearly had me covering my ears. I'd avoided confrontations with my mom all my life because it was easier to give in than argue. "You think he ever *gave* us anything?"

Was she fucking serious?

But Kathy's petulant expression said it all. It was easy to believe your own lies if you repeated them endlessly.

Concentrating on keeping my voice even, I replied, "He gave us plenty when he thought Molly was his daughter, before you moved her across the country, after you tired of him. You ruined his marriage, and then you ripped away his daughter."

My mother let out a belabored sigh. "You have no idea what he was like, Brenna."

I tilted my head, motioning to myself. "Enlighten me."

"It's too difficult to speak about."

"Well, when you gather the strength," I replied, my voice dripping with sarcasm, "let me know. In the meantime, I'll keep the money. Gordon would roll over in his grave if I shared a cent with you."

My mother started her whole woe-is-me spiel, but I blocked her out. One of the survival mechanisms I'd mastered while living with Kathy Quinn.

But then it dawned on me. I had one hand left to play. I wouldn't need to take Molly from her if she freely signed over her parental rights. I'd never considered simply asking, because most mothers wouldn't sign away their daughters, not unless they couldn't care for them or didn't love them.

Kathy Quinn couldn't be the kind of mother Molly deserved, but Kathy didn't recognize that. She loved Molly—and me—in her own toxic way. And now that her cheating married boyfriend was back with his wife, Molly was all she had. If there wasn't another metaphorical punching bag around, who would she spew her ugliness to—herself?

But I had something she wanted. I turned my back, retreating to my bed, thinking about how to broach the subject.

"Are you even *listening* to me, Brenna Rae Quinn?"

"Yeah, of course." I chewed my lip. Making this offer could go very, very wrong. But on the off chance it went right, I had to take it. "I was thinking maybe we can come to an arrangement."

Her furrowed eyebrows smoothed at the prospect that her little rant worked. "I'm listening."

"I'll give you the money from the sale of the house..." I paused. "If you make me Molly's guardian."

Kathy reared back like she'd been slapped. I thought she'd appreciate the opportunity to reclaim her life, having heard her complain about how Molly and I prevented her from doing anything she wanted.

"How *dare* you." Her quiet fury unnerved me.

I jumped when she slammed the door so hard a picture fell off my nightstand, shattering the glass.

A metaphor, if there ever was one, for my relationship with my mother.

47

NATHAN

Now

"So this is the famous Middlebury?" Leo mused, his gaze out the window as I drove to my orthopedic appointment.

Not having to face this alone brought me massive comfort.

While I got dressed, my stomach threatened to upend my dinner from last night. Despite extensive advancements in surgeries, repairing a torn labrum took down about half the pitchers who had it. They never recovered to their preinjury form, even with the best surgeons. That statistic alone had me trying every strategy known to man, because the idea of losing baseball—my first love, my only talent—terrified me.

"Everything you imagined?"

Leo's head swiveled toward me. "A bit disappointing, but maybe because the reason you love Middlebury isn't here."

He might as well have stabbed a fork straight into my chest. "Is that why you came? To meet Brenna?"

"It's one of the reasons. I've known you for five years, man, and no woman has stuck around longer than a few months."

"I could say the same for you."

"But that's all I want. You're not like me. You want all the crap that comes with love."

I did want it, but it wasn't like Leo and I sat around talking about our feelings. He knew me better than I realized. Or maybe I was fucking obvious.

"I wanted to meet the woman who had locked up your heart. She must be special."

I blew out a breath, as if I could rid myself of the emotion, but nope, still there, a vice around my heart. She was a seven-hour flight and three time zones away from me. All I knew was pain. "You have no fucking idea."

Before I knew it, we pulled into the parking lot at the surgeon's office, the drive passing in a blink. A generically bland building with dark tinted windows and tan brick. No one would think their life could change inside of it.

Leo patted me on the arm. "Whatever happens, I've got your back."

I replied to Brenna's text that her flight landed safely.

Nathan
I miss you so fucking much, Bren.

Then I sucked in a breath and climbed out of the car to meet my fate.

Dr. Martin's office ran like a well-oiled machine, and I was invited into an exam room within a minute of my arrival. The fluorescent lights burned my eyes, forcing me to shut them as we waited for the doctor. Leo word-vomited into the silence while I counted in my head, something that steadied me on the mound when my body temperature spiked.

I'd reached one hundred and two when a knock sounded.

"Nathan Sharpe?" a man said as the door swung open. "I'm Dr. Martin."

This renowned surgeon, who had served as the team doctor for the Palmer City Wolves for twenty years, looked way too young to have accomplished all that the website said he had. He was also too good-looking to be so brilliant, but no one ever said life was fair. His dark hair and mahogany-toned skin contrasted starkly with his white coat, the only color in his stitched name below his right shoulder. The singular sign of his age was a distinguished dusting of gray peppering his hair.

Deandra—and her employer, a professional hockey team, plus hundreds of reviewers online—said he was the best doctor in North Carolina to see about my injury, so I should stop being presumptuous.

"Good to meet you," I said.

"I'm Leo McGinnis." Leo immediately jumped in after me. I tossed him a look he pretended not to see. "His catcher."

Dr. Martin took a seat on a stool with wheels, propelling himself forward until he was squarely in front of me. "I understand you're having shoulder pain. When did it start?"

I looked up, trying to trace the pain through my memories. "Uh, maybe three years ago? I had a similar issue in high school, but I had physical therapy and was able to pitch again. This time around, it keeps getting worse."

Dr. Martin nodded, intently focusing on my words. "Tell me what it feels like."

I explained the pain as best I could and answered a litany of questions. After, he asked me to stand so he could physically test my shoulder. He put my right hand on my left shoulder so my pitching arm jutted out in front of me like a chicken wing, then he pressed down. My shoulder shuddered. Not the same pain I experienced while pitching, but it was still there.

He ordered an arthrography CT scan to confirm the labral tear. A fun procedure involving a long needle to inject a numbing agent followed by color-contrast material into my shoulder before imaging it.

Leo was asleep by the time I returned to the room. He jerked awake when the door closed behind me.

Dr. Martin entered moments later, taking a seat on his stool and wheeling himself in front of me. He pulled up the first image on his tablet and turned it to face me. "All right, you've got a clear labral tear, Nathan. You can see it right there." He pointed to an obvious gap in the thin line surrounding the circular core of my shoulder. "So we've got two options—you can try physical therapy for a month to see if it helps, or we can go in and fix the tear arthroscopically."

Dr. Martin's words, *You've got a clear labral tear,* boomeranged around my mind. Leo took over the conversation, asking about recovery time and how the surgery would affect my ability to pitch. My mind whirled with each new piece of information and the decision I needed to make.

More than anything, I wanted to go home and talk to Brenna.

Except she wasn't fucking there.

"Nathan, call my office when you make a decision." Dr. Martin opened the door, pausing before leaving the room. "Good to meet you."

"You too." After the door clicked shut, I slumped in my seat.

Leo tapped my knee. "I don't know about you, but I need a stiff drink… or ten."

"You got that fucking right."

⸻◆⸻

Leo drove us back to the house because he could tell how distracted I was, then we took a rideshare to the bar we'd gone to after the baseball game. It'd be cheaper to get shit-faced at the house, but I didn't want to be there. Not without her.

Leo clapped me on my nonpitching shoulder and guided me to a two-seat high top in the corner. "I ordered enough booze to forget our names. And food."

"Food defeats the purpose." I parked myself in a wooden chair, looking at the large crowd of people packing the bar, more than I'd expected on a weekday. Maybe they were celebrating the new year. At that moment, I hated them all.

"I haven't eaten all day," Leo explained. "If I need to drink more, I'll drink more."

A woman in her fifties arrived at our table, carrying a tray with no fewer than ten shot glasses. She lifted each shot, one-by-one, and placed it on the table between Leo and me.

She narrowed her eyes, fixing a look at me for a beat before shifting to Leo. "Neither of y'all are driving tonight, you hear?"

Leo flashed a dazzling smile, the one that won over every woman he set his sights on. "Wouldn't dream of it."

She pointed at him. "Oh, you're trouble, hon, but don't *cause* trouble."

Leo saluted, giving the server confirmation he wouldn't get plastered and ruin the bar. She left with a half smile on her face. I rolled my eyes. Leo apparently appealed to women of all ages.

"Dealer's choice." He upturned his palms and swept them across the top of the drinks.

"We're mixing alcohol tonight?" Never advisable, but I took a shot of brown liquid and tossed it down my throat. The delicious burn eased some of the anxiety brewing inside me. I took another one, clear this time.

"Slow down there, champ." Leo swiped a shot glass and placed it against his lips for a moment before swallowing it down. His eyes locked on a woman behind us as he did so. What the fuck else was new?

I didn't want to slow down. I wanted to forget today—watching Brenna walk into the airport, hearing the doctor confirm I tore my labrum. I didn't want to be conscious in case things somehow got worse. Bad news tended to come in threes.

And when I got back to the house later, I didn't want the emptiness to register.

"Don't even think about picking someone up at this bar."

Leo's attention landed back on me. "It's called flirting, and it never hurt anyone. This Brenna chick must be a saint to put up with you. Tell me *how* exactly you managed to win her over. I thought she was engaged."

The idea of Brenna engaged to another man—even though she wasn't any longer—still made me want to punch a hole in a wall.

"Technically, she was engaged, but they didn't have much of a relationship, living long-distance from each other." I'd be lying if that bit of her history didn't fuel my present concerns.

Leo smirked. "And now she's with you?"

"As much as two people who don't live anywhere near each other can be together."

"What the fuck does that mean? You have an open relationship?"

I scoffed. "Hell, no." I'd rather swallow boiling water than know Brenna was out with another man. "But we didn't exactly figure out how we'd make it work, or for how long. I thought we had more time, but her fucking mother showed up early, and I only had one last night with her. After talking got us nowhere closer to a plan, we enjoyed the time we had."

"Can't say I wouldn't do the same," Leo said before taking another shot.

The server dropped off our food, eyeing the empty shot glasses on our table. She left with a pointed stare at Leo.

"If you get the surgery, you could do it anywhere, right? Or get it here and recover close to where she lives?"

The alcohol swimming in my veins raised my body temperature to bathwater levels. My mind wasn't slow yet, but the rest of my body was loose. I wanted to plunge into that feeling, leave my worries behind.

But his question brought every worry to the forefront again.

"What if the surgery doesn't work, Leo?" The anxious words suddenly ripped out of me. "What can I offer her?"

"You think she's with you because you play baseball? She knew you before all of that."

I shook my head, trying and failing to clear the fears. They'd lingered beneath the surface, momentarily forgotten thanks to the intoxication of being with her. Now she was gone, and they wouldn't leave my mind.

"She wants to become her sister's guardian. She shouldn't have to take care of me too."

"Fuck off, man. You honestly think all you bring to the table is the potential payday of making it to the big leagues?"

"You don't get it," I mumbled, the right side of my face resting on my open palm. "There's a difference in what you look for when you're hooking up or dating and when you're building a life. Brenna's focus is on creating a life that's worthy of Molly. She's going to want a partner, not some loser with nothing to offer."

Leo scrubbed a hand over his face. "You want to be her partner, Nathan? Then, be her fucking partner. Show up for her. Be what she needs. I guarantee it's not an ATM." His hand smacked the table as he barked out a laugh. "Fucking hell. You know you've hit rock bottom when *I'm* the one talking sense."

Shit, Leo was right. Staying here in Palmer City and drowning my sorrows, worrying I might not be good enough for Brenna guaranteed I'd fail her. That our relationship wouldn't survive. That I would lose her... again.

I thought losing baseball meant the end of my life. It was my dream, the only thing I'd had for so long... but it wasn't all I *could* have. Brenna Quinn made me realize that even if I lost my ability to pitch, I could still have a great life. With her.

I wanted a life with her more than anything else. This second chance came at the exact moment I'd needed it most. I suspected when she needed me most too.

I would not let her down.

"I need to go to California." I shot out of my seat, heading toward the exit as I looked for a rideshare and a flight.

Leo snatched the phone from my hands. "You're in no shape to sort this now. We'll go in the morning."

48

BRENNA

Now

THE TEMPERATURE IN MY mother's house rivaled the nasty blizzards I experienced all too often in Chicago.

I ducked out the morning after my disastrous conversation with Kathy to beg the physical therapy practice I used to work for to give me my administrative assistant job back. Someone had to pay the bills. At least the job was related to what I eventually wanted to do. My employers were also kind, allowing my shift to start later so I could take Molly to school. Thankfully, they'd used only temp labor and hadn't filled my position yet, so there was a chance. They'd let me know later this week.

Maybe I could find a way to be happy here, taking care of my sister, building friendships with coworkers, working tangentially in the field I studied at school. I'd still see Nathan through video chat, and he could visit in the offseason.

All the good feelings dissipated as soon as we sat down to dinner in agonizing silence aside from the clacking of silverware against plates. I only lasted a few minutes before I didn't think I could take it any longer.

"Did you have a nice day at school, Molly girl?" Kathy shocked me by breaking the silence.

I fought the instinct to look up from my plate, to interpret her expression. Any sudden movement could send this conversation vaulting in a different direction.

"Yes, we're reading *Charlie and the Chocolate Factory*, and everyone in class gets to read a different part. I was Violet today."

My heart squeezed, thinking about the resilience of this kid. Even with her complicated home life, she still exuded joy over the simplest things. Surreptitiously, I patted her knee, communicating my pride and love without tipping Kathy off.

"Which one is Violet again?" Kathy asked.

"She's the one who chews gum, Mom."

Molly soaked in this kind of attention that she so rarely received. She clearly craved it. I recognized the joy lighting her eyes. The key to emotional manipulation was moments like this, when the person received what they desired. It couldn't be poor treatment all the time, because they'd become disillusioned with the manipulator. But give them crumbs, and they'd keep coming back.

Molly added, "I wish I could make gum bubbles."

"You will one day, I'm sure." Kathy's voice sounded wistful. A first.

"What did you do today, Mom?" Molly asked.

For the last three months, the answer would have been the same. Kathy stayed in bed eating chips, watching soaps, and feeling sorry for herself. But she'd kept up her appearance these past few days, which meant she was prowling for a new man or rendezvousing with her married boyfriend again.

It was ironic that Kathy found herself manipulated by crumbs too.

She dropped her fork to her plate with a clang. "Funny you should ask, munchkin. I got an interesting job offer today."

I paused my spoon halfway to my mouth, sure I was hallucinating or I'd fallen into another dimension.

"A friend of mine owns a boat and wants to travel around the world for the next six months. I've been offered a job as a crew member."

A crew member. Right. I suspected her duties involved things most HR departments would deem *not allowable* in a job description.

"Molly..." My mother paused, waiting until she had Molly's undivided attention. "What do you think about staying with your sister for a while?"

My world tilted on its axis.

It *couldn't* be... could it?

Molly glanced at me. I expected to see unabashed joy, especially after she'd sobbed when our mom took her away from our Christmas holiday. Instead, her wary eyes found mine, her lips pinched into a line.

Because I had been Molly, I knew what was upsetting her. She worried her mother would leave and never come back. Even with the ups and downs Molly had experienced all her life, Kathy Quinn was her main caretaker, and from what I could tell, she hadn't completely failed. Molly was a national treasure, and that didn't come from *nowhere*.

"It'd be for the rest of the school year," I added when Molly hesitated. Six months would get us through June. "Then Mom will come home for the summer, and we can spend it together. Go to the beach and build sandcastles. Maybe hit up a baseball game..."

I nudged her in the side, and she darted away from me.

She shook her head and finally gave a small smile. "No baseball."

"We'll see about that."

Looking at my mother stopped me dead. She watched us intently, her expression soft, thoughtful. What the hell was causing this change in her demeanor? Was she trying to keep the peace before she up and left for six months? Or now she was leaving, did she realize what her selfishness would make her miss? Because Molly and I were pretty damn awesome.

"Sounds like a great plan," Kathy said before refocusing on the spaghetti in front of her.

I waited for something more—a snarky comment, an exposition of all the amazing things she'd see over the next six months—but she fell silent for the rest of the meal, leaving me to carry the conversation with Molly. It wasn't difficult to keep Molly talking, not after I asked her about *Charlie and the Chocolate Factory* and the latest Wolves game. My mother kept her gaze down, but she was listening.

Molly soon left the table to watch hockey, giving me an opportunity to talk to my mother alone. I found her scrubbing plates, a sight I hadn't stumbled upon since moving back. She usually headed to her room after dinner, taking a bath before settling into bed, leaving me with the cleanup.

"Is she all right?" Kathy kept her back to me, continuing to wash plates and utensils.

"She's fine," I said, voice tight.

My mother allowing me to become Molly's guardian didn't erase the garbage she put us through. It certainly didn't erode my bitter feelings.

"Did you mean what you said?" I asked.

"Which part?"

She damn well knew.

I took another step into the kitchen, positioning myself to the side of the sink, where she could see me. "You're leaving?"

She didn't pause her movement. "Richard invited me to sail with him. Now that he's divorcing his wife, he's free to do what he's always wanted. She was bleeding him dry, you know."

I suppressed an instinct to roll my eyes. She fully intended to do the same.

"He's asked me to travel with him before, but I could never go... with Molly. It's one of the reasons he stayed with his wife."

"Molly was?" I whisper-yelled, the instinct to protect her at all costs flaring to life.

My mother paused her chore, turning to face me. "Oh, don't use that tone, Brenna Rae. I won't have you implying he isn't a good man. He already raised his kids. It's not a sin to not want to parent another child. This is the time in his life to finally do what *he* wants."

I shuffled my weight to the other foot. "Why didn't you go with him when he asked before?"

"How can you ask me that? She's my *daughter*. I know I'm not a perfect mother, but did I not provide for your entire life? For her entire life? You both had a roof over your heads and food on the table. I drove you to school. We celebrated holidays, birthdays. I loved you both from the moment you were born."

"You also brought men into our lives to pay your bills, even when they were shitty. We would've been fine in apartments, but you wanted a house, and the best makeup, stylish clothes—"

She dried her hands on the rag beside the sink, never dropping eye contact. "I also wanted those things for you!"

"All I wanted was your attention, Mom. I wanted you to sit in the stands at my baseball games. To help me with my homework. To not make me feel like a colossal failure when I made a mistake or cried or because I wanted to play sports. I *never* wanted you to break up a marriage."

She took a step toward me, her voice rising. "It was always about *that* boy."

I never understood her disdain for Nathan, but my relationship with him, my love for him, had always threatened her.

I scoffed. "No, it was about *me*. That's what you've never understood." I heaved a sigh. "I loved living next to the Sharpes. They were the family I always wanted. So you just had to ruin it. Take away your best friend's husband to prove that you could, that you were better than her. You lit the match that destroyed my relationship with Nathan. But I didn't lose only him. I lost all my friends, baseball, my reputation. And you never apologized or cared how depressed I was. You got Gordon, your shiny new ring, a new baby to fawn over. While you were happy, I lived in misery."

The words exploded out of me like soda with pop rocks. I cursed myself for putting this new tenuous agreement in jeopardy. I'd hate myself forever if my temper or sensitivity ruined my chance of giving Molly the childhood she deserved. But I had to say the words I'd swallowed down my entire life. Even if they wouldn't make one bit of a difference.

"Don't pretend you didn't do the same thing when you were in my position, daughter."

So like Kathy Quinn to ignore every valid point and home in on the one where she thought she could win. In her mind, I cheated on Derek with Nathan, which made me as bad as her.

"I was in high school, and I grew from my mistakes. Made sure I didn't repeat them. You're still fine being the *other woman*."

She placed a hand on her hip. "I'm not. That's why we came back from our trip early. His wife called to wish him Merry Christmas, and because I'm not the dead-inside villain you make me out to be, I told him we couldn't do it anymore. He ended his marriage to be with me."

"Better late than never, huh?"

"Brenna." She sighed. "We should be talking about Molly, don't you think?"

That tone. I gritted my teeth, resisting the urge to hurl another retort at her, giving her what she wanted. The chance to make herself look like the bigger person. Needing space from her, I took a seat at the table. "Sure, let's talk about Molly. What did you have in mind?"

"I need to know you won't completely push me out of her life," she said. "And Molly can never know about our... arrangement."

"I will never cut you out of her life or tell her about the money." *Even though she's better off without you.* Molly would need to decide whether she wanted a relationship with our mother when she was older. I wouldn't take that choice away from her. "We can come up with a schedule for video calls."

She crossed her arms over her chest. "And... the money?"

"I'll wire it to you when the sale goes through in April. Obviously, I have to split the profit with Nathan."

"Obviously."

A knock at the door stopped me from saying something I might regret. I glanced at the clock over the stove. *Eight p.m.* "Are you expecting someone?"

She shook her head, turning back to the sink. "It's probably another one of those damn Girl Scouts. Like I need more cookies."

"I guess I'll get it," I announced, heading to the front door.

My knees weakened when I looked through the peephole.

"Hey, Quinn," Nathan said when I pulled the door open, the sight of his gorgeous face knocking the wind right out of me.

"Hey, Quinn," Nathan said when I pulled the door open, the sight of his gorgeous face knocking the wind right out of me.

49

NATHAN

Now

THE TENSION IN MY body deflated the moment I laid eyes on Brenna.

She gaped at me, her lips parted in the most distracting way. She wore leggings and a sleepshirt, like she often had around our house. So many moments pressed against each other, savoring the closeness, never wanting to move even an inch.

Leo let out a whistle. "Okay, now I get it." I cringed, waiting for an out-of-pocket comment, but he only smirked. "I've never seen you look at anyone else like that before."

I stuffed my hands in my pockets. "Brenna, this is Leo, my teammate and roommate. Leo, this is Brenna."

"What he means to say is that I'm his friend." Leo held out his hand to Brenna. When she placed her hand in his, he lifted it to his mouth, kissing the back.

I smacked his arm. "Knock it off, man."

Leo laughed. "Oh... this jealous side is new too."

"Who is it?" A voice called from deep inside the house—one I recognized as Kathy Quinn.

Brenna didn't respond. Instead, she took a step onto the porch and shut the door behind her. "Nathan, what are you doing here?"

"You're here, Bren. I belong wherever you are."

Leo cleared his throat. "I'll give y'all some space. Very nice meeting you, Brenna," he said before reopening the door and strolling inside, as if it wasn't his first time here.

Brenna pointed behind her. "Will he..."

I waved a dismissive hand. "He'll be fine. He can charm anyone."

Without warning, Brenna jumped to me, wrapping her arms around my neck and her legs around my waist. After shaking off the initial surprise, I clutched her to me, breathing her in, running my fingers through her hair, convincing myself she was real. She was here.

We were together.

"I've missed you so much."

The knot in the center of my chest unfurled at her words.

"Me too, Bren." I held her tighter. "Me too."

"Why are you here?"

I sucked in a breath, ready to put it all on the line. "I tried life without you, Brenna. It doesn't work."

The door swung open to reveal my least favorite person on the planet. Brenna wriggled out of my grip. Kathy crossed her arms, curled her lip in distaste, and locked her eyes on me. Thank fuck looks couldn't kill.

"Nathaniel," she said. It wasn't even my name. "I believe *this one* belongs to you."

I smothered a laugh. We'd found the one woman immune to Leo McGinnis's charms.

"We are not in a position to host unexpected guests," Kathy said, looking at Brenna.

"I'll make space in my room, if it's an imposition," Brenna replied.

"No need to make space." Leo winked at Bren and me. "We can squeeze."

Brenna gripped my hand and pulled me past Kathy into the house. I smacked Leo lightly on the back of his head as we passed.

"Nathan!" Molly's voice rang out from the top of the stairs. Her face fit snugly in the banister as she watched us in the foyer. "Come see my room! Wait—who's that?"

I toed off my sneakers and gestured for Leo to do the same. "This is my friend, Leo. We play baseball together."

"Ack!" Molly fake-gagged. "Another baseball player?"

Leo snorted. "I'm real popular in this house."

"I'll heat some food." Brenna's hand landed on my forearm. "Go on up."

Leo and I headed up to Molly, not bothering to glance in Kathy's direction. Her name might be on the lease, but Brenna paid the bills. The gravy train would cease running if she tossed me out on my ass.

Molly gripped my hand and tugged me down the hall until we reached a pink room covered in hockey posters. I recognized some of the Palmer City Wolves we'd met when Deandra took us to their locker room after the game.

"It's *always* hockey, isn't it?" Leo bemoaned, inspecting the posters.

"Are you here to stay?" Molly's big eyes stared at me with so much hope.

The stab in my gut returned as I thought about how I'd shunned her as a baby. I'd sat across the table from her at meals, slept in the same house two weekends every month, and watched Brenna care for her. Molly was perfectly innocent in the entire mess that was our family history. She didn't deserve anything that happened to her—not my shittiness, not losing her father, not moving across the country away from the sister who loved her most, and not an unstable life with Kathy Quinn.

She deserved the kind of love and happiness Brenna and I could give her.

"That's up to your sister," I said.

Her smile reached those big eyes. "Yay!"

I wished I had Molly's unshakable confidence. Eight years ago, I flew home to tell my best friend I had feelings for her. I suspected she had them for me, too, but if I'd read it wrong, I risked our friendship.

And now, I'd risk anything for a chance with Brenna by asking her to invite me into her life, the one she planned to build with Molly. She'd been clear about her priorities. Brenna had to decide whether she could see our lives fitting together and whether she could trust me to stick around, to care for her sister, to be her partner.

I swallowed down my nerves and took a seat beside Molly. She held out a book to me—*The Little Engine That Could.* I read it to her, letting the words distract me from my racing thoughts.

50

BRENNA

Now

My mom leaned against the counter, arms crossed tightly against her body. "So this again."

I kept my attention on the stovetop, where I was reheating spaghetti and meatballs for Nathan and Leo. The delicious smell of garlic wafted toward me every time I opened the oven to check the progress of the bread.

"What does it matter to you?" My tone remained carefully neutral. I wouldn't pretend we had a relationship we didn't, but I didn't want to jeopardize our agreement.

She *tsked*. "You haven't had your fill of heartbreak yet, huh?"

"You don't even know Nathan."

"But I know *you*," Kathy pressed. "The way you cried and cried over that boy. The amount of money I shelled out to pay for therapy to help you cope."

My arm froze midstir. All this time she knew?

Kathy's ambivalence to anyone's feelings wasn't new, but still, it stung, this realization my mother had known my struggle and never once asked me about it.

"I thought you would've grown up by now, but nothing's changed. You still have that weakness—"

I spun to face her. "It's not a weakness!" Kathy opened her mouth, but I barreled forward, tired of pretending she wasn't wrong. "I'm not weak. It took me a long time to accept myself, but I'm happy as I am. You're not going to make me feel differently, so I recommend you stop talking now."

"I'm your mother, I know—"

My cold laugh silenced her. "You don't know me, Kathy. You've *never* known me. And it's your loss. You'll never recognize it, and that's fine. You can blame me or Nathan or Gordon or whoever you want for our lack of relationship. It's your choice. But I know the truth. That therapy you shelled out money for—Gordon's money, by the way—helped me understand I'm not to blame for your inability to be a good mother. We either choose to show up for people or we don't. It's as simple as that."

A proud smile graced Nathan's perfect lips when he appeared in the kitchen, effectively ending the conversation with my mother. I returned his smile, my silent thanks for his interference.

Kathy strode out of the kitchen, mumbling something about rewriting history and bumping Nathan's shoulder as she passed him.

"You are amazing," he said.

I turned back to the food. "You're getting this dinner whether you compliment me or not."

"Yeah?"

"Its temperature might change based on the compliments though." I tossed him a cheeky grin over my shoulder.

Nathan closed the distance between us, wrapping his arms around my waist, fusing my back to his front. "In that case," he said, his voice low, his breath tickling the shell of my ear. "Have I told you how gorgeous you look today? How tempted I was to push you against the house and remind you of exactly how well we fit together?"

The words made me quiver.

"Stop distracting me." I bumped him with my ass, and he loosened his grip, taking a step back. "Or you might eat burnt spaghetti."

"To see that blush on your cheeks? Worth it."

I held a plate out to him, steam billowing up from the food. "Is Leo joining us?"

"Nah, he's watching hockey with your sister."

"Oh, I like him already. I'm surprised he flew out here with you."

"Same. But Leo's full of surprises. He went to my doctor's appointment with me yesterday too."

My heart stopped dead. "Wait—what doctor's appointment?"

"Let me take this to Leo, then I'll tell you about it. There's a lot I want to talk to you about."

Part of me wished we didn't have to talk about the future, to save these conversations for later. Maybe date for a bit. But with our lives on separate coasts, we had to figure out whether we could move forward and how we'd manage the obstacles in our way if we did.

I didn't need any more time with Nathan to know what I wanted.

When he got back, he settled on the opposite side of the table and dug into his dinner, taking a couple of bites while I waited on pins and needles for him to answer my question. His throat worked down a mouthful of food, and then he dropped his utensils on the plate with a clang.

"I went to an orthopedic surgeon."

"You what?"

I'd given up trying to convince him to get his shoulder assessed. I never thought he'd accept that his arm needed intervention. Nathan didn't like to be away from baseball, so he pushed through every injury, grinning and bearing it, regardless of what anyone said.

Apparently until now.

"You were right. I knew it the moment my arm popped at the end of last season. I have a torn labrum, and I need surgery if I want to keep playing baseball."

"I'm sorry, Nate. Are you... in pain now?"

He shook his head, taking a sip from his beer bottle. "No, and it's only certain motions."

"Your pitching motion?"

Nathan laughed humorlessly. "When I pitch, it feels like someone is ripping my shoulder from my body. Not the entire time, but eventually. Rest and ice and physical therapy exercises aren't doing shit anymore. I take the mound, and my shoulder hurts."

The notion that Nathan's favorite thing in the world was causing him the most pain was unfair in epic proportions. There were always people who had it worse—it was one of the things I told myself whenever my mood plummeted. Nathan and I, despite the messiness of our lives, were extremely lucky.

And yet, this twist of fate was especially cruel.

"I went to the doctor because of you."

"I can be very convincing."

He snuck in another bite of food, swallowing it down before continuing. "It wasn't that, although you're scarily good at convincing me to do things." One side of his lips tugged up briefly before returning to a flat line. "I've avoided facing this because I don't want to lose baseball. I love it, but also… I didn't have anything else in my life to look forward to if I lost it. Then my father, of all people, brought you back into my life."

My heart galloped in my chest. I understood why he flew here to have this conversation face-to-face.

"I hated him at first, Bren. I watched you agree to marry another man, and my father trapped us together? Talk about a fucking nightmare."

Tears stung the corners of my eyes. "I hate that you saw that."

"I don't. I *needed* to see it. To realize my feelings for you hadn't gone anywhere. I hated seeing that ring on your finger and that look on your face, like you'd rather be anywhere else than trapped in Middlebury with the person who had broken your heart, made your life hell, even if I thought it was the right thing—"

Every instinct shouted to smooth his pain. "Nathan, it's okay—"

"It's not—"

"It's all in the past."

"Ever since the night of the snowstorm," he continued, "I started to hope I'd have another chance at a life with you. Bren, these last three months—I've never been happier."

Tears streaked down my face as I heard my thoughts echoed in his words. "You remember the day I fell off the treadmill and you caught me?"

"It's not every day you save someone's life." Nathan broke into a smile, his face losing some of its seriousness.

"You were frustrating that day too." I laughed through my tears. "It all came rushing back. It hurt to see you, knowing what we used to be and no longer were. When I learned I had to stay in Middlebury with you, I knew it was only mattera of time..."

"Until?" He rose from the table and approached me.

"Until I was in love with you again." I stood on wobbly legs, taking his outstretched hands. I took a steadying breath. "And I was right."

"I'm so fucking in love with you, Brenna. That's why I'm here, to tell you I'm all in. I will build my life around you and Molly. I've never been more sure of anything."

When real life ambushed the fantasy we'd lived these last three months, I worried we'd break under the pressure. But here he was, ready to bend to make our life work.

"You mean that?"

Nathan wiped away my tears with the sleeve of his sweatshirt. His fingers lingered on my jaw, tracing back and forth. "I meant every word. But which part?"

"About Molly." I sniffled, trying to calm my emotions. I loved that it hadn't fazed Nathan. He'd been one of the only people in my life who accepted me, sensitivity and all. "You'd be okay taking care of her?"

His fingers moved to my hair, playing with the ends. "Christmas with both of you was the most at-home I've felt in years."

"Kathy agreed to sign over custody of Molly to me," I whispered, still shocked at the turn of events.

Nathan straightened. "What? She did?"

I leaned forward, not wanting to risk Molly hearing. "I offered her my part of the profit from the sale of the house. I was going to use it to fight for custody anyway. It's a small price."

Nathan shook his head. "It's not a small price. You have no idea how rare you are. I don't deserve you."

"I don't think there are any two people in the world who deserve each other more than us."

Nathan pressed his lips to mine, placing both hands on the small of my back. I melted into him, savoring the urgent way his mouth moved. Nathan held me close without an inch of space between us, the way I liked it. Warmth bloomed in my chest, happiness to the point of pain.

Not many people found lasting love at such a young age. We'd gone through so much to get back to each other, but maybe it's what we needed to do to make it work. Relationships without fight died. Nathan and I learned that the hard way.

His teeth raked over my bottom lip as he pulled back, sending a delicious zap of desire deep into my gut.

"So," he rasped, "where are we headed next?"

"Well, what about baseball? Your shoulder? Where do you need to be?"

"I need to be with you." He kissed my forehead. His arms, this safety, they were what I needed. "Tell me where we're going and I'm there. We'll figure it out together."

If he kept saying things like that, someone would need to scrape me off the floor.

"I was thinking Middlebury," I said. *Home.* Middlebury felt like home again, especially with Nathan by my side. "I don't want to sell the café, Nathan. I love it there. It's *ours.*"

Nathan's brow wrinkled. "You sure?"

His skepticism was understandable. Nathan knew that before the mess with our parents, I'd wanted to move back to Middlebury after college. But living there hadn't been easy toward the end of high school, and I abandoned my plan. These last few months, though, we replaced the tough memories with new ones as we fell in love with each other all over again.

Middlebury was the first place I called home, not because I lived there the longest, or because the house was the nicest place I'd stayed as a kid. Or that my favorite person in the world lived there. I liked that the town was small enough for people to know each other. It meant nosiness but also genuine caring. A strong community. And we would need that to raise Molly.

"I'm sure." I leaned my forehead against Nathan's. "I cried after you left me at the airport."

"I'd like to think it had something to do with me," he said wryly.

I pulled back to stare him in the eyes. "It had *everything* to do with you and the life we're carving out in Middlebury. But we'll need to find a new home."

"I'll live wherever you want." His voice was saturated with emotion. "As long as I wake up next to you every morning."

"You're giving me an awful lot of power."

Nathan leaned his forehead against mine again. "I trust you with it, Bren."

Trust was the last thing to come back. Trust was more logical than love, less instinctual than attraction.

"I trust you too," I said, fighting more tears.

"We're going to be happy, Brenna Quinn. *I'm* going to make you happy."

"Oh, back to calling your shot, are you?"

He threw his head back and laughed. "You loved it when we were kids. It's why I kept doing it. I lived to make you smile."

I tilted my head to the side. "Oh? I thought it was because you were a cocky little shit."

Nathan kissed me, knocking the floor out from under my stomach. He was breathless when he released me. "Nah, that was me showing off for my girl."

We had many details to sort as we embarked on this new life together. We needed to find somewhere to live, a place big enough for three people and four cats. Molly needed a school and activities that would help her make friends in Middlebury. Nathan would undergo surgery and rehabilitation to get another shot at this dream. I wanted to reenroll in a master's program for physical therapy.

But none of that stirred my usual anxiety, because I wouldn't be doing it alone. I had Nathan. We were partners. A team.

Family.

I thought then of the girl who looked out her window after moving to her fifth city in five years. She watched a boy tossing a baseball to himself, zipping it high in the air and catching it with his glove. Her heart skipped a beat when he spotted her and motioned her to come outside. An introvert at heart, she shied away from people but not him. Never him.

It was the start of a friendship unlike any she'd known. The kind of love story she'd read about in books, a soul-deep connection.

Connections like that never died.

Our story proved it.

Epilogue

BRENNA

Two months later

"CAN YOU ZIP ME up?" Nathan smirked, enjoying his dependence on me far too much.

He'd been in a sling for the week and a half since his surgery, only escaping it to do physical therapy and to take a shower—with my help. Those first few days postsurgery had been tough, with Nathan's shoulder constantly hooked up to an ice machine to keep the inflammation down and to ease the pain. I filled it with ice and water every few hours, including during the night when Nathan woke with discomfort. Sleeping sitting up in a sling was no one's idea of a restful night.

I squatted in front of him, eye level with his crotch, and smirked right back. "Anything for you, my liege."

Nathan groaned. "Don't you think I've been tortured enough?"

This week, he'd taken longer walks and started living out of the sling around the house. The physical therapist gave him permission to push himself within his comfort zone, which left me in the position of reining him in. I refused to do anything that could put his recovery in jeopardy, even though Nathan liked to make tempting offers like *I don't need my hands to get you off.*

The torture had gone both ways.

I pulled the zipper up to his chest, leaning forward to give him a chaste kiss. "Better?"

"Well, I'm not cold anymore, if that's what you mean."

I returned to my seat beside him on the bleachers at a hockey rink in Palmer City, where Molly took hockey lessons. Practices were held once a week on Thursday nights, which made it possible for Nathan and me to watch. We hadn't missed one since she started, except for last week when Gemma brought her while Nathan was early in post-op recovery.

"I hope we're not interrupting anything," Gemma trilled, making me jump.

I hadn't expected her. She sometimes joined us at practices when caring for her friend Connie's kids. Gemma used to nanny for them, before she had her daughter—as a test run, she said—and she missed Mason, Izzy, and Silas terribly. She volunteered often to help Connie while she and her husband were at work. Gem's bakery closed early, giving her flexibility.

She lightly placed a hand on my shoulder. "Sorry about that."

Gemma and I had grown close since we moved back, often having lunch when we were both working. When I told Gemma I was an HSP, she asked how she could make me feel more comfortable. If I hadn't already liked her, that would've sealed it for me.

"Hey." I stood to hug her. "What are you doing here?"

Gemma motioned behind her. "Just hanging with my girls."

"Hey, Brenna, Nathan, good to see you again." Connie smiled before easing onto the bench. Gemma's daughter slept soundly on Connie's chest in one of those strapped-to-the-body contraptions. "Molly's famous in the Callahan household."

I grinned. "Molly loves Izzy too. We should get them together more often." Connie's kids went to a super pricey prep school I'd never be able to afford in my wildest dreams.

"Oh, she'd love that," Connie said, then winked. "So would Mason."

Nathan leaned forward, his left hand supporting his sling. "She has another decade before I need to worry about boys."

I flicked his ear. "Do you remember what we were doing when we were sixteen? What we would have been doing before then if you hadn't been oblivious?"

"Molly is *seven*," Nathan said, stress rising in his voice. He was taking his role as Molly's guardian very seriously, which made it immensely satisfying to rile him up like this.

I leaned into him, whispering, "Relax, babe, we're not serious. Besides, I fully believe in your ability to keep the boys away from our girl."

The tension in Nathan's posture eased. "In another decade," he repeated.

We turned our attention back to the ice where the kids—all under ten years old—did drills, skating with hockey pucks around cones to learn handling skills. Molly stood beside Connie's daughter, Izzy, talking away while they watched the players in front of them skate. Suddenly, Connie's son, Mason, turned to glare at them. He must have said something Molly didn't like because she crossed her arms—and stick—over her chest.

Gemma laughed. "Oh, they are a *best friend's brother* trope in the making."

Nathan raised a brow. "I don't know what that means."

"Best if you don't," I muttered.

Mercifully, Gemma changed the subject before Nathan asked questions that would have his overprotective nature shifting beyond the point of *adorable*. "How's the arm, Sharpe?"

"So far, so good." He hadn't taken his eyes off the ice. "But we won't know until I start throwing."

The waiting made him anxious. Uncertainty often burned more than bad news. At least once you knew what you faced, you could deal with it.

"Kennedy said you'll be working out with some of the Wolves this summer," Gemma continued. "I hope you know what you're in for. Volkov is *seriously* unhinged when it comes to training."

Nathan had asked Deandra to connect him with anyone from the Wolves who'd be training in the summer—their offseason—when he'd rehab his shoulder. She knew, like I did, that Nathan would work relentlessly after shoulder surgery, singularly focused on building strength. He'd do whatever was necessary to return to baseball. Apparently, Alexei was the Wolf who put in the most time at the gym, and he would push Nathan the hardest.

"Unhinged is his speed," I said at the same time Nathan told her, "I'm not worried."

Gemma shrugged. "You should meet him before you decide. How about dinner at my place next Friday? The guys are in town and don't have a game. Con, can y'all make it?"

Connie slipped her phone from her pocket, jabbed a few keys, and stared intently at the screen. "After six, we can."

Gemma clapped her hands. "Great, it's a date." She bumped my shoulder. "Have I told you recently how happy I am y'all stayed?"

I smiled at her. "Not today."

"Well, I am."

"Me too, Gem."

Nathan's left hand reached for mine, squeezing once. "I've never been happier."

"Surgery and all?"

"I've had you waiting on me night and day." The love simmering in those turquoise eyes still made my chest tight. It always would. "Being with you and Molly is everything I never thought I'd have. Our family, our life, they're perfect. Even if I never get to throw another pitch professionally, I've got my favorite catcher right here. Nothing else can live up to that."

I took a deep, steadying breath before I made a spectacle of myself at the hockey rink, and Molly would never let me come to another practice.

I met Nathan's gaze as I answered. "I wouldn't change anything—not one damn thing—because it got us here. Teammates for life."

Nathan kissed my cheek. "Teammates for life, Bren."

NATHAN

Four months later

My mom carried the birthday cake with eight burning candles to the porch from the kitchen while singing the happy birthday song.

Brenna wrapped a towel around Molly's shoulders as she made her way from the pool to the porch, her eyes wide as saucers. Brenna planned this months in advance to ensure everyone could be here. My mom took two weeks off work to fly here from England to visit us for the first time since we'd moved back to Middlebury.

Leo was able to be here because we chose all-star weekend. He made the major league team, the Nashville Blitz, this season and moved out of Houston, vacating the apartment we'd lived in for years. I couldn't have been happier for him. Playing on the Blitz meant his dream had come true, and it brought him closer to North Carolina.

"Nathan," Gemma called, waving me over. "Picture time!"

Molly sat in front of the cake, barely holding herself back from blowing out the candles. I threw an arm around Brenna's shoulders, a smile stretching across my face that had nothing to do with the picture. Gemma took a few regular photos before ordering us to be silly, which had everyone except my mom sticking tongues out at each other.

Brenna took the lead on cutting the cake and handing plates to Gemma to deliver to Molly's friends from school, hockey, and the neighborhood.

"I'm so proud of you, Nathan." My mom joined me a few steps away from the chaos. She'd been wary about returning to Middlebury, had talked with me about making the trip here for weeks before agreeing to it. Her hesitation primarily came from the prospect of seeing Kathy Quinn again. Even though Kathy had been invited, she was still sailing the world with her boyfriend. She regularly checked in with Molly, though it was far less often than she'd agreed to.

I scanned the party proudly. "This party was all Brenna."

Well, Brenna and her new group of friends—Gemma, Kennedy, and, to my absolute shock, Deandra.

Brenna used to tense up or bolt anytime Deandra came around, but they were forced into proximity by Gemma. Bren slowly started to warm to her, making little mentions of things she'd said. It was even her idea to invite Deandra to this party. And now that Brenna would be working with the Palmer City Wolves' athletic trainers for an internship this fall, I only expected them to grow closer.

My mom smiled, revealing laugh lines. It was a relief to see them on her face, to see she wasn't uncomfortable being here. "I always loved Brenna, you know that."

"It means a lot to me that you accept us, that you came. Especially for Molly's birthday. I know it wasn't easy."

Her hands landed on my shoulders. "I'll always be here when you ask, Nathan. I'm sorry if I made you feel like I wouldn't." She heaved out a watery breath. "You've created a lovely life here, and you deserve every bit of this happiness. I admire the man you've become."

"Thank you, Mom," I said, hugging her tight to me. "You're part of that lovely life, you know? You're welcome anytime."

She stepped back to look me in the eyes. "I love you, son."

"I love you too, Mom."

Across the deck, Brenna held up a plate, looking in our direction. "Leah! Do you want cake?"

I nodded toward her. "Go ahead. I've got some people to catch up with."

Brenna laughed, tossing her head back, at something my mom said as she approached. The two of them crowded together, staring at Molly, who'd run off with her friends to eat cake. This trip couldn't have gone better, though I wasn't the one with doubts. Brenna thought my mom would hold a grudge because she was Kathy Quinn's daughter. But like I'd told her, she had nothing to worry about.

"So when are you going to make that woman your wife?" Leo clapped a hand on my shoulder.

Wife. I loved the sound of it.

I tried to shake off the emotions stirring in me. "We just moved in together a few months ago."

Leo adjusted his backward baseball cap, lifting it once before repositioning it over his shaggy blond hair. Women went crazy for it, like everything else about him.

"You're practically married already, Sharpe. Don't you want it all official and in writing?"

I shook off his hand and rolled my eyes. "It's already official. I don't need a piece of paper to tie us together."

He nudged me. "But you fucking *want* it. I know you, man. You haven't thought about it?"

Of course, I'd thought about it, but I wasn't about to let Leo spread that news around the entire party. He wouldn't do it on purpose, but get a few drinks in him, conversation flowing, and he couldn't help himself.

"Oh, it won't be long," Deandra said from the top step of the patio behind Leo. "If it were up to him, it would've happened years ago."

Leo scanned Deandra, from the strappy sandals wrapped around her tanned calves to the short blue-patterned thin-strapped dress until he reached her face. She wore dark eyeshadow and dark red lipstick, even at this casual party. Since she'd reentered my life, I hadn't seen her without that armor once.

"And *who* are you?" Leo drawled.

She crossed her arms over her chest, which emphasized her cleavage and drew Leo's attention. She snapped her fingers. "I'm up here."

"Leo, this is Deandra," I jumped in before she verbally ripped him to shreds. "We went to high school together. Leo's my friend from the league."

"His catcher," Leo clarified. "I play for the Nashville Blitz."

"Good for you." Deandra turned her attention to me. "I've gotta head out."

"Where are you going?" Leo asked, undeterred by her lack of interest.

She would've made out with him on a couch in high school, but she'd raised her standards since then.

Deandra squared herself to Leo. "If you must know, I have a date."

"You should blow him off." Leo gave her a roguish grin, the one that usually made women agree to whatever he wanted. "Go out with me."

Deandra smoothed her dress. "He's a successful, handsome lawyer, and he's taking me to one of the best restaurants downtown. I think I'll pass."

Leo took a step toward her. "Bet he won't give you what you need."

"Yeah, what's that?"

He tipped her chin with one hand. "Being bent over—"

"Do *not* finish that sentence," I cut him off, scrubbing a hand over my face. "Jesus Christ, this is a *child's* birthday party."

"Relax, Nathan. I was only having a little fun." Deandra winked at Leo. "There's no way he could handle me."

She started walking to the house, then turned, a sultry grin on her face when she found Leo still staring. "See y'all later."

Leo spun back to me. "I think I'm in love."

"You're an idiot," I said, shaking my head slowly. "And she is totally out of your league, dude."

I clapped him on the shoulder, then headed to Brenna and Molly floating in the deep end of the pool.

I discarded my shirt and cannonballed into the water, soaking them with my splash. Molly and Brenna screamed, then splashed me as soon as I surfaced. I threw Molly over my shoulder. She shrieked, begging me to put her down, calling to Brenna for help. After a few minutes of swimming, Brenna managed to dunk me under water, freeing Molly from my grasp. She smoothed Molly's wayward blond hair back from her face.

"Do you like your party?" I asked Molly.

She grinned so wide, I could see the gap where she'd recently lost a tooth. "It was the best." She launched herself around my shoulders. "Thank you, Nathan." She moved to Brenna next, settling in the crook of her neck. "I love you, B."

It wasn't only pool water reflecting in Brenna's gaze. "Oh, Molls, I love you more than you will ever know."

Bren's hand found mine beneath the surface. We remained like that—this little family we'd created against all odds, soaking in the gift of each other's company.

Eventually, Molly's friends called her to the other end, leaving Brenna and me alone.

She hooked her legs around my waist, and I went willingly, finding her waiting lips. With Brenna in my arms, the rest of the party fell away, leaving only her lips sliding against mine, her contented sighs every time my tongue swiped hers. It was always like this. A fucking *relief.*

This week, I'd start throwing pitches for the first time since surgery. They would all go to the woman who knew me best, who owned my heart. My life started when I met her, and she'd remain with me until the end.

The two of us could take on anything, as long as we did it together.

If you enjoyed Call Your Shot and...

... want more of Nathan and Brenna, visit my website by scanning the QR code below to sign up for my newsletter and receive a free bonus scene.

Acknowledgements

It's surreal to be back here writing acknowledgments for my second published book!

Thank you to everyone who read my debut, *Play Your Part.* You gave me the validation (which I personally crave, darn sensitivity) and confidence to keep going. Sharing my stories with the world has been the ultimate act of vulnerability since they are so deeply personal to me. Words can't express how much every like, comment, message, and review means to me. The book community is absolutely the best part of the internet.

Thank you to **my parents** who have always had my back and never made me feel badly about my sensitivity. My best was always good enough for you. I can't imagine where I'd be if that wasn't the case.

And to **my husband, Mike**, who is on the opposite side of the sensitivity spectrum from me. It isn't easy for either of us to relate to how the other experiences the world but we love each other enough to always keep trying. I'm grateful every day to have you in my life.

Call Your Shot benefited from the careful read from my lovely beta readers/critique partners — **AnnaMaria, Becky, Cristina, Hope, Rose, and Sarah.** I appreciate you sharing your honest thoughts. I know it's not easy to share a critique, but it's invaluable to me. There's so much that changed in this story thanks to your feedback.

Becky – I am so glad that we've become writing besties. I never thought I'd have someone to vent, brainstorm, and support on this writing journey. What are the odds that I'd find someone who likes my writing, writes their own amazing stories that I love, gets my sense of humor, and also grew up in love with Pacey Witter?

To my editor, Rachel Shipp – thank you for making *Call Your Shot* shine. Your edits were once again fantastic, sharpening my writing while keeping my voice. Working with you has helped me grow as a writer.

Mary Scarlett LaBerge – I'm so in love with this cover. Thank you for making the cover design process a wonderful experience once again.

And thank **YOU, dear reader,** for reading my book. I will never get over hearing from readers or connecting with other writers. My DMs are always open.

Also by Kathryn Kincaid

<u>**All In series**</u>

Play Your Part
Call Your Shot

About the Author

Kathryn Kincaid writes contemporary romance featuring sports and characters finding the love they deserve. She lives in North Carolina with her husband and four adorable but high-maintenance cats. When she's not working or writing, she spends her free time devouring books, binging TV shows, cheering on the Carolina Hurricanes, and getting her butt kicked at OrangeTheory.

goodreads.com/author/show/31022409.Kathryn_Kincaid

instagram.com/authorkathrynkincaid

amazon.com/stores/Kathryn-Kincaid/author/B0C2K59RGZ

tiktok.com/@authorkathrynkincaid